EAST END
A FAMILY OF STEEL

By Kim Hunter

Kim Hunter

This is a work of fiction.
Names, places, characters and incidents originate from the writers imagination.
Any resemblance to actual persons, living or dead is purely coincidental.

Table of contents

OTHER WORKS BY KIM HUNTER

WHATEVER IT TAKES
EAST END HONOUR
TRAFFICKED
BELL LANE LONDON E1
EAST END LEGACY
PHILLIMORE PLACE LONDON

Web site www.kimhunterauthor.com

Dedication

To Josie. The paperweight was invaluable!
X

FOREWORD

"Heaven has no rage like love to hatred
turned,
Nor hell a fury like a woman scorned."
William Congreve 1703

CHAPTER ONE
JUNE 2012

Sandra Steel had resided in the council semi on
Boreham Avenue since the day she'd married forty
three years earlier. Although the rent hadn't been
extortionate it was at times still a struggle to pay.
Her husband Kenneth wasn't lazy by any means but
his fondness for the drink and women had seen the
family go without on many occasions. Ken was
handsome and that had been the initial attraction. It
wasn't that he was nice to her, even when they were
a courting couple he had a knack of belittling her in
front of others but whenever he had taken her in his
arms Sandra seemed to melt like butter. The
wedding was nothing posh just a simple ceremony
down at Canning Town registry office. Sandra had
hoped for some kind of honeymoon but she'd been
in for a big disappointment. There was no after
party, no traditional East End knees up and before
the ink was dry on their marriage certificate
Kenneth Steel had almost frogmarched his new wife
home to Boreham Avenue. With the front door only
just closed he had pushed her to the floor and
violently raped her. When he was at last sexually
gratified, Kenneth Steel checked his appearance in
the hall mirror before leaving to join his mates
down the Kent Arms on Albert Road for a few
celebration drinks. Sandra had grasped hold of the
newel post and managed to pull herself to her feet

1

Pain seared through her and she instantly placed her hands on to her stomach in a protective way. Climbing the stairs she prayed that she wouldn't miscarry and that for tonight at least there wouldn't be a repeat performance. It seemed that for once God answered her prayers as Kenneth came home slaughtered. After falling over on the path and trying to get his key in the lock for several minutes he finally fell into the hallway. Managing to make it into the front room he staggered forward onto the couch, where he spent the rest of the night in a drunken stupor. This incident along with many more that occurred over the years was never mentioned and the next day her husband would act as if nothing had happened.

Early on Sandra had learnt to riffle through his trousers each night in the search for any loose change but never before he was snoring heavily. She didn't know how but Kenneth Steel had a knack of watching her even when his eyes appeared to be closed. He only caught her in the act once and even though shed been heavily pregnant with Vic it hadn't stopped her husband from punching her hard in the stomach. Luckily no damage was done to the child but it was a constant reminder, to always be on her guard. The years passed slowly and painfully and even though Sandra had produced three strapping sons for her husband and ran a good house to boot, it didn't stop the beatings which mostly happened on a Friday and Saturday night.

Monday was always wash day with time set aside for her to try and hide the bruising with heavy foundation. It wasn't something Sandra was very successful at but no one ever asked if she was alright. Her family had turned their backs on her when she had first announced she was marrying Ken Steel. All those years ago Sandra's father warned her that she would rue the day but he hadn't been privy to the fact that she was four months pregnant and so didn't have much choice in the matter. God if the same scenario arose today and it was her own daughter, then she would tell her girl to run as fast as she could but that was now and back then in the sixties it was still a stigma to be an unmarried mother.

Years later when her old man was no longer on the scene her boys had clubbed together and bought the house when the right to buy scheme was introduced. Boreham Avenue was now Sandra's castle and she defended it fiercely. Her sons always provided well and it had been years since she'd had to take in washing just to put food on the table. The Steel home stood out above any other on the avenue and it was something Sandra was proud of. Her windows glistened, the lace nets were a brilliant white and her small front garden was immaculately kept unlike many of the other houses in the road. No one threw litter onto her garden, not if they Knew what was good for them. Every resident in the avenue was only too aware of the Steels reputation and what they were capable of.

Sandra Steel stepped from the bus laden down with six bags of shopping. She didn't mind as it was only a few hundred yards to her house and the fact that the whole of her family were coming to Sunday lunch the next day made all the hard work worthwhile. What pleased her even more was that she'd been able to knock the local butcher Manne South, down a few quid on a nice leg of lamb. Lamb was her boy Kenny's favourite and just the thought that she was giving him what he liked pleased Sandra. Michelle her youngest and only girl was a different kettle of fish altogether. She was probably on one of her fad diets and wouldn't touch a scrap but that was Shell all over and a weekly occurrence in the Steel household. All in all Sandra was happy with her life. At sixty one years of age she was healthy and had three strong boys who provided well and loved her dearly, she was sure of that but her daughter was a different matter. Struggling to unlock the gate she felt his hand on her shoulder as he bent down and relieved her of three of the bags.

"Here mum let me give you a hand."

Sandra peered up into the most amazing blue eyes and even though he was hers she couldn't deny that Kenny was a handsome sod but then it wasn't something he didn't already know himself.

"Thanks love, nice cup of tea?"

"Lovely. You know the way to a man's heart and no mistake."

Sandra laughed; her eldest could charm the bird's right out of the trees. For a moment she thought back to when he told her he was joining the army. To Sandra it had felt like she was about to lose a limb, though it wasn't something she had voiced at the time. Now looking at his strong handsome face she knew that somewhere along the line something had been lost, something special that he would never get back and it scared her.

Inside the pristine kitchen which had set Kenny back over ten grand; Sandra placed the shopping onto the granite work surface. After switching the kettle onto boil she began to put the groceries away and chatted to her son as she did so.

"So, what you been up to son?"

"Oh you know mum this and that."

Sandra had known for years that for the majority of the time her boys worked outside of the law but it wasn't something she cared to dwell on.

As long as they were all healthy and happy then as far as Sandra Steel was concerned everything was alright with the world.

"You still alright for lunch tomorrow?"

"I wouldn't miss one of your roasts for the world mum."

"What about Charlie and Vic? Don't tell me that bitch Deidre has come up with some excuse or another?"

"Not as far as I know. Anyway it don't matter if she has mum, I mean it aint like she's really family now is it?"

Sandra smiled warmly at her son, he always knew the right thing to say and on this occasion he was right once again. Deidre Kegan might think she was a Steel but it would only ever be in the eyes of the law. A Steel had to have the right blood running through their veins and the only thing Deidre Kegan had contributed to the family was little Vic. He was only five and just about to start school but Sandra had known from the day he was born that he was a Steel through and through. You only had to look at him to see that, though she had often thought he looked more like Kenny than her middle son Vic.

"You seen our Charlie today?"

"No mum not since last night. One of the boys phoned and said he'd seen Charlie hanging round a piece of skirt and by all accounts she was a right dirty little slapper."

"Kenny!"

"Oh come on mum you know our Charlie; hell screw anything that fucking breathes. He's only interested in two things, how good he looks and the next slag he can fuck. I've told him time and time again that he's going to end up with a dose but he don't listen. It'll serve the dirty little bastard right if he does get the clap."

"Not a lot different from your old man then."

At the exact same time Kenny and Sandra steel began to laugh. They shared a bond so special that at times it had caused resentment from Vic, Charlie and Michelle but they just didn't understand. Vic had been nine, Charlie just three and Michelle hadn't even been born when Kenny announced at the age of eighteen that he was joining the army. Coming out of the Para's seven years later had been difficult for Kenny. On his first night back in London his father Kenneth had arrived home drunk and as usual had started on Sandra as soon as he set foot through the door. It wasn't something Kenny had never seen before but his father's act of violence as he'd slapped Sandra's face, coupled with the atrocities that he'd witnessed in the Gulf tipped him over the edge. With one punch he had knocked his father to the floor but when he'd continually put the boot in it was Sandra who had eventually pulled her son off of the bloody mess that was her husband. Kenny roughly shrugged her arm away and for a split second she saw a coldness that had never been there before.

"You alright mum?"

His words jolted her back to reality and for a moment she was silent.

"Sorry Son just daydreaming a little."

"What about?"

Sandra laughed as she sat down at the table to pour the tea.

"I was remembering the night you kicked the old

7

man out. I can still see the look of shock on his face when you threw him out the front door."

"He never came back mum did he? That aint why you're thinking about it is it?"

"Not on your Nelly. The old bastard was too scared of you to darken my doorstep again. He's still shacked up with that Gaynor Wilson over in Whitechapel. Pam McKenzie from up the road says she sees them most Saturday nights down the Mecca. She reckons Gaynor has a face like a smacked baby's arse and always has a shiner to boot, poor cow."

"Don't bother you after all this time does it?"

"No chance! I'm just glad it's her getting the back hander's and not me."

Kenny drank the last of his tea and stood up. "Well Id better be getting off now said Id meet Vic and Charlie down the office."

Sandra stood up and walking over to her son tenderly placed her hands on his cheeks.

"Now you take care boy because I don't know if I could go on without you."

Kenny Steel removed her hands and laughed as he did so.

"Leave it out mother you'll probably be around long after any of us."

"Oh don't say that boy not even in bleeding jest."

"Anyway where's Shell?"

Sandra proceeded to clear the cups away as she spoke. Keeping the place like a show house was her main priority and she was only truly happy with a cloth or duster of some description in her hand.

"Oh don't even go there. She's round that daft mare Julie Sullivan's. Said she might go to that Sugar Hut tonight. I noticed she took a change of clothes with her so she probably won't come back here much before the milkman. Heaven knows why she wants to go to that place its nothing but tits and heels but you know our Shell."

Kenny smiled. He didn't know her as well as he'd like too but no one else would ever be privy to that fact. From the moment shed been born Kenny had a weird fascination with his little sister. He knew it wasn't natural and did his
best to hide it.

"I worry about that girl. With your old man disappearing from the scene before she was born she aint exactly had a father figure to look up to." Kenny gave his mother a quizzical look that said what about me but when she frowned he knew not to argue the case.

"What time tomorrow mum?"

"About two alright? You know Vic likes a pint on a Sunday lunch time and Charlie won't be out of his pit before one. As for Shell well your guess is as good as mine whether she will turn up or not. You going over to the house tonight?"

"Yeh thought I'd just pop in and make sure everything's ok. I'll probably stay the night so I'll see you tomorrow ok?"

"Ok love."

Kissing his mother gently on the cheek Kenny walked from the kitchen to begin his work. He needed to call in at the office before heading over to the house. Shortly after leaving the army Kenny Steel had purchased his first property. For some reason everyone referred to the Georgian pile as the house. It was back in nineteen ninety five and still several years before Notting Hill would become a trendy place to live. Kenny had used the ruse that he'd met a girl but nothing could be further from the truth. Now worth over five million pounds it was a nice little nest egg for the future and somewhere he was proud of but didn't want to live in. His true home would always be with his mother and the house was only kept for what Kenny liked to call his special parties. Parties that would take place as regular as once a week but there was nothing conventional about them.

When she heard the front door close Sandra Steel took a seat at the table and sighed heavily. Surveying her beautiful surroundings she knew she was lucky but still a dark cloud seemed to envelop her. It wasn't depression, Sandra had a strong will and nothing much got her down. No this was different and she wouldn't really have been able to describe it if she'd been asked. The sensation had happened many times over the years but recently it was becoming more frequent. She loved her family dearly, would die for them in fact but there was something about them all that she couldn't put her finger on. True they were all as different as chalk and cheese but that wasn't the problem it went much deeper than that. Sandra had a feeling of foreboding and it didn't make her happy in the least. Standing up she grabbed a duster from her domestic supplies cupboard and set about giving the place a good clean. A clean house meant a clean mind and just maybe it would make her feel a bit better.

CHAPTER TWO

The office was nondescript and situated two miles away from the family home on Poplar High Street. Above a kebab shop it didn't lend itself to anything other than a plain street door. There were no company details advertising its line of work, it wasn't needed and Kenny liked to try and keep a low profile as much as possible. In the early days there had been some trouble with other firms trying to muscle in and wanting a piece of the action but Kenny Steel, with the help of a few heavies, had soon put them straight. Lately there seemed to be a new security firm starting up each week and it was imperative to keep your eye on the ball if you didn't want to lose a contract. With such a good reputation that wasn't the case for the Steels, luckily things were running smoothly and that was exactly how Kenny wanted it to stay. The security firm that the Steels ran employed over two hundred doormen who worked mainly over in Essex. It was standard practice in the industry to work outside of your own manor. It saved receiving aggro and meant that the families of those carrying out the work could sleep soundly at night, for most of the time at least. Payments for the various shifts were made once a week in arrears and always in cash. Several men who Kenny called shift leaders would collect all the wages from the office on a Thursday afternoon. Vic was in charge of checking the time sheets and not one penny would be handed over if there was the slightest discrepancy. If any of the staff had a grievance or wanted to speak to their boss then it was strictly via his mobile. The world in which they worked was a dangerous one and there was always someone ready to take a pop at them, reason or not. Walking up the steep flight of stairs Kenny entered the single room that was the Steel brother's company headquarters. Furniture was minimal with just a desk, swivel chair and a couple of stools. A large map filled the back wall and every pub and club that used the firm's services was clearly marked with a red pin. Vic sat with his feet up on the desk and a copy of The Sun covered his face. The door opening startled him and the newspaper shot all over the floor. Vic rubbed at his eyes with the back of his hands and yawned.

"Sorry Kenny, just grabbing forty winks. Deidre was on one again last night. She was fucking nagging away until the early hours and she was doing me bleeding head in. Most of the time I'd rather not even be there. I tell you if it wasn't for my boy Id have cleared out long ago."

"I can't understand why you don't just give her a fucking slap. What was it over this time?"

Vic Steel shook his head.

"The greedy bitch only wants another fucking sofa. I wouldn't mind but that's three in as many years. As soon as her mate replaces anything she wants the same. I tell you, she'll bleed me fucking dry and when I'm dead shell still be nagging away at me wake. Sometimes I think she's only with me for a meal ticket."

They both laughed but Kenny knew that his brother's words weren't too far from the truth. At thirty four Vic was nine years younger than Kenny. For a Steel Vic was a nice man but his older brother sometimes saw him as weak. Not in the sense of taking care of himself, Vic was more than capable of a good row. What really riled Kenny was that his younger brother was to an extent, under the thumb and hen pecked. As Kenny walked around the desk Vic instantly got up from his seat. It was an unwritten rule that the leather swivel chair was Kenny's. When he wasn't in residence then it was alright to use it but as soon as he walked through the door you moved your arse and fast. Kenny Steel took his seat and opened up the big leather diary. Anyone who telephoned the office was written in the book, a book that was referred to as the bible. It logged any item of business carried out by the firm, even down to menial tasks such as buying a fresh roll for the toilet. Kenny liked to be aware of every single detail and would become irate if anything was missed out, which if it was left up to Charlie Steel, it undoubtedly would be.

"I see Romford Ron's been on the blower again. What's wrong this time?"

Vic Steel walked to the back of the chair and staring over his brother's shoulder began to scan the page.

14

The writing was scrawled and only just legible, again down to Charlie.

"Oh that was last night. Charlie took the call so I aint exactly sure what was said."

"Where is he?"

"He phoned about an hour ago, said he'd be here soon so my guess is hell turn up about four."

Kenny Steel wasn't amused.

"He takes the piss and its starting to get more frequent. I think it's about time I had a word with that kid brother of ours and put him straight on a few things. If he don't start towing the line he can sling his fucking hook."

"Alright Bro calm down. You know as well as I do that you aint going to change him now."

Kenny was angry and snatching up his mobile began to scroll down looking for the number of his youngest brother."

Charlie Steel was still in bed. He'd picked up Zena Cartwright just before the Mayhem club over in Southend had closed for the night. Zena wasn't bad looking but she wasn't much to write home about either. As far as Charlie was concerned she only had two things going for her, big tits and the fact that she had her own place. A nice little one bedroom flat on the new Dryden Avenue development made her seem all the more appealing. She had spent a small fortune kiting the place out and he had to give her one thing, her taste was smart and right up to the minute. As a cabin crew member on one of Heathrow's long haul flights she only made it home for a couple of days once a fortnight and Charlie liked to make the most of her time off. Zena Cartwright idolised the ground that Charlie Steel walked on, had done for years. Deep down she wasn't fooling anyone, least of all herself and knew that out of a long list of many she would probably come almost at the bottom. That didn't stop her informing all her work colleagues that she was Charlie Steels girl. Most didn't have a clue who she was going on about but then they didn't frequent the Essex pubs and clubs like she did. Struggling to open the bedroom door she finally walked in with a breakfast tray just as he answered his phone. It was the signal to Zena that her little dream was about to abruptly come to an end, at least for the next two weeks.

"Ok don't fucking go on Kenny, I'll be about an hour ok! Why? because I'm still in fucking Southend that's why."

Charlie Steel ended the call and smiled up at his own personal servant.

"Alright girl? Now that's what I call service, the fucking punters on your planes must love all this?" Zena Cartwright giggled as she placed the tray containing fresh coffee, hot buttered toast and a romantic single rose beside him. Seeing as he was in a good mood she seized the opportunity to ask the question that deep down she already knew the answer to.

16

"Charlie?"

"What babe?"

Zena twirled a few strands of her long hair between her thumb and forefinger. She imagined it looked sexy but to Charlie it was anything but. As far as Charlie was concerned a woman didn't need to be attractive, he never had a problem in that department and would have been able to get it up for the bride of Godzilla.

"Next time I'm home my Mum asked if you'd like to come over to dinner. My Dads always saying that he wants to meet you and I think over a meal would be nice, don't you?"

Inwardly Charlie groaned, this was all he needed. He liked Zena but only as a fuck buddy. He wasn't about to settle down and even when he was it wouldn't be with a plain Jane like Zena Cartwright.

"It's a bit difficult babe."

He instantly saw the look of disappointment in her eyes.

"Come over here you silly cow. I aint saying no but you know the kind of work I do. I aint got a clue what's happening from one day to the next.

Tell your old lady thanks and as soon as I get a free night well all get together. Now did you iron that shirt for me?"

Zena walked over to the wardrobe and sliding back the door removed an immaculately pressed Armani shirt.

"Good girl! You'll make someone a brilliant little

17

wife one day."

His words hurt her deeply but she didn't let him see that. Zena Cartwright would have given up her career and married Charlie in a heartbeat if he'd asked but she knew deep down that he never would. Still she was content just having him once a fortnight and kidding herself with the idea that he loved her. Not wanting to disappoint her further Charlie forced down the coffee and toast and then jumped from the bed. After a quick shower he was dressed and in his Porsche without a second thought for the poor little mare that he had just spent the night with. Today was a new day and tonight would see Charlie hone in on another fresh conquest. The drive over to Poplar took just under an hour and after finding a parking space he climbed the stairs to the office ready to receive the onslaught that he knew was inevitable. His brothers were again studying the diary when he entered but Kenny didn't even look up as he spoke.

"Wonders will never cease, you took your fucking time!"

Charlie could only grin which made Vic shake his head and roll his eyes upwards. Finally Kenny lifted his head.

"By the state of your dress I gather it was the Cartwright bit of skirt?"

"I never kiss and tell you know that."

Kenny couldn't help but laugh. His kid brother usually arrived home or to the office in a really dishevelled mess, except for once a fortnight when he looked just as he had the previous night.

"Right! Stop fucking larking about we've got work to do. Charlie what's this here about Romford Ronnie?"

Charlie Steel screwed up his face as he answered the question.

"Oh he aint been on the bleeding blower again has he? That prick is a right tosser Kenny. He's only saying that the blokes on the door are skimming. That's the second time this month. He says he wants a total replacement of bodies or hell get a new firm in. I say we tell him to fuck off or better still give the cunt a good slap."

Kenny stood up and placing his palms flat on the desk leaned in close to where his brother was standing.

"Well you would twat! That's why I'm in charge instead of you. The Romford Ronnie's of this world are who keep you in your posh clobber and give you enough dosh to sweet talk the tarts into your bed. We will give Ronnie what he wants and no arguments. Now Vic as you're on duty tonight I want you to trawl round a few of the pubs and make sure everything's pukka. I'll do the first few before I clock off. I know it'll take a while but you should get round the most troublesome ones by closing. As usual Charlie you do the clubs and I mean the clubs and not the dirty whores who frequent them. Mums expecting us all by two

19

tomorrow so make sure neither of you are late."
Charlie smirked which instantly riled his brother.
"I fucking mean it Charlie, wherever you end up
kipping make sure you aint late tomorrow!"
With that Kenny Steel left the office and slammed
the door as he did so. Charlie looked in Vic's
direction and the smile on his brother's face got his
back up.
"Who the fuck does he think he is?"
"Whether you like it or not little brother that is our
boss and you'd do well to remember that fact."
"Well I'll tell you something for nothing Vic, I'm
getting sick and tired of his regimented orders.
Anyway I'm thinking of starting up my own firm,
then no one will tell me what I fucking can and can't
do."
Vic knew that his brother was just running off at the
mouth but he still didn't like to hear the disrespect
that he was showing towards Kenny.
"Do you know Charlie, sometimes you can be a
right ungrateful little bastard. You think it's easy
running a firm like this? I'd give you six months at
best and you'd probably end up down some ally
with your fucking head kicked in. We both owe
Kenny a lot so show a bit of respect and get your
bleeding head out of your arse."
Charlie continued with his moaning, although now
it was more low key because deep down he knew
his brother was right and maybe that was the reason
he was mouthing off in the first place. He knew he

was useless and would always be chasing his brother's shirt tails and it was something he struggled to accept. Vic Steel ignored Charlie's continuing remarks because when it came down to it neither of them would have amounted to anything if it wasn't for Kenny. Vic knew that he would probably be working in some factory or another on just above minimum pay, while Charlie would be a no good ponce relying only on his looks until the day they ran out and then only god knew what would have become of him. Unlike his younger brother Vic didn't struggle with it and was just grateful he had a job that paid as well as it did.

CHAPTER THREE

Michelle Steel sat perched on the edge of her friend's bed painting her nails. From time to time she would stop and glance around at the room. All the furnishings and wallpaper throughout the house were old and outdated and she knew she could never live in a place like this. Mrs Sullivan kept the maisonette clean but it was a far cry from her home over on Boreham Avenue. For a start this was a council house and hers was owned, something Michelle took great pleasure informing anyone of when she met them for the first time. Now Michelle's mum really knew how to keep house and Shell had never worried about taking friends home. Reloading the brush with acid yellow polish she carefully drew it down her long nail. Suddenly the door flew open and Julie Sullivan struggled in with a heavily laden plate.

"OMG Jules! That lots well fattening you know." Julie was only five feet tall and although she hadn't ventured onto a set of weighing scales in a long time, must have weighed at least fifteen stone. Flopping down onto the bed with a doughnut in one hand and a plateful containing more in the other she sighed as she took a large bite. Michelle Steel made a huffing sound as she snatched up the bottle of acid yellow nail varnish before it had a chance to spill.

"You aint going to scoff all those are you?"

Julie surveyed the plate and raised an eyebrow.
"Probably. My mum says I'm a growing girl."
"Yeh well you've only got to look at your old lady to
see how you're going to end up. Honestly Jules!
You aint ever going to get a fella if you eat and act
like a pig."
Her friend's words were spiteful and it hurt her
deeply but Julie knew better than to disagree. All
through school Michelle Steel was the only one who
had given her the time of day. Julie wasn't stupid,
she knew Shell only hung around with her because
it made her look good standing next to a fatty but
friends of any sort were hard to come by when you
resembled Princess Fiona out of Shrek.
"You watch Towie last night Jules?"
"Nah. My mum had some documentary on about
Hitler whoever that is. Proper boring I can tell you.
I ended up walking down Dominos to get a twelve
inch pepperoni."
Michelle Steel could only shake her head. The
conversation was momentarily halted when Ruby
Sullivan called up the stairs.
"Julie!!! You up there girl?"
Her friends reply was equally as shrill and it sent a
shiver down Michelle's spine.
"Yes mum and Shells here as well."
Ruby sighed and shook her head. She didn't like
the Steel girl, she'd met too many of her type over
the years but she never voiced her opinion for fear
of upsetting her daughter. Julie meant the world

to her mother and she wouldn't hurt her feelings for anything.

"You staying for tea Shell?"

Michelle got up from the bed and walking over to the door opened it just enough so that she didn't have to shout.

"No thank you Mrs Sullivan I'll get a Panini while we're out."

Ruby knew that was a lie but she wasn't about to argue the point. The girl was stick thin and you didn't stay like that without starving yourself. She just hoped this starving yourself thing wouldn't rub off on her precious girl.

"Up to you but I've offered. Julie it will be ready in five minutes so get your arse down these stairs."

"Ok mum."

Michelle Steel turned to her friend and frowned.

"You're never going to eat more food after you've just scoffed those doughnuts are you?"

"It's my favourite! Macaroni cheese with extra cheese but my mum will put a baked spud on the side so it is kind of dieting I suppose."

"Oh I give up with you Jules. Anyway while you're filling your face I'm going to start getting ready."

Julie Sullivan smiled to herself. She knew that when Shell got ready it was a mammoth task and would take ages. Give or take ten minutes she would have time to eat her dinner, chat to her mum, get ready herself and she would still end up having to wait for her friend.

24

"Where we going tonight?"

"Sugar Hut, my Kenny has just took over the door and said I can get in anytime I want. Someone said on face book that a few of the girls from Towie are going to be there."

"No!"

"Straight up and I've just got to see what that Laurens wearing and guess what....."

"It's ready Julie!""Ok mum I'm on my way. Sorry Shell but if I don't get me arse down there shell get the right nark."

Without another word Julie Sullivan left the room much to her friend's disgust. Michelle Steel hated being cut off mid sentence. Everything she had to say was important, at least as far as she was concerned. Lifting up the small Louis Vuitton weekend case Michelle slowly unzipped it and savoured every second.

Carefully she removed the new bandage style dress that just happened to be the same acid colour as her nails. It had cost Kenny just over a grand but Michelle hadn't given it a second thought.   Her strappy Jimmy Choo's were the exact same shade as her dress, though much to her disgust had already been worn by her a couple of times. Still Michelle Steel knew that she was going to look fabulous.

Three hours later and the girls were at last ready. Julie Sullivan had to the best of her ability, tried to copy her friend but had come out a very poor second. Her dress was similar in style but where

25

Michelle's had been purchased on Oxford Street
Julies had come from Chapel Street market over in
Islington. Where Shells outfit smoothly caressed
her figure Julies fought tooth and nail with the roles
of fat underneath which were desperately trying to
escape. Silently she prayed that the seams would
hold out at least until the morning.
"You're not wearing those, OMG!"
Julie was trying to squeeze her foot into a pair of flat
black jellies but wasn't having much success.
"Shell I just can't wear them heels. They bleeding
kill me feet and make me feel like I'm going to fall
over."
"Well all I can say is thank god my Kenny runs the
door or we wouldn't get in period! Come on get a
move on the cab will be here in a minute."
From the kitchen Ruby Sullivan watched as they
descended the stairs. Michelle Steel really was a
stunner but to Ruby her Julie with her mane if
flaming red hair was just as beautiful. In all honesty
Julie's hair was a ginger fuzzy mess but to her
mother she was gorgeous. The twenty plus mile
journey had taken just over thirty five minutes, had
cost fifty eight pounds and was courtesy of Kenny
Steel of course. Michelle hadn't even bothered to
ask Julie for her half as her friend never had any
money so it would be a waste of her breath. It had
been the same when Michelle had the idea of
enrolling in a beauty course at the Newtec College
in Stratford. Of course she wanted Julie to enrol as

26

well but she hadn't had the money for the compulsory kit of beauty equipment. Once again just to keep his sister happy Kenny had come to the rescue and paid for not only his sister's equipment but her friends as well. As the girls got out of the cab they could see a long queue which had formed outside The Sugar Hut. The sound of Rihanna was blaring out from inside and Michelle instantly became excited. Ignoring the line of people who had been waiting for over half an hour the two walked straight up to the front. Larry Tennant and Rob Asker were on the door and they instantly recognised the junior member of the Steel clan. Ignoring the snide remarks from the other hopeful club goers the girls walked inside. Instantly all eyes were on Michelle but fat Julie in her jellies brought nothing but sniggers. The looks and jibes cut Julie Sullivan like a knife and she wiped away a tear that had formed in the corner of her eye.

Her supposedly best friend didn't stop for a second to reassure her, instead Michelle headed straight for the VIP area with Julie almost having to run just to keep up with her. The room was decked out in crimson velvet with low round stools surrounding glass topped coffee tables. There were just three booths and Michelle had her eye on the one that was directly next to the roped off entrance. If she couldn't actually be among the celebrities she was going to make sure she was as close to them as she could get. Michelle made a mental note to have a word with her brother in the morning, it was disgusting that they couldn't gain access to the VIPs and she was sure he could sort it out for her. Before taking a seat the girls made their way to the bar and ordered two cocktails and again they were naturally put onto Kenny's tab. Taking their seats in the booth Michelle ignored her friend and focused her attention on the entrance. Julie almost necked her cocktail in one swig until she saw the look of disgust on her friends face.

"I'm thirsty!"

"If you get pissed well have to leave and then I'll be well angry Jules. Just sip it like a lady ok? OMG I think I just saw Arg come in, he's so reem."

Michelle strained her neck to such a degree that Julie thought she resembled a giraffe. Instantly she stifled the giggle that was trying to escape. It didn't bode well if you laughed at Shell and besides Julie was enjoying herself too much. She knew it would all come to an abrupt end if Michelle got into one of her strops. Five hours later and the last song of the night began to play. There had been no sign of the stars from Towie and Michelle had given up looking a couple of hours earlier. For the last thirty minutes she had totally ignored Julie as she was too busy on Face book via her mobile phone. It hadn't bothered her friend as while Shell was engrossed looking at the small screen Julie had been able to replenish her drink several times. Now more than a little tipsy, she had just taken a large swig of her sex

28

on the beach, when Michelle shrieked out, causing the liquid to reappear down Julies nostrils.

"OMG! OMG!"

Julie Sullivan desperately tried to wipe the liquid away with the back of her hand. Her eyes were now watering which caused her mascara to run. Julie now resembled a panda but she was oblivious to the fact.

"What Shell? What is it?"

"Only a media leak. Listen and I'll read it to you. Stars of Towie are set to begin filming this month in Marbella."

Julie Sullivan couldn't see what all the excitement was about. She liked to watch Towie but not to the point of obsession like Shell.

"So?"

"So! How do you fancy a little trip to Spain?"

"Sounds nice but you know I aint got no spare cash at the moment Shell."

Michelle Steel laughed at her friends words.

"And when has that ever stopped us Jules?"

"True but your Kenny will never let you go to Spain."

Michelle Steel stood up and smoothed down the nonexistent wrinkles in her dress.

"You leave Kenny to me. As far as his baby sisters concerned I can have anything I want. I might have to work on him a bit more than usual but as far as Spain goes it's a done deal. You just start packing Julie because in two weeks time we're off."

Julie Sullivan grinned from ear to ear. Her mum wouldn't be happy about it but she wasn't about to miss out on a free holiday to Spain for anyone.

The cab pulled up outside the Sullivan residence and Julie in her intoxicated state almost fell out of the door. Turning round she waited for her friend to join her.

"What you doing Shell? I thought you was stopping the night?"

"I was but now I'm going home. We've got a big family dinner tomorrow and I want to be bright eyed when Kenny gets there. I'm need to start working on him straight away over dinner. Early dog catches the worm and all that."

The cab door slammed shut leaving Julie Sullivan standing on the pavement. Not the brightest bulb in the box even she had to admit that Shell was a bit thick. Whatever was all that about dogs and worms, even Julie knew it would be a cat never a dog. Shaking her head she decided to ask her mum when she got inside.

When Michelle Steel arrived at Boreham Avenue she placed her key in the lock and tiptoed as quietly as she could to her room. Her mother had ears like Dumbo and whereas everyone else seemed to let Michelle do whatever she wanted her mother was the complete opposite. Shell supposedly loved her mother but it was a strange relationship and fraught with tears and arguments. The only one who could sort the pair of them out once they really got going was Kenny and he mostly came down on the side of his sister. Closing her bedroom door Michelle silently made the sign of the cross on her chest. She had managed to get home without her mother mouthing off about what time it was, or at least she thought she had. Sandra Steel had been standing behind her bedroom door listening. She wanted to make sure her daughter wasn't trying to smuggle some boy into the house. Satisfied that all was well she noted the time from the bedside clock and then climbed back into bed. If Michelle thought she was going to get away with coming home at this hour she was mistaken. Sandra would tackle her girl first thing in the morning and long before the others arrived for lunch.

CHAPTER FOUR

After leaving the office Vic Steel quickly went home
to change and grab something to eat. Deidre and
little Vic were nowhere to be seen and he knew that
she was probably round at her mothers slagging off
some poor cow she hardly knew. Still it gave him a
few minutes rest and he took a seat at the table to
enjoy a cup of tea in peace. Fifteen minutes later
and as he glanced up at the wall clock, knew that he
really should get a move on. Reluctantly he
snatched up his car keys and began the journey over
to Essex. He hated the place, a place where he
would spend most of the evening driving from one
pub to another. In total the Steel firm had over
seventy on their books and most of them weren't
any bother and only required two men on the door.
Only a handful of the places were known to cause
trouble on a regular basis and required more bodies
especially on a Friday and Saturday night. These
were the ones that Kenny had wanted him to visit
but as yet everything was relatively quiet. Driving
out to Romford Vic quickly called in at Brannigans
and The Bull. Moving onto Basildon it was The
Edge and The Honey pot. Again there was nothing
to worry about and at this rate Vic thought he might
actually get an early night. His last port of call was
Chinnerys over in Southend.
It was accepted by all in the firm that out of
everywhere this was the venue that gave them the

most aggravation. For some reason the pub
attracted the worst of Southend's society and
anyone who had recently been released from a stint
at her majesties seemed to want to hold their
coming out parties here. There were a few blokes
milling about outside with glasses in their hands
and Vic was on his guard as he approached the
entrance. Matt and Aaron who regularly worked
the place were standing on either side of the door.
Occasionally they would be joined by Tommy Bex
but tonight Kenny had other work for him. Tommy
had been in the army with Kenny and the pair went
way back. Known for being able to take on three or
four men at the same time he was always first
choice if they thought there was going to be bother.
It appeared that tonight he thankfully wouldn't be
needed.

"Evening Mr Steel."

Vic smiled. He had a particular fondness for Mattie
Singer. The bloke was as straight as they came and
could be trusted. That said he wasn't as white as the
proverbial driven and was known to deal a few Es
from time to time but none of that concerned Vic so
he didn't pass judgement.

"Alright Mattie? Had any aggro tonight?"

"Nothing yet Mr Steel and let's just hope it fucking
stays that way. Just as well really as we aint seen
neither hide nor hair of Tommy. There have been a
few rumours flying about that Carlton Jenson got
out today and that he's baying for your Kenny's

blood but he aint turned up as yet."

Vic laughed.

"Mattie, there's always someone after our Kenny. You know Carlton as well as anyone and he's all fucking mouth. The wankers probably already been tucked up in bed by his old lady, the soft twat!"

All three men laughed. Vic wasn't worried about Carlton Jenson in the least but he was glad that Tommy wasn't working the shift. The two had never hit it off and Vic was always nervous when he was in Tommy's company. He couldn't put his finger on exactly what it was about the man but there was definitely something. Vic patted Mattie on the shoulder as he turned from the exit.

"I'm going to call it a night. It aint long until closing but if you do get any bother Kenny's off for the night so you'll have to give Charlie a call ok?"

"Ok Mr Steel but we should be alright."

"Oh and Mattie I don't think you should let them outside with glasses so have a word. If Kenny saw it he'd do his fucking nut."

"Ok Mr Steel well sort it."

Mattie Singer had been with the firm for a little over five years and he loved his work. He looked on both Kenny and Vic as his bosses but Charlie was a different matter all together. He hoped there wouldn't be any trouble as the youngest Steel was about as much use as a chocolate teapot and that was if he even bothered to turn up. Mattie remembered back to a couple of years ago when he'd been working the door at The Prince of Wales over in Basildon. It was a really cold Christmas Eve and he couldn't wait for the shift to end. Inside someone threw a glass and suddenly it was as if world war three had kicked off. Charlie had pulled up in his car just as a body came flying out of the doors and had immediately driven off. The two doormen didn't stand a chance and were left to fend for themselves. Mattie had taken a blade to his left shoulder and ended up spending Christmas two thousand and ten in the University hospital thirty miles away from his family. The incident had never been mentioned by the Steels but Mattie had heard that Charlie received a good slap from his brother but no apologies were ever made. Since the incident Mattie hadn't given Charlie the time of day and he knew that it deeply riled the bloke but after what had occurred Charlie hadn't dare complain. In fact it was over a month later when the youngest brother had finally plucked up the courage to show his face again. Mattie had been on shift and Charlie Steel couldn't look Mattie in the eye.

Vic Steel now got back into his car and began the journey home. He hoped Deidre had gone to bed as he wasn't in the mood for another ear bashing. If her mother and sister had been round and they'd started on the wine then the three would gang up on Vic. It had been a long day and he was tired and not in the mood for an argument with the witches of Canning Town. Vic loathed his mother-in-law almost as much as Deidre hated Sandra but whereas Deidre had no real reason Vic had plenty. Since the day he'd got married Merle Kegan had constantly been round at the maisonette. She nagged him as if she was the one married to him and was constantly telling her daughter that she had married beneath her. That was a joke as far as Vic was concerned. For a start the old cow had never had a serious man in her life and both sisters had different fathers. Louise Kegan was no better. She was as jealous of her sister as any human being could be and although she was at his home as much as her mother, Vic could tell that she wasn't that fond of Deidre. The endless fags and bottles of wine that his wife dished out was her only incentive to visit. Glancing at his watch he saw that it was ten minutes to midnight and if the three women were still together in his home then the chances of them being sober and still awake was minimal. For once Vic might actually have a peaceful end to his day and be able to go to sleep with ease.

Charlie Steel had been doing much the same as his brother only his visits had been to the clubs. There were fourteen in total and it had taken him what seemed like hours to get round them all. For the most part he would just drive up and wind down his window. On being told that everything was fine he would then drive onto the next. Three clubs were in Brentwood, five in Basildon and six in Romford. Charlie had actually been at the Sugar

Hut at the same time as Michelle but hadn't bothered to seek out or speak to his sister. There wasn't a lot of love lost between the two and he tried to avoid being in her company whenever possible. With all the will in the world he couldn't see what his mum and Kenny saw and though he was loath to admit it, he didn't actually like his sister. At times he had tried to speak to Vic about her but as usual his brother always sat on the fence and didn't want to get involved. To Charlie Michelle was no better than the Towie wannabes he shagged round the back of one club or another two or three times a week. Now that Kenny had given her a free hand at most of the venues he knew it wouldn't be long before she brought trouble to their door. Reaching Yates over in Romford which was his last port of call for the night Charlie Steel glanced at his watch. In half an hour the pubs would be calling time and he would be able to start enjoying himself. Compared to the clubs it was the pubs that caused most of the trouble but once they had shut for the night things would ease up a bit. Yates, like the rest of the places he'd visited tonight had dance music thumping off of every wall and the punters were well oiled and in high spirits. It smelled strongly of sweat and stale beer and could have done with a good clean. Unlike The Sugar Hut which traded on its name and the celebrities that frequented it this place had been doing well for years. When Ronnie had taken over he hadn't seen the point in splashing out on a refurbishment and it was now starting to show in more ways than one. Apart from the two men at the entrance the outside was now deserted but four more of the Steels doormen were milling about inside in case of any trouble. They were all, as Kenny liked to put it built like brick shit houses and it took balls or plenty of alcohol to take one of them on. The latter were the easiest to deal with as a drunks coordination left a lot to be desired. Occasionally some lad would have a go when he was sober and would end up receiving a beating but thankfully that didn't happen too often. As Charlie neared the bar his eyes scanned the dance floor trying to seek out a piece of skirt that would nicely top off his evening. At the moment no one caught his eye even though he was known for not being overly fussy. He decided to leave it a while and when the place started to wind down he'd have another look. Reaching the bar he saw his usual tipple was already sitting waiting for him and he downed the Jack Daniels in one. Ordering a refill he spied Romford Ronnie out of the corner of his eye. Charlie let out a low groan. Ron Ashton had owned Yates for the last ten years. The place was a goldmine and when on the premises Ronnie thought he was king, not only thought it but acted the part as well. The man was very overweight, in his mid sixties and had the worst comb over Charlie had ever seen. With all that going against him it still didn't stop Ronnie having two beauties on his arm most of the time. Charlie knew these types of skirt well and for a second the thought crossed his mind that if it wasn't for Kenny then Shell would have probably ended up exactly the same. Hoping that he hadn't been seen Charlie stood at the bar with his back towards Ronnie but knew that he hadn't got away with it when he suddenly felt a hard slap on the shoulder.

"Charlie boy! How you doing mate?"

Wearing the most convincing smile he could muster Charlie Steel slowly turned round.

"Hello Mr Ashton, I'm fine thanks how are you?"

Ronnie put an arm around the girl's waists and pulled them to him. As they placed a kiss on each of his cheeks his eyes never once left Charlie's. Ronnie was the epitome of a letch and any decent girl wouldn't have gone within a mile of him. Ronnie could tell that the young man disliked him and he never missed any opportunity to rub Charlie up the wrong way.

"Good, now did you speak to Kenny about the problems I'm having boy?"

Charlie took a swig of his drink before answering. The tall brunette standing to Ronnie's left stared at Charlie Steel and seductively ran her tongue over her top lip. She wasn't bad looking but Charlie Steel wasn't about to go near anything that had had Romford Ronnie's cock inside it and there was no doubting the fact that this one had definitely had more than one portion. When the girl didn't get the reaction she wanted she turned her attention back to Ronnie and playfully ran her hand across his chest. "Yes Mr Ashton and he said he would sort everything out tomorrow."

"Fucking tomorrow? you cunt! I pay your brother a shed load of cash every month so I expect any fucking problems to be sorted out straight away. You tell him from me that I aint fucking happy."

"No worries Ronnie."

"Fucking Ronnie! Listen to me you little cunt I'm Mr Ashton to the monkeys and you certainly aint the organ grinder so show a bit of respect."

With that Ronnie and his girls walked off in the direction of the office and Charlie turned back to the bar. He knew that within a few minutes the fat old bastard would be half naked and banging away at one of them if not both. The thought disgusted him but he couldn't help a snigger as he pictured it. One thing was for sure, Ronnie shouting his mouth off in public about money wouldn't please Kenny.

Charlie again smiled to himself; he would take great pleasure in repeating the conversation over Sunday lunch the next day.

CHAPTER FIVE

Before going over to the house Kenny Steel had stopped off at Heroes Gym. The owner Andy Grant had phoned Kenny a couple of days earlier and informed him that there were three or four members who were up to the standard Kenny required and who were showing an interest in security work.

As soon as Kenny left the army he'd applied for his SIA security licence and because of his forces history quickly went on to become a trainer himself. It was a brilliant idea as he was then able to get his own men to the exact standard he required. They were all certificated and shown the correct procedures so that the police never questioned their professionalism. Once out on the doors it was a different story but Kenny was still very selective regarding which of his men were asked to do the special work. A man had to be employed for at least six months by Steel Security before they were even approached. Some wanted door work purely for financial reasons and some for the Kudos that being a doorman brought. Kenny Steel didn't care what their reasons for doing the job was as long as they kept fit and did their work. As far as he was concerned anything else was irrelevant and none of his business.

Heroes was hardcore and there were definitely no gym bunnies in tight leotards watching themselves in the mirrors. The smell of sweat hung in the air and massive free weights covered most of the floor area. Andy Grant sat behind a counter at the bottom of the gym and when he spied Kenny, smiled and raised a hand in recognition. Making his way through the gym Kenny individually eyed up the eight or so men who were training. Only one really caught his attention and he walked over to where Jock Denman was about to bench press a bar holding a hundred and ten kilos.

"Alright Pal?"

Jock nodded but didn't speak. He was overly weary of people since being released from the scrubs a couple of weeks earlier.

"You one of the boys that Andy says wants a job?"

Jock Denman realised who was speaking to him and as he rose from the bench, instantly offered his hand which Kenny accepted.

"Yeh Mr Steel and sorry I didn't realise who you were. The only problem is I've just come out of nick and I didn't know if that would affect me chances?"

"Maybe to some firms it would but not mine. There's a boot camp over on Beckton district park just off Stansfeld Road, know it?"

Jock nodded his head vigorously.

"Meet me there tomorrow at eleven. If you make the grade I'll take you on."

"Thanks Mr Steel and I really mean that."

"I wouldn't be thanking anyone yet son, you aint seen how fucking tough it is."

Before he left Heroes Kenny went over to the counter where Andy handed over a small bag containing bottles of steroids and several syringes. In exchange Kenny gave Andy an envelope of cash. Neither man bothered to check the contents as they had been doing business together for so many years and had built up a mutual trust with each other.

"Is he any good to you Ken?"

"Looks ok but I'll know more tomorrow. How many others did you say there were?"

"Hopefully there's at least two but possibly three. Let me know when you're coming in again and I'll make sure they're here."

"Nice one mate, probably be early next week. I've got a few problems over at one of the clubs so I need to do a bit of a swap around."

About to leave Kenny was stunned at Andy's next sentence.

"You heard about Bethnal Green Barry. Got sent down this morning on a fifteen stretch. They reckon the way he plays up that hell end up doing the whole lot as well."

Kenny was shocked; he knew it was on the cards for Barry to do some time but not that long. He would pay his contact a visit in the next few days as a matter of urgency. Party drugs were big business in the clubs and Bethnal Green Barry had supplied Steel Security for the last five years with all that they required. Now he was off the scene Kenny would have to source another supplier which he

wasn't happy about. It took time to trust someone
and as demand was high, time wasn't something
Kenny Steel had much of. Back in his Range Rover
he set off on his journey to the house. The ride was
smooth and he mulled over Romford Ronnie's
accusations. Kenny was well aware that his blokes
skimmed the odd entry fee but it was now
becoming so regular that it was getting out of hand
and he would have to put a stop to it. Steel Security
had a good reputation and he wasn't about to see
that reputation go down the pan for the sake of a
few greedy slag's who didn't know when to stop.
Turning onto Ladbroke Walk Kenny pressed his key
fob and the electric gates slid effortlessly open. It
was just starting to get dark and the security lights
switched on as he pulled into the drive. Built on the
site of an old warehouse the place was less than
twenty years old but was designed in a neo
Georgian style with two large pillars flanking either
side of the front door. When Kenny had first
purchased the place it had cost a pretty penny even
by today's prices. At only twenty five years old no
one had questioned where the money had come
from. During his army career Kenny Steel had been
a model soldier and swiftly rose in the ranks. What
his commanders and comrades were not aware of,
was the fact that towards the end of his career
Kenny had worked out a way to smuggle large
amounts of heroin from Afghanistan into Iraq and
then, with the use of forces aircraft, into England

without being detected. Many would have seen
Kenny as a hypocrite for buying heroin from the
terrorists he was supposed to be fighting but to him
it was just business. By the time he entered Civvy
Street the young man had over five million pounds
stashed away in a Swiss bank account. It was now
sixteen years since he'd first bought the house but it
still didn't feel like home. Kenny felt nothing for the
property; he only cared about the hard cash that it
represented. Entering the marble floored hallway
he placed his car keys and steroids onto the fine
antique table before heading upstairs to take a
shower. Emerging ten minutes later with just a
towel wrapped round his waist he admired himself
in the full length mirror. Standing six feet tall, he
was tanned and with a shaven head. Rugged good
looks had been the only thing his father had ever
given him but Kenny was glad of the gift all the
same. Every muscle stood to attention as he turned
this way and that in different poses. He would
always smile as he touched the cap badge tattoo of
his platoon that was emblazoned on his right upper
arm. Most would have thought that the little ritual
was due to the fact that Kenny was proud to have
been a soldier. Nothing was further from the truth
and it was purely down to the fact that the army
had set him up financially for life and he'd gotten
one over on the establishment. Without her
majesties army Kenny Steel would never have been
able to accumulate the wealth that he now had.

Dressing in nothing more than a silk robe he descended the stairs and made his way into the kitchen. Alcohol, glasses and a few nibbles had been neatly arranged on the granite work surface by Mrs Brooks. She was the only person Kenny trusted totally to come and go freely, at least where his house was concerned. Lilly Brooks had looked after the place since the day he had collected the keys. Her son Joey had been good friends with Kenny Steel and up until his death they had both been determined to serve and protect their country. It was during the Gulf war that her son had died and afterwards Kenny had visited her and made sure she was alright financially. Now his full time housekeeper, she cared for the property and would one day each week get everything ready for his party. Lilly Brooks wasn't naive but as far as Kenny was concerned, well in her eyes he could do no wrong. She wasn't interested in what went on but would have to admit that when she came in on a Monday morning to clean up even she was shocked at some of the things lying around and the state the bedroom was left in. At nine pm the buzzer sounded and Kenny pressed the entry button. Tommy Bex emerged from behind the blacked out windows of a people carrier. Following closely in his footsteps were three young girls who were no more than sixteen or seventeen years old.
"Evening Boss. These do you?"
Kenny grinned. Walking back inside he left the

front door open and they followed him in. The girls hadn't been put under any duress and were, as far as he was concerned, all willing participants. Chrissie Wallace was a regular at Kenny's parties and tonight shed brought along her mate Bev and a girl called Lorraine Morgan that she'd met at her local while waiting for Tommy to collect them. Chrissie had warned Lorraine in advance about what to expect and had also told her and Bev about the handsome payment they would all receive if they did a good job. Tommy led the young women through to the kitchen and poured each one a large measure of vodka. Following their friends lead Bev and Lorraine necked three of the drinks in quick succession before Tommy snatched the bottle away from them.

"Slow down you lot, there'll be time for drink after you've all performed."

Lorraine made a bee line for the nibbles and lifting the bowl to her chin began to shovel handfuls of peanuts into her mouth. Bev and Chrissie knew nothing about the girl, didn't know that she was about to lose her flat as she couldn't make the rent. Six months ago she wouldn't have dreamed of agreeing to something like this but now she was hungry, had no heating and she was in a desperate state. As he watched her Tommy wore a sickly grin which didn't go unnoticed by Lorraine.

"Now get your skinny arses up to the bedroom."

As they entered Kenny stood totally naked at the

back of the room and was staring up at a ninety two inch plasma television that was silently screening a hard core movie. Chrissie knew exactly what to do and the others copied her to the letter. Slowly she removed her clothes and when she was down to her bra and panties lay down on the bed. Her friends were beside her in seconds. The girls began to fondle each other and Chrissie gently parted Bev's legs. Slowly she rubbed her friends mound through the silky fabric of her panties before placing her long fingers inside her moist warm hole. Lorraine suddenly stopped and stared wide eyed. True Chrissie had told her what would happen but deep down she naively thought that they wouldn't have to go through with it. Lorraine slid from the bed and began to gather up her clothes. Walking towards the bedroom door she was stopped from going any further by Tommy Bex.

"You know the score love! Now get back on that bed and do what you're being fucking paid to do. I've spent good money on you lot and the boss wants to see some action."

Chrissie and Bev were now in the deep throes of passion. Neither were lesbians but touching each other so intimately, saw them both orgasm at the same time. Still clutching her clothes Lorraine sat on the edge of the divan and tried to avert her eyes but as her friends groaned and wriggled on the silk bedspread she couldn't help but get aroused.

All the while a naked Kenny Steel stood watching

but said nothing. Chrissie now straddled her friends face and Bev's tongue was duly obliging. Lorraine couldn't take her eyes off of the two women and was now pleasuring herself as she watched Chrissie begin to rock back and forth in ecstasy. When at last all three girls had come Tommy Bex walked over to the wardrobe and removed what Kenny liked to call his box of tricks. Tommy threw the largest dildo that Lorraine Morgan had ever seen onto the bed. It was black, sixteen inches long and three inches wide. Lorraine, who had been reluctant at the beginning started to get scared and suddenly stood up. As far as she was concerned a bit of rug munching though it still turned her stomach, was ok as she was so financially strapped but this thing looked like it could really hurt.

"Look mate I aint into fucking depravity I ..." Lorraine didn't get to finish her words as Tommy's hand flew up and grabbed her by the throat. Thrashing her arms about she tried to scream and Bev and Chrissie were instantly by her side. "Alright Tommy mate, calm down there aint no need for that."

Tommy Bex pushed Chrissie hard in the chest and it was enough to tell her to mind her own business. The girl seemed a nice sort but in this game no one was worth getting a beating for. Confident that he wouldn't get stopped again Tommy turned his attention back to Lorraine.

49

"You'll do as you're fucking told if you know what's good for you. Now hold her down."

Reluctantly the girls both grabbed one of Lorraine's wrists and pulled her down onto the bed. Chrissie winked at Lorraine and whispered in her ear.

"I'm so sorry but just try and be quiet until it's over then we can all get out of here."

Tommy Bex kneeled on the bed and using his knees forcibly parted Lorraine Morgan's legs. Picking up the monster of a dildo he positioned it and as he slowly fed it inside her she let out a piercing scream. Kenny Steel nodded his head then left the room. It was the signal to Tommy that the party was over. Although the sight sometimes turned him on, for Kenny it wasn't a sexual thing but one of pure domination. Except for his mother, sister and Lilly Brooks Kenny disliked all women and loved to see them endure pain. He hadn't always been this way but things had changed at the end of his third year of active service. Standing only a hundred feet away from Joey Brooks when he got blown to bits had damaged Kenny Steel far more than he would ever admit. His platoon had been out on a reconnaissance mission and as they entered a small village Joey was approached by a woman. She was dressed from head to toe in a black burqa. Even though only her eyes were visible, Joey could tell that she was smiling and he reciprocated the gesture. It was the last image Kenny would have of the young man before Joey and the woman were blown to kingdom come. What the soldiers didn't know was the fact that under her dress she was wearing a suicide vest packed with twenty kilos of screws, nails and bolts to cause maximum damage. The choice of explosive to detonate the bomb was acetone peroxide known as Mother of Satan because of its instability. As pieces of Joey Brooks body lay strewn upon the ground Kenny's loyalties changed from his country to himself and he soon began to hate army life. He decided that until he was discharged, instead of giving he would take as much as he could get. Since that day Kenny Steel saw almost every woman in the same light and enjoyed inflicting pain upon them. With the current war in Afghanistan now well under way and with so many soldiers being killed on a weekly basis, Kenny Steels loathing of women had seemed in the last couple of years to have escalated from loathing into a real hatred.

In the bedroom Tommy had removed the sex toy and there was now a heavy amount of blood on the covers. Chrissie was trying to comfort the girl but she wasn't having much success as Lorraine sobbed uncontrollably. The sight didn't make Tommy feel good. Unlike his boss he didn't hate women and hurting young girls for no reason weighed heavily on his conscience. Each week after he had dropped the different women home he'd parked up the car and gone and got completely rat arsed in an attempt to feel better about what he'd taken part in. It never worked but something, possibly the large wedge of cash he was given by his boss still made him return the following week.

The girls were ushered out of the house as quickly as possible. In the back of the people carrier Chrissie handed the other two a hundred pounds each and warned Lorraine Morgan that if she knew what was good for her she wouldn't breathe a word of what had occurred. Chrissie had been given five hundred pounds by Tommy but she reasoned that as she was the most regular girl and the one who always had to procure others, then it was only fair she should have the lions share.

Back at the house Kenny had gone to sleep in the master suit and the mess in the spare room was left for Lilly Brooks to clean up after the weekend. He didn't see it as anything disgusting for a woman of her age to see; after all she was paid handsomely. All in all it hadn't been a bad day and Kenny Steel would now sleep like a baby in readiness for the following day.

The next morning and waking at just after ten Kenny showered and dressed in his army fatigues. After a vigorous workout he would shower again once he reached his mother's house. Due to it being a Sunday morning the journey from Notting Hill over to Canning Town would take just seven minutes. Pulling into Beckton district park Kenny was a little early for his usual training session. There were a couple of blokes milling around but no one he was overly familiar with. Switching on the stereo he tuned into Capital radio and reclined his seat. Beginning to drift off he was startled back to reality by someone tapping on the widow. Jock Denman had been up since the crack of dawn and couldn't wait to meet his prospective boss at the park. Although he knew of the boot camps reputation he wasn't overly worried. His time inside had mostly been spent in the gym and he was, as far as he was concerned, at the peak of physical fitness.

Kenny Steel stretched out his arms and rolled his shoulders in both directions before getting out of the Range Rover.

"Morning Mr Steel, I'm right looking forward to this."

Kenny could only laugh. By his estimation Jock was no more than twenty four or five and his willingness to please was comical. Soon several cars pulled up and a selection of people from all walks of life now stood ready to participate. Most were just your average punters who were happy to pay a tenner on a Sunday morning in the hope of getting fit but who in reality were never going to achieve anything near their dream goal. They all knew Kenny Steel was the exception; they were also aware of who he was and although they smiled and nodded their recognition, kept as far from the man as was possible. When a clapped out Astra van pulled into the car park everyone knew it was time to begin. Jake Barsham had started up the camp a couple of years earlier and he was proud of his achievement even though its success had been limited. Jake liked to make out he was fit but no one ever actually saw him participate in any way. Short and slightly portly he had an enormous bubble bum that on first meeting him had everyone mesmerised. With the grin of a Cheshire cat he falsely greeted his clients while holding out his hand for the ten pound note that they all, except for Kenny Steel, had to produce.

"Right guys let's get started. Up that hill as fast as you can then I want twenty push ups followed by twenty squat thrusts. Come on now what are you all waiting for!"

Kenny was the first to begin and had completed the task before the others had reached half way. Jock was a close second but as the session progressed even he began to lag behind. It was no less than Kenny expected, in fact the lad had done far better than he'd imagined and would be taken on by the firm at the end of the workout. One hour later when everyone was panting for breath, all except Kenny Steel that was, the session was complete. Jake Barsham was a hundred pounds better off and his clients all felt as though they were on their last legs. Kenny was about to get into the Range Rover when Jock approached him.

"So Mr Steel how did I do?"

"Good enough. Drop by the office tomorrow and

we can begin your training."

"Thanks Mr Steel."

Kenny again smiled but didn't speak; instead he climbed into his car and drove the short distance home, eagerly anticipating the marvellous roast that he knew his mother would be preparing.

CHAPTER SIX

Vic Steel placed the rubbish into the wheelie bin and for a second gazed out into Rutland Road. His Jack Russell Nibby who had been lovingly named by little Vic was sniffing round a pile of dog shit that no one had bothered to clean up and he angrily shouted for the dog to get away.

"Nibby! Nibby! Get the fuck out of it you dirty little cunt."

The dog ignored Vic and it wasn't until his toe made contact with Nibby's arse that it finally obeyed his command. This wasn't how he had envisaged living his life and he could feel the frustration begin to build up inside. He didn't realise how hard the palm of his hand was pressing down on the lid of the bin and suddenly he heard a cracking sound. The plastic was nipping his skin and when he released his hand a purple welt had begun to form in the centre. He was still rubbing at his hand when the kitchen window of his maisonette opened and Deidre poked her head out.

"Are you going to stand there all bleeding day dreaming or are you going to come and get little Vic ready?"

Deidre Steel was a complete nag of a wife. Vic knew that except for Kenny she hated his entire family and only had anything to do with the other members so that she could keep her comfortable lifestyle. Now with a family lunch on the horizon

Vic was dreading the day before it had even got started. He looked upwards and the window was now firmly closed but he knew that if he didn't go inside immediately then she would once more start shouting like a fishwife. Rutland Road was very run down. On a scale of one to ten of the most deprived areas in Canning Town it had to be number two, at least as far as Vic was concerned. For the first few years of his marriage he'd worked the night shift down at the Evening Standard. The pay was good and Vic felt a sense of freedom driving around the city in the early hours of the morning. An added bonus was that he didn't have to see that much of his wife which suited him down to the ground. Then out of the blue Deidre had begun to moan that they weren't earning enough money but she still sat on her arse all day drinking coffee with her mother. When Vic couldn't take the constant ear bashing any longer he had set out to find a better job but at that time there wasn't much about. It had been his wife's idea that he should try and join Kenny at Steel Security but at first Vic had been reluctant. Accepting that he wouldn't get any peace until he gave her what she wanted, he approached his brother who had been only too glad to help. The business was relatively new on the scene and the brothers worked hard to build it up. Within six months his wages were three times more than he had been earning at the Standard and Vic Steel now wanted to move house but Deidre wouldn't hear of it. Born in the East End she didn't want to be very far away from her mother and sister. When the three of them got together he didn't stand a chance and had pretty quickly given up on the idea. Suddenly the window flew open again and this time it was clear for all to see that Deidre's face was red with rage. She didn't care that the neighbours could hear every word, didn't care what they thought of her and it embarrassed Vic deeply.

"If you don't get up these fucking stairs now and sort this little bastard out you can forget about going to your mothers!"

Vic sighed out loud but dutifully did as he was told. He was just grateful that Kenny wasn't here because Vic knew that he wouldn't have had to worry about giving her a slap, Kenny would have done it for him. Nibby came charging up the stairs and disappeared down the hall just as Vic made it onto the landing. The maisonette had a decent sized living room and kitchen with two bedrooms on the second floor. It was furnished with the best that money could buy but Deidre Steel wasn't particularly house-proud. As Vic liked to put it, she wasn't well acquainted with the vacuum cleaner and her husband would be forced to use it once a week just to keep the place half decent. It had been over two years since Sandra Steel had set foot in her son's home. She couldn't stand the mess and sometimes just the sight of her daughter-in-law made her skin crawl. To begin with it had hurt Vic deeply but he had never made an issue of it. Instead he resigned himself to the fact that it was best to just visit his mother's home and save a full scale row between Deidre and Sandra. His wife had a spiteful tongue and she would only end up saying something that could never be forgiven.

"About bleeding time!"

"Where's little Vic?"

"Still in his room. He aint even washed and changed yet the lazy little sod. Tell him from me, if he's got that fucking dog on the bed again I'm going to kick its arse out of this house for good."

Deidre sat at the kitchen table with a fag in one hand and a glass of wine in the other. After taking a drag of her cigarette and then a sip of wine she picked up her pen and began to fill out the Suns crossword. For once at least, she had managed to get dressed and out of the pyjamas that she usually spent all day in.

"What time does the old cow want us there?"

Vic clenched his hands and stopped the urge to strangle her right there and then in his own kitchen. Deidre was nothing but mouth and he knew she would be all sweetness and light when they got there, she wouldn't dare be anything else.

"Dinners at two. I'll come back and pick you up when I've been for a pint."

"Oh that's right you bugger off and leave me to look after his nibs."

59

Vic Steel ignored her and climbing the next set of stairs entered his son's room. Little Vic was just five years old and the apple of his father's eye. He had recently started infant school in the reception class and by all accounts was doing really well even though it was only five mornings a week. A bright boy, he loved mixing with other kids and couldn't wait to start full time in September. His eagerness was no surprise to his father, not after he'd been forced to spend day after day with his poor excuse for a mother.

"Hello Son what you up to?"

Little Vic was lying on the bed and he gave the warmest smile to his father. The small scruffy Jack Russell that was now nestled by his side looked up as his young master spoke.

"Just reading me book to Nibby dad."

"That's pukka boy. Are you going to take it for your Nan to see? Maybe read her a bit you know she likes a good story."

Little Vic was off the bed in seconds. He loved his Nan and the idea that she would be proud had him chaffing at the bit to get round to Boreham Avenue. The sight made his father smile.

"Hold your horses we aint going yet. Now I'm just going to pop out for a pint then I'll come back and collect you and mum."

The mention of his mother's name instantly wiped the smile from little Vic's face. It shouldn't be possible for a child so young to hate anyone but at

this early age the boy already loathed his mother.
Vic laid out some smart trousers and a crisp white
shirt onto the bed.

"Now while I'm gone I want you to have a wash and
I mean a wash, not just a lick and a polish like you
normally do. You know how much Nan likes to see
you clean and tidy. Can you do that for me Son?"
Little Vic nodded his head.

"Good boy, now I'll see you in a bit."

Vic left the room ginning. He knew his last request
regarding having a wash would do the trick as his
boy would move heaven and earth to please his
Nan.

After a swift pint down at the Durham Arms Vic
Steel was back home by one thirty. He'd told
Deidre to be ready by twenty past but knew she
wouldn't be. Beeping the car horn it was another
five minutes before his wife and son emerged. Even
from the car he could see that Deidre's face was full
of hell and he shook his head. She had hold of little
Vic's hand far too tightly and was almost dragging
him along. Normally Vic would have given her a
mouthful but today he held his tongue in the hope
of calming her before they arrived. As she got into
the car he handed her a box of chocolates that he'd
picked up at the local garage on his way back.

"Thanks a fucking bunch! As if I aint fat enough
already. I suppose you just want me to look like a
bloater and be a laughing stock in front of your
family."

"No Dee I just thought it would be a nice gesture that's all. You could always give them to me mum which would also be nice. Now can we get going before we're late?"

"You've got to be bleeding joking aint you; I'd rather throw them in the bastard bin!"

Little Vic sat silently in the back. He had learnt early on that silence was the best policy when his mother was in one of her moods. Sometimes he wished that he and his dad could go and live with his Nan but he supposed that would never happen. The drive over to Boreham Avenue was taken in silence and when Vic parked up and turned off the engine Deidre couldn't just get out of the car she had to say something.

"Here we bleeding go!"

Vic looked over his shoulder towards his son and at just five years old the boy already knew the score. He gave his father a feeble grin that spoke volumes. Sandra was busy in the kitchen as they walked in but instantly stopped what she was doing and picked up her grandson. She gave him several wet kisses and he wrinkled up his face in protest but secretly he loved the attention. Deidre hated having to be here and hated her mother-in-laws company even more. Walking through to the front room she flopped down into one of the ornate armchairs and turned towards her sister-in-law.

"What you watching Shell?"

Michelle had been warned in advance to be pleasant

towards Deidre. Normally she wouldn't give the woman the time of day but she was already in her mother's bad books. Reluctantly she had agreed to a truce just to get her mother off her back and possibly make Sandra drop the constant remarks regarding last night's lateness.

"A rerun of Towie."

"Not that fucking rubbish. You'd have to be as thick as two sort planks to not realise that it's all put on."

Michelle could feel her hackles start to rise and was just about to give Deidre a mouthful when the front door opened and Kenny walked in. Deidre was out of her chair in seconds. Walking over to him she planted a lingering kiss on Kenny's lips as she pushed her body close to his and held him tightly.

"Hello there, nice to see you."

"Kenny Steel patted her on the shoulder but slightly pushed her out of the way as he did so. Sitting down next to his sister he took her hand in his.

"So what you been up to darling?"

Deidre was enraged and rather than watch the sickening act going on right in front of her eyes she flounced in the direction of the kitchen to see what aggro she could cause there.

"Not a lot really. Oh me and Jules did go over to The Sugar Hut last night."

"Any good?"

"It was ok but they said some of the Towie lot were going to be there but they weren't and I couldn't get into the VIP area."

Kenny Steel placed an arm around his sister's shoulder and pulled her close.

"Never mind darling better luck next time and leave it with me regarding the VIPs and I'll see what I can do."

Sandra Steel was in the middle of dishing up the dinner when she started to get one of her hot flushes but Deidre just leant against the doorframe and didn't offer to help. Big Vic and little Vic were setting out the placemats and cutlery and the sight pissed Deidre off big time.

"I'm going out for a fag."

Although dinner was only a couple of minutes from being ready Sandra didn't inform her daughter-in-law of that fact. As far as she was concerned if the lazy cow couldn't help out, then it was her fault if she came back to a cold meal. Sandra called Kenny and asked if he'd go upstairs and get Charlie out of his bed. The task was done in seconds as Kenny walked straight
into his brothers room and stripped the bed bare. A naked Charlie steel was instantly awake and clambering to cover himself.

"I want you down them fucking stairs and sitting at that table in a minute. God help you if I have to come back up here. The old lady's spent hours doing your dinner and you can't even be bothered to get out of your pit."

Kenny slammed the door as he went and Charlie knew he would be in big trouble if he ignored his brother. Five minutes later and they were all, including Deidre, seated at the table. Sandra had put on a fabulous feast, there were four different kinds of vegetables roast and mashed potatoes and it was all topped off with a whole leg of lamb.

"Kenny will you carve Son?"

Kenny Steel sat at the head of the table and taking the carving knife and fork in his hand stood up.

"I most certainly will and I have to say mum you really know how to put on a blinding spread."

Seconds later and they were all helping themselves to the serving dishes as Kenny handed round the meat. Sandra was busy chatting to little Vic and making sure he had a healthy serving of vegetables. Deidre wasn't speaking to anyone and Vic made small talk with Charlie. Just as she'd hoped Michelle now had Kenny's undivided attention.

"Kenny."

"What babe?"

"Me and Jules are thinking about getting some Botox and maybe having our tongues pierced as well. What do you think?"

She knew he wouldn't be pleased but when he slammed his knife and fork down and everyone stopped talking to see what the problem was, even Michelle was surprised."

"Over my fucking dead body! You will not do anything to yourself do you hear me?"

Sandra Steel didn't know what her daughter had said but she hadn't seen her son this angry in a long time.

"Come on you two, pack it in!"

"I aint being rude Mum but can you butt out of this."

Kenny grabbed Michelle's hand and he wasn't gentle. She winced and he immediately let go.

"Promise me?"

Michelle Steels devious little plan was coming together exactly as she had hoped.

"Ok I promise. It was either Botox or a week in Marbella and I suppose you're going to say no to that as well!"

Kenny took a moment to think. He didn't like the idea of her being away from him but he could relent on a week in Spain if it meant she wouldn't touch her beautiful face.

"Just a week though!"

Michelle was out of her seat in a second and as she wrapped her arms around her brother's neck, she kissed him on the cheek. Sandra smiled; all was well again with her brood.

"Now can we please just eat our dinner you lot?"

"I aint that hungry mum and besides I've got to phone Jules and tell her the news."

As she watched her sister-in-law disappear into the hall Deidre could feel her blood begin to boil and this time she didn't hold back her anger.

"Fuck me you don't have to do a bleeding lot in this house to get a free holiday or do you?"

Everyone knew what the insinuation was referring

to but unusually it was Vic who spoke.
"For once, why don't you shut your nasty fucking
trap? Now get your coat were going. Mum can
little Vic stay with you and I'll pick him up later?"
Vic didn't wait for his mother to answer and
grabbing his wife by the wrist almost dragged her
from the room and frogmarched her out to the car.
No one at the table thought anything of the rumpus
that had just occurred it was normal for at least one
fall out during a family dinner. Charlie who was in
the mood to shit stir, turned towards his older
brother.
"Here Kenny! I had a bit of a face to face with
Romford Ronnie last night. The bastard was
running off at the mouth about money and
switching firms."
If Charlie Steel thought his brother would blow up
he was sorely disappointed. Today was for family
and he was enjoying his sisters company
too much to worry about business.
"Leave it out will you. You know I don't talk
fucking shop when I'm at home, now eat your grub
and shut the fuck up."
Outside Vic opened the passenger door and threw
Deidre inside. As she landed on the seat he
slammed the door which banged heavily on to her
arm and she screamed out in pain. Vic Steel took no
notice and after driving home at well over the speed
limit he again marched her into the house. With the
front door closed he proceeded to rein down blow

after blow on his wife. It had been a long time coming and all the pent up anger that he had held deep within for years showed itself with every punch. Deidre was now a bloody mess and whimpered as she cowered in the corner. The sight of his wife brought about no remorse and he made his way upstairs to the kitchen. Pouring a large measure of whisky Vic Steel downed it in one. He felt the emotions of shame and pride both at the same time. Hitting a woman was something he'd never done before nor wanted to do again but for once he had stood up for himself. Strangely the emotions made him feel liberated and he liked it. As far as he was concerned things were about to change, at least in this Steel household. It would all start tomorrow when he would, with great pleasure, forcibly expel his mother in law.

CHAPTER SEVEN

Kenny had stayed home on Sunday evening and after little Vic had been collected all was now calm in the house. Charlie had left for a night out and when his mother had gone up to bed Kenny joined his sister in the front room to watch a film. Michelle liked to watch daft movies but it didn't bother him. Even when the closing credits had rolled he wouldn't have been able to tell anyone what the film was about, as unbeknown to her he'd spent most of the evening staring at his sister. Kenny loved it when she giggled and the way her hair would fall onto her face, god he wanted her and it took all of his strength to stop himself laying down on the floor beside her.

Now in the cold light of day he felt a little calmer but as Sandra prepared his breakfast his eyes never left the kitchen door in the hope that Michelle would make an appearance.

"Got a busy day Son?"

Kenny Steel rubbed at the back of his neck. It wasn't yet nine and already he could feel the tension beginning to build up.

"A bit I suppose. I've got to go and see Bethnal Green Barry today and I aint looking forward to it I can tell you."

"Oh I heard about that from Mavis Lambert when I was down the market. She said he got a fifteen stretch, is that right?"

69

"Yeh and they reckon hell end up doing the lot but then again you know Barry!"

"I do indeed, nasty little bastard or he was when he was a kid. He always had two green candles of snot hanging down on his lip. Mind you his old lady weren't much better."

"Mum!"

"What! I aint saying nothing that aint true.

Maureen Abbott was about as dirty as you could get and I don't just mean in the cleanliness department. The whole of Canning Town knew what she was up to. I suppose poor old Barry never stood a chance. Anyway where are they holding him?"

"Pentonville."

"Oh nasty. Here Kenny if you're going over to north London stop off at Chapel Street market and get some of that stinky cheese I like. Silvio runs a stall about halfway down the first aisle. You can't miss it on account of the fucking smell but he don't half stock some nice cheese. Now let me think what it was called again, Rockingham or was it Rockington something."

"You mean Roquefort."

"That's the one."

"I'll see what I can do but only if I get time."

Sandra Steel smiled at her son. He always said he'd see what he could do but to date he had never let her down. In fact Sandra knew he would move heaven and earth to get her whatever she asked for.

"Anyway what did Barry really get done for? Only

there's been all sorts of rumours flying round Canning Town. He's been everything from a big time drug dealer to a kiddie fiddler."

"Fucking kiddie fiddler! The bastards, I tell you mum it never ceases to fucking amaze me what people will make up. For the record it was smuggling but there weren't even any drugs involved. He got mixed up with some Chinese geezers who were smuggling of all things fucking Rhino horn."

Sandra Steel began to laugh; she laughed so hard that her eyes began to water and she could feel the onset of pee as it started to escape.

"Bleeding Rhino horn? Well I aint never heard nothing like it. Why the hell would he get caught up with a load of chinks and dodgy animals from Africa?"

"These people know what they're doing mum. Barry thought he could make a few grand and he could have if the daft twat hadn't been caught by the Old Bill walking down Whitechapel high Street with a whole horn under his arm!"

Sandra began to laugh again and she knew it wouldn't take much more before she would have to change her knickers.

"I'm sorry son but I can just picture the great lump. I bet he won't be getting the fucking horn for a long time to come."

"Mum!"

"Oh come on Kenny even you've got to see the

funny side."

Kenny had to admit that she was right and he couldn't for the life of him understand why Bethnal Green Barry had taken that route. The man had always been a successful supplier of party drugs but Kenny supposed he'd got greedy like so many before him.

"Still I do think a fifteen stretch is a bit bleeding harsh Kenny."

"Well if the silly sod hadn't hit the copper over the head with it then maybe he'd have got less. Old plod got concussion and they ended up doing Barry for attempted murder. Never thought it would stick myself but there you go, the CPS ended up getting a conviction and poor old Barry's looking at four small walls for the foreseeable. Anyway mum Id better be going. I'll call in later today with your cheese."

With that her son disappeared from the kitchen and once again Sandra Steel started to laugh at the absurd story shed just heard. In fact she laughed so hard that she finally did wet herself as she pictured Barry hitting the copper on the head with a huge horn.

After Kenny turned onto Aspen Road it was a straightforward journey. He was dreading going to the prison but he was enjoying the bright sunshine and he realised that his impending visit was probably the reason he was appreciating the weather. Poor old Barry wouldn't get much chance to see a clear blue sky, not for the next fifteen years at least. For a Monday the traffic was relatively light and after stopping off to collect his mother's cheese he arrived in just under twenty five minutes. Pulling into the car park Kenny looked up at the huge arched gates and a shiver ran through his body. Even in the army he'd never seen the inside of the glasshouse and he couldn't begin to imagine how Barry was feeling. The visitors centre was situated at the front and reluctantly he entered. Wives and off springs were milling about and the incessant screaming by the kids instantly pissed him off. After registering he took a seat and waited to be called through. Kenny didn't look anyone in the face; the last thing he wanted was to be recognised or for someone to try and strike up a conversation. His visit had been booked for ten forty five and exactly ten minutes before his appointment his name was called. Entering through the arched Victorian gate a shiver again ran down Kenny Steels spine. He was searched, asked for identification and then ushered through just like the rest of the bodies who were on their weekly visits. With the security checks finally over he was then led through to the visiting room. Kenny purchased two teas and a Kit Kat from the canteen and then took a seat at one of the tables. It was only a couple of minutes later when the prisoners were at last filtered into the room. Barry Abbott was second from the front and when he saw Kenny he beamed from ear to ear.

It wasn't the first bird Bethnal Green Barry had been faced with prison but it would certainly be the longest. Tall and lean he had a gormless look about him and no one would ever guess that he had a fantastic brain for business. The only trouble was, he didn't stick to what he was good at and was always looking out for a new scam hence the reason he was now being visited by Kenny Steel. Taking a seat at the table he reached out and shook his old friend's hand.

"Nice to see you Ken. What a fucking mess I've got myself into this time!"

"You're going to have to get your head round it and soon pal, that or you'll go off your nut. Here I got you a cuppa and some chocolate."

"Thanks Kenny. Now down to business, because I know you aint here to catch up on old times or to enquire after me health."

"Well the problem is since your incarceration I aint got a regular supplier. Now I could source someone new but you know me Barry, it's all about trust and some of them fucking little toe rags would grass me up as soon as look at me. Besides I'm thinking about branching out, on a bit bigger scale so to speak."

"And where do I come in all of this?"

"Well I was hoping you'd put me in touch with your contact. I mean it aint as if you've got any need for him now. There'll be a nice little earner in it for you of course."

Barry Abbot took a moment to think it over but even he had to admit that a few grand for when he eventually got out was better than a contact he couldn't use for god knew how long.

"I see where you're coming from Kenny. Ok what shall we say ten grand?"

Kenny laughed.

"You'll get five and fucking like it you slag."

"Can't blame a bloke for trying can you?"

Both men heartily laughed. Suddenly Barry's smile disappeared from his face as quickly as it had formed.

"Right go get a pencil and a bit of paper from one of the screws. If you ask nicely they'll lend you one but will watch you like a fucking hawk in case you try and do anyone any damage."

Kenny did as he was told and a few seconds later was seated back at the table.

"Write this down and be quick his names Joginder Choudhary."

"Who?"

Barry took the pencil from his friend and from memory quickly scribbled down a phone number before the guards came over and took the pencil away from him.

"You'll need to go to Delhi though and don't phone him until you get there. That's about all I can tell you."

"Fuck me it aint much is it."

"Don't need to be. If you phone as soon as you

land I can guarantee you will be meeting him within an hour but watch him Kenny, he's a slippery bastard."

"What, you mean hell try and con me?"

"Well no not exactly. In fact I can honestly say that in all the years I've been dealing with him he's never tried that on. I mean watch him on the price you shouldn't be paying anymore than a hundred and twenty five a kilo but the greedy little fucker will try and get three hundred out of you, maybe more."

"Fuck me Barry that's peanuts."

"That aint the point Ken. If you're going to buy a couple of kilos he will be eager to sell so just walk away if he ups the price and believe me he will!"

"So what should I be making out of it, remember I've only ever bought the tabs from you."

"Come and see me again when you get back and I'll sort you out with a contact who'll turn it into tabs for you but you should be talking about five hundred K."

Kenny Steel sat with his mouth wide open, he couldn't believe the figure he'd just been told.

"Did I hear you right?"

Barry laughed. He usually sold to Kenny for a fiver a tab. Kenny then moved them in the clubs for about twelve fifty each.

"You did. Look I don't usually buy any more than a quarter of a kilo but if you are going to do it you might as well go large. Make sure when its cut that they don't do it with anything nasty and be there when it's done because again the greedy bastards will mug you off if they get a chance but that's a bit down the line from here. You need to get the stuff here first."

Before there was time for anymore conversation the bell went signalling the end of the visit. As Kenny neared the door he heard Barry call out Watch your back mate, oh and thanks for the chat and the Kit Kat. Kenny could only shake his head and laugh as even now, after receiving a stretch that would finish a lot of men Bethnal Green Barry was still beaming from ear to ear.

In the car park Kenny took a moment to digest what he had just been told. He knew Barry made a good mark up and he made even more selling them on in the clubs but the realisation that he was now going to make vast sums of money was unbelievable. Even back in his army days when Kenny had been importing heroin it had taken him a few years to amass the amount of money that he could now earn with just a few trips to India. Bringing his mind back to reality he realised that he had to find a way of getting the Ketamine into the country and that would take some planning. There was always a snag and this snag was just bigger than usual. Deciding to deal with one thing at a time he drove over to Golders Green. Joosef Metzer ran a small independent travel agency on Woodstock Road. The man had a knack of being able to get flights to anywhere in the world on short notice and with no questions asked. He wasn't always the cheapest but Kenny didn't fancy sitting in one of the large travel agents and having all and sundry know his business. Joosef was stereotypical of most people's idea of a Jew. He always had his hands clasped together and he slightly bowed his head as he spoke. Kenny Steel liked the old man as he never pried into your business and always went the extra mile to help.

"Good day Mr Steel. It's been a long time since you last visited my shop."

"It sure has Joosef."

"And how can I help you today?"

Kenny took a seat on the sofa that sat in front of the window. There was no counter or formal chairs, just an old desk with a laptop and printer.

"I need a flight out to Delhi either tonight or sometime tomorrow at the latest."

As Kenny spoke Joosef smiled and sagely nodded his head.

"Give me a moment to see what I can do for you Mr Steel. Is it a return you are after?"

Kenny nodded his head as the old man took a seat at the desk and began to tap away on his computer. Suddenly the printer burst into life and a few seconds later Joosef Metzer walked over to Kenny clutching a piece of paper.

"This is a flight leaving Heathrow tomorrow at three. That will be five hundred and fifty pounds."

Kenny knew he was being slightly stitched up and

that the little Jew had probably added an extra ton on for himself but removing a wad of notes he paid for the e ticket and thanked the old man.

"Nice doing business with you again Mr Steel." Kenny waved a hand as he left the shop. Deciding to call it a day he headed home to pack a small bag. Working out that he had to be at the airport by just after noon the following day, he decided that he would make his weekly journey over to Vic's on the way. Deidre needed to be taught a lesson for her rudeness and insinuations yesterday. Getting rid of Vic wouldn't be a problem; Kenny would just send him over to sort out Romford Ronnie. All in all it had been a good day and with any luck tomorrow would be even better.

CHAPTER EIGHT

Kenny Steel had been awake for over an hour and was now sitting at the kitchen table when his mother came in. Knowing he wasn't one to lay about in bed she wasn't surprised to see her eldest up so early but he didn't normally get up before her. "Morning son, couldn't you sleep?"

"I slept fine mum but I've got a lot on and need to make an early start. Now I'm going to be out of the country for a couple of days so I'm leaving Vic in charge."

Alarm bells began to sound for Sandra and for a moment she studied her son. He didn't look worried about anything; maybe he was just tired and wanted to get away for a while. Sandra Steel decided not to pry too much further. If Kenny felt the need to tell her anything then she was sure he would do so in his own good time.

"Where you going to son, anywhere nice?"

"India."

"Bleeding India! Well just you take care and don't go getting mugged. What time you off?"

Kenny laughed at his mother's words; she thought everyone was out to mug you especially foreigners. "About ten."

"Then you'll need a good breakfast inside you. Cant travel on an empty stomach it'll make you throw up."

Kenny smiled and as his mother removed the frying

80

pan and began to prepare one of her gut buster fry ups he lifted the phone and called his brother. Vic had just dressed his son, was in the middle of tipping cereal into a bowl and trying without much success to stop little Vic pouring out his own milk when his mobile rang. As he answered the phone with one hand, he removed the carton from his son with the other hand before passing the dish to little Vic. His tone sounded stressed as he spoke.

"Yeh."

"Vic its Kenny, you alright?"

"Just the pains of being a dad, anyway what can I do for you?"

"I aint going to be around for a couple of days so keep an eye on things will you? I told Romford Ronnie you'd meet him at the club about ten today."

"Ok mate, I'll shoot off as soon as I've dropped the boy off at school. Where are you going anyway?"

"Just a bit of business I've got to sort out. Now if Ronnie kicks off just tell him anything to keep him sweet and I'll sort the rest out when I get back."

With that Kenny hung up. Continuing to make small talk with his mother he was surprised when the kitchen door opened and Michelle entered. She was washed and smartly dressed in her college tunic. Kenny thought she looked stunning.

"Morning sweetheart, you look nice. I've got to go out in a bit, do you want a lift?"

"Nah thanks. I'm going to walk round to Jules and then we'll get the bus. We've got lots to talk about;

81

going to Marbella takes a lot of planning you know. If we bump into the Towie lot I want to look me best."

"Babe you always look good."

Michelle didn't reply or bat an eye lid at the comment from her brother; she was so used to receiving them that it went straight over her head. Sandra placed a large plate in front of her son. Sausages, bacon, two eggs, a fried slice and beans filled the surface; in fact it was so full that you could hardly see any white of the plate.

"Gawd help me mum, you don't expect me to eat all this. Here Shell give us a hand will you."

Michelle Steel felt sick just looking at the greasy mess.

"Not a hope. That lots full of calories not to mention the fact that it's a cardiac waiting to happen."

Bending down she kissed her brother on the cheek before disappearing from the room. Kenny Steel did his best to finish the breakfast but even he couldn't consume that much food.

"Thanks Mum that was blinding nosh."

Placing his plate in the sink he kissed his mother, collected his holdall and made his way to the car. It was only a short drive and as he turned into Rutland Road he surveyed the parking spaces just to make sure that his brother's car wasn't there. Kenny Glanced at his watch and knew that Vic would now be long gone. He'd made sure the schedule was tight so that his brother had no time to

return for anything. The paintwork on the front
door was peeling and Kenny knew that inside
wasn't much better. His brother did his best but the
poor sod must be knackered what with work and
everything. He placed a key Deidre had given him
into the lock and climbed the stairs. The smell of
cigarettes was strong and the handrail was sticky
with grease which made Kenny grimace. Walking
into the kitchen he saw Deidre standing at the sink
wearing a worn out dirty dressing gown. When she
turned and saw who it was she beamed from ear to
ear. Kenny Steel had been calling at his sister-in-
laws since shortly after she had married his brother.
He didn't like her or find her attractive; in fact she
actually repulsed him. For Kenny it was a
dominance thing and he liked nothing more than to
treat women as whores. Since leaving the army his
libido had been low and he wasn't interested in
having sex with a woman, not unless he ever got the
chance to sleep with Michelle but Kenny accepted
that scenario wouldn't and couldn't ever be allowed
to happen. Deidre's facial bruising was clearly
evident but he didn't ask how it had happened.
Kenny actually liked the look and thought that for
once his brother might have grown a set of balls
where his wife was concerned. Deidre didn't speak
and walking over to where he stood she dropped to
her knees. Releasing his penis she set to work on
him. Deidre knew he used her but his one visit a
week kept hope alive in her heart that one day he

83

would be hers. As she took his penis in her mouth Kenny violently grabbed a handful of her hair. He pulled so hard that she whimpered in pain. After yesterdays outburst she was going to pay and with every thrust into her mouth he pulled harder and harder on her hair. When he had at last ejaculated Deidre looked up into his face and her eyes were full of tears. She knew why he had done it and she accepted her punishment without question. Kenny zipped up his trousers and was about to leave the maisonette when she spoke.

"I suppose that's it then until next week?"

Kenny didn't reply and only gave her a look of disgust.

"Is this all its ever going to be, me just giving you a blow job once a week?"

Still he didn't answer and could only turn up his face as if there was a bad smell in the room.

Walking down the stairs Kenny could hear his sister-in-law begin to sob but the sound made no impact on him whatsoever.

The drive over to Heathrow took three quarters of an hour. In that time Kenny mulled over many thoughts in his head but not one of them were about Deidre Steel. After parking up and making his way to terminal five, Kenny was booked in and free of his luggage by noon. He wandered about as he waited for his flight to get underway and spent quite a while in duty free as he selected a couple of bottles of perfume for Michelle. Finally the call was announced that flight AF1089 was about to board. Kenny wasn't looking forward to the eight and a half hours of being in a confined space but the end reward was going to be so great that he would have readily endured much longer. Time passed slowly and every half an hour he glanced at his watch willing his journey to be over. When the seat belt light finally flashed on he looked out of the window and by the mass of twinkling lights over the city, could tell how vast it was. He hoped Barry had written down the correct telephone number because if he hadn't it would be like looking for a needle in a haystack. Touching down in Delhi it was now four am local time and he was tired and uptight. Thankfully his bag came through quickly but as he exited the airport Kenny was at a bit of a loss as to where to go. He didn't have a place to stay and so jumping into the first colourful auto-rickshaw he came across, he asked to be taken to a decent hotel. The drivers English was surprisingly good as he replied.

"Jolly good Sir."

Entering the city Kenny was amazed at the noise and traffic even at this hour. Car upon car filled the roads and they were not the sort he was used to seeing. Old Morris Oxfords, Minors and the likes jostled with newer makes and car horns were sounding constantly. The smell of spice was overpowering and there seemed nothing clean about the air. It took about ten minutes to reach the destination and from the outside the Royal Plaza hotel looked grand. It wasn't as opulent on the inside but much to Kenny's pleasure it was clean. His small room overlooked the garden area and was quiet, a blessing in this vastly overpopulated city. Remembering Barry's words he was about to telephone Joginder Choudhary when he thought better of it. If the bloke wanted to meet within the hour then Kenny knew it would end up being a whole day without any sleep. Deciding that he had to get at least a couple of hours shut eye he climbed into bed.

Someone banging on the door at nine the following morning woke Kenny but he ignored it. Surprisingly after only three and a half hours rest he felt refreshed. Before washing he scrolled down his phone and selected Joginder's number. The men arranged to meet at Connaught Place at ten thirty. Unexpectedly the hotel laid on a lavish breakfast which Kenny ravenously consumed as he hadn't eaten since the food at his mother's some twenty hours earlier. Exiting the Plaza he once more jumped into a rickshaw but this time the drivers English wasn't so good and it took several minutes for Kenny to make the man understand where it was he wanted to go. The rickshaws engine spluttered into life and for the entire journey Kenny was either coughing or feeling he was about to regurgitate his breakfast as the diesel fumes from the exhaust seemed to fill the whole back seat. As

the rickshaw came to a halt Kenny was surprised to see that the area was a business district. He had agreed to meet Joginder outside the Regency cinema but he didn't have a clue what the man looked like. He needn't have worried as Kenny stood out like a sore thumb and a few seconds later he was approached by a middle aged portly man.
"Mr Steel?"
Kenny looked the man up and down and eyed him suspiciously. Barry hadn't given him a description and he was constantly on his guard about being set up. His mother's last words regarding being mugged sprang into his mind and he wanted to laugh but did his best not to show it.
"Please Mr Steel do not look so worried."
The man spoke perfect English with just the slightest hint of an Indian accent. Joginder Choudhary held out his hand and Kenny shook it. Pointing towards a relatively new Volkswagen the two men crossed the road and got inside. Joginder drove to the east side of Delhi arriving in a suburb known as Preet Vihar. The car stopped at a dilapidated building that instantly had Kenny on his guard again. Joginder opened the padlock on a corrugated tin door. Kenny was shocked at the sight that greeted him on the inside. The walls and floor were covered in high gloss white ceramic tiles. Several tables were dotted about and each had four women sitting at them dressed in clinical clothing. The workforce were all busy with different tasks

and didn't look up. Some were counting pills, others were weighing out powders and Kenny guessed that it was cocaine.

"Please follow me Mr Steel."

Joginder walked towards a small office at the rear of the building and sat down behind one of two desks that almost filled the room.

"Please take a seat. Now how can I help you?"

"Well as I explained on the phone, Barry Abbott aint going to be around for a long while and he's happy for me to take over, though it will be on a much larger scale so can you cope with that?"

Joginder Choudhary laughed.

"Mr Steel this may appear to be a back street operation but it is anything but. I was educated at Cambridge and have built this business up, with the help of my uncle's money of course. It now has an annual turnover in excess of ten million dollars. We smuggle and I reluctantly use the word smuggle, drugs to all corners of the world. Some of our clients place big orders and some like your friend Barry's are relatively small. But as they say in your country business is business. Now what exactly are you after and what quantities are you wishing to purchase?"

Kenny was amazed at the scale and magnitude of the man's company but he didn't ask any questions.

"Ketamine and that would depend on the price."

Joginder laughed heartily but it was a false sounding laugh that Kenny had heard a hundred times before.

"And the price Mr Steel would depend on the quantity."

"Look let's not beat about the fucking bush. I want two kilos so how much do you want."

Joginder Choudhary puffed out his cheeks in an over exaggerated manner and Kenny knew that if he didn't push things along then this deal would take hours to agree.

"Well Mr Steel you are looking at three hundred dollars a kilo."

Remembering what Barry had told him, Kenny stood up and asked to be taken back to his hotel.

"Mr Steel why the rush we have only just begun our negotiations."

"Look pal, I've got a long flight ahead of me and I aint in the mood for doing a long drawn out deal, not when there's no need. Now you may do things differently in your neck of the woods but I don't barter. We both know what the price is, now you either want to sell to me or you don't. Either way I aint that fussed because I imagine there are plenty more little set ups out there just like this one who would welcome my business."

Joginder again laughed but this time it was genuine.

"It was worth a try Mr Steel and you cannot blame a man for trying. How does two hundred dollars a kilo sound?"

"That sounds about right to me."

It was still more expensive than the hundred and

twenty five Barry had said he should pay but Kenny wasn't about to argue over a few dollars.

"Now I have to arrange collection and I'll need to send you a message regarding a date. If all goes well it should be within the next two weeks."

Kenny was given another telephone number. Joginder explained that it was used solely for texts. The men shook hands on the deal and Kenny was swiftly returned to his hotel. After checking out and heading to the airport he boarded the afternoon flight back to London. The trip had been more than successful but it was a journey Kenny hoped he wouldn't have to be making again. If everything went to plan then any future deals could be carried out via the telephone. While in the forces he had seen enough of the world to last him a lifetime. As far as he was concerned there really was no place on earth that could compare to good old London Town.

CHAPTER NINE

Kenny was seated in the office by eight thirty the following day. He was eager to get the ball rolling and had told Vic and Charlie to be there early. As usual Vic was on time but when they'd been waiting for Charlie to appear for over an hour Kenny started to lose his patience.

"I've just about had a gutful of that little toe rag! He's really taking the fucking piss now Vic."

Zena Cartwright was home for a two day rest period and Charlie, having spent the night with her had overslept. Reaching over to the bedside table he snatched up his Rolex and let out a loud groan when he saw what time it was. Zena was still asleep beside him and he roughly shook her awake.

"Make us a coffee babe I'm running late."

Dutifully Zena hauled herself out of the bed. She was still half asleep but not once did she complain. He was her whole world and whatever Charlie wanted from her he could have without question. By the time she returned to the bedroom he was dressed and ready to go. Charlie Steel took one small swig of the coffee before pecking Zena on the cheek and heading out of the door. His Porsche clocked up a speeding ticket as he tried to make up time but it didn't faze him in the least. Running up the stairs he burst through the door and perspiration stood out on his brow. If he thought his cheeky grin would cut any mustard with his oldest brother he was in for a rude awakening. As soon as Charlie Steel closed the office door he felt the back of Kenny's hand as it made contact with his cheek. The assault was swift and over within seconds but Charlie was left under no illusion that he had well and truly over stepped the mark.

"When I say be here at a certain time, I don't mean two fucking hours later. Now you can either start to fucking knuckle down Charlie or find somewhere else to work. I'm getting sick and tired of people telling me you aint pulling your weight!"

Charlie gave Vic a look of daggers.

"And don't look at him like that because he aint the one who's been complaining. Charlie all you seem to do is ponce about in your designer gear and worry about getting laid."

Kenny now felt slightly guilty about his action but somehow his youngest brother knew just how to rub him up the wrong way.

"If we all acted like you then the fucking firm would go down the pan. Now pull your fucking socks up and don't let me have to tell you again."

It was the norm that when Kenny spoke you listened but once he had dished out a reprimand he didn't hold a grudge and it was instantly forgotten. Taking his seat behind the desk he beckoned for his brothers to sit. As Charlie dragged a chair over to the desk he was still rubbing at his cheek and Vic wanted to laugh at the sight. He held back knowing that if he let out the smallest snigger then Charlie would go off like a bottle of pop.

"Right! I've been to India."

"India!"

"Don't interrupt Vic. You both know that since Bethnal Green Barry got banged up we've lost our supplier of Super K. Well Barry, for a price of course, kindly let me in on his operation and you wouldn't fucking believe how much money there is to be made."

Kenny Steel proceeded to tell his brothers all that he had learned and the conversation he'd had with Joginder Choudhary. Charlie was all ears but Vic didn't like what he was hearing. He hated any kind of drugs, he always had and even refused to do any dealing at the clubs no matter how much Kenny moaned about it.

"Fuck me Kenny we're asking for trouble if we start smuggling. I mean you lot moving a few tabs on in the clubs is one thing but what you're suggesting is a whole new ball game."

Kenny stared at his brother like he was from a different planet. Vic was always apprehensive when it came down to anything new but he must be off his trolley if he couldn't see what was on offer here.

"And just when do you think we'll get another opportunity to turn a hundred and twenty five nicker into a half a million? I've ordered two kilos so it's actually a million and I aint talking about long term, maybe just a couple of deals. If you want out Vic that's up to you but when the reddies start Rolling in and believe me they will, don't then say you want a slice because it'll be too fucking late." Unlike his brothers Vic wasn't greedy. All he wanted was a quiet life but deep down he knew that in the world they lived in that was an impossibility. He remained silent and decided to hear his brother out, though his decision to have no part in it was already made. Charlie on the other hand was chomping at the bit to know more.

"So what's the risk?"

Kenny smiled. Now happy that at least one of his brothers was on board he proceeded to explain that the risks, to them at least were relatively small.

"I've done the deal and paid for the stuff. The only problem now is getting the gear into the country. Charlie that's where you come in."

"Now hold on a minute Kenny! I run the fucking doors I aint no drugs mule."

"Did I say that? Correct me if I'm wrong but didn't you once say the Cartwright girl flies to India?" Suddenly Charlie Steel understood and he smiled. Getting Zena on side would take a bit of doing but it wasn't unachievable.

"Do you think you can get her on board?"

"Piece of piss Bro. She's off for a couple of days and I think if I have that meet with her mum and dad that she's always on about she will be putty in me hands. I can probably talk her into it over the next day or so but then she won't be back again for a fortnight, does that leave us enough time?"

"Perfect. Now here's what I want you to do." Kenny started to inform his youngest brother in detail about the plan he hatched and exactly what he wanted Charlie to say.

"Let me know how it goes and well take it from there."

Charlie Steel left the office and drove home to get washed and changed. As he lay in the bath he phoned his sometimes girlfriend. Zena Cartwright was about to go shopping when her mobile burst into life. Seeing who the caller was her heart skipped a beat. Usually after he'd slept with her Charlie didn't bother getting in contact again for a fortnight when she would once more be at his beck and call.

"Hi Babe, you ok?"

"I'm fine Charlie thanks."

"Good. Now I know its short notice but you remember when you said about a meal with your mum and dad? Well I can make it tonight. I don't expect your old lady to cook as I aint exactly given her much time, so what if I take you all out to a nice restaurant?"

Zena couldn't believe what she had just heard and felt like all her Christmases had come at once. She also knew that her mother prided herself in her cooking and she would be heartbroken if she couldn't prepare a meal for Charlie, not after her daughter had talked about him nonstop for the last six months.

"Oh Charlie you don't know what this means to me and mum but she would be devastated if she didn't cook for you. I'll give her a ring now, what time should I say? About seven alright?"

Charlie Steel rolled his eyes upwards. He wasn't looking forward to this one bit but he had to get back in Kenny's good books somehow and the amount of money that had been mentioned was too good an opportunity to pass up.

"Seven would be great, I'll pick you up about half six."

With that he was abruptly gone but it didn't matter to Zena as she felt on top of the world. Phoning her parents she explained about Charlie and the call and it was then one mad rush by her mother to get everything ready.

Stan and Linda Cartwright had moved to Southend when Zena was a toddler. After working as a cabbie in the city, Stan wanted a quieter slower pace of life to raise his only child in. It had been many years into their married life before Linda had fallen pregnant and now they both doted on their one and only daughter. Whatever she asked for, she got without argument and her parents had even given her a huge deposit to put down on her flat. That said Zena wasn't a spoilt girl and she loved her parents dearly. Since the Cartwright's had been in Southend they had moved home three times. Finally realising their dream they now lived in a smart semi on the leafy Burgess Terrace. The house was immaculate and every penny Linda earned from her job as a kitchen assistant at Thorpe Greenways School was spent on the property. At six fifty five the table was set and the aromas coming from the kitchen were mouth watering. Linda Cartwright was dressed up to the nines in her best blue dress that shed only worn once before to her nieces wedding. She was apprehensive; Linda knew how much this Charlie meant to her daughter but she was also aware that Stan wasn't keen on the boy. They had never even met but her husband had taken an instant dislike when his baby had on several occasions come home in floods of tears. When the doorbell at last rang Linda could feel the tension begin to build at the base of her neck. Just as Stan went to answer the door she grabbed his arm.

"Please be nice love, our Zena has been waiting for this meal to happen for weeks."

Stan Cartwright gave his wife a look but she wasn't able to tell if it was one of I'm going to watch the little shit like a hawk or it will be fine she prayed it was the latter. With the formal introductions over and when Charlie had handed Linda a massive bunch of flowers the men went into the dining room and Zena helped her mother to dish up the food. Charlie sat beside Stan at the table and from the off you could cut the atmosphere with a knife. It took all of Charlie's resolve not to just get up and walk out but he knew that without Zena Kenny didn't have a safe way of getting the K into the country. The meal was delicious and from time to time Charlie would wink in Zen's direction or pay her a kind compliment. By the end of the evening Linda Cartwright was smitten with the young man. Stan's opinion hadn't changed in the least but he had shown willing and was making polite conversation with Charlie which was about as much as Linda could have hoped for.

"Stan why don't you show Charlie some of your photos. You wouldn't believe our girl was once a keen angler when she was younger, would he Zena?"

"She wasn't too bad at hitting the odd clay pigeon either."

"Too bad Dad? I was always better than you."

The family's idle chit chat was boring Charlie to tears but he smiled and nodded at all the right times and Stan took this as a real show of interest. Walking over to the sideboard he removed not one but five different photograph albums and inwardly Charlie Steel groaned. Spreading them out on the dining room table Stan Cartwright proceeded to go through them one at a time, page by page. Each was labelled and dated and showed either Zena or Stan doing some sort of hunting, fishing or shooting. An hour later when they had reached the last page of album five Charlie could feel his eyelids drooping. He knew he couldn't openly show his boredom but he couldn't help but stifle a small yawn. Zena saw he was tired and after thanking her parents the couple set off for Zena's flat.

When the front door was at last closed Stan turned to his wife and she could tell that he wasn't happy.

"What a twat!"

"Stan!"

"I don't care what you say Linda he's an arsehole. What the fuck is our girl getting mixed up with a wanker like that for?"

Normally Linda was a mild mannered woman but her husband's attitude really angered her and for once she didn't hold back.

"Now you listen to me Stanley Cartwright! You've spent the last hour boring the poor little sod to tears and then you have the cheek to call him all sorts."

"It was your idea to get the photos out."

"Not five bloody albums it wasn't. They were here for dinner not one of your old boys get together's where you spend the whole night
lying about who caught the biggest bloody fish! Now Charlie Steel might not be who we would have chosen but it's not our choice its Zena's. Didn't you see how happy she was? If this relationship does go the distance then you will have to like it or lump it, that or we lose our girl and I tell you this Stanley Cartwright, if that happens I will never forgive you."

With that Linda stormed up to bed. The kitchen was a mess and the dishes were piled high in the sink. It was something unheard of in the Cartwright household and Stan knew he had overstepped the mark. Back at her flat Zena felt as if she was floating on air. Expecting Charlie to stay the night she was taken back when he kissed her gently on the cheek at her front door.

"Where are you going?"

"I've got to check on one of the clubs but I'm coming back as soon as I've finished because I've got a surprise."

With tears in her eyes Zena let herself into the flat and took a seat on the sofa to begin the wait. It was a further two hours before he returned but when he did she couldn't believe what she was seeing.

Carrying the biggest bunch of roses that she had ever clapped eyes on Charlie Steel bent down onto one knee and took her hand in his.

"Will you marry me Zena?"

Nipping herself hard in case she was dreaming Zena Cartwright flung her arms around Charlie's neck as she began to sob uncontrollably.

"You soppy mare whatever's the matter?"

"Oh Charlie you've made me the happiest girl in the world."

As she clung to him Zena buried her head in his chest but all Charlie Steel could do was roll his eyes upwards. That night even he had to admit that the sex was pretty amazing. Zena performed every trick in the book and by morning Charlie was worn out. Over breakfast he began to reel her in, regarding Kenny's plan but he took things slowly. "Babe as soon as I can I'll get you a ring but in the mean time you can think about setting a date." Zena Cartwright beamed from ear to ear.

"As soon as possible and I don't care if it's just a registry office as long as I become Mrs Charlie Steel."

"No way babe! You are having the fucking works or nothing."

Zena could feel panic begin to build. She knew her parents had used up their life saving when they helped her with the deposit on her flat. There was no way she could ask them for more. Slowly she explained her dilemma to Charlie and she watched for any sign that he may be trying to back out.

"Then we'll just have to pay for it ourselves. Let me have a think, I'm sure I can come up with something. When are you home again?"

"Well as luck would have it next weekend and then my shifts are all over the place. I've swapped with Suzie Lampton as she needs the following week off. It will mean that I then have to do three weekends straight before I get a break but I don't mind doing Susie a favour she's such a nice girl. The only trouble is two others also want time off so it's going to be a bit manic for a while."

Wiping his mouth Charlie placed his serviette down onto the table. As he pulled on his jacket he bent down and placed a kiss on her cheek.

"I'll be back later but don't you worry your pretty

101

little head about anything alright? I aint never let you down before have I?"

Zena smiled and shook her head but deep down she knew that Charlie had continually let her down for the whole of their relationship.

At four o'clock and just as she was thinking about leaving for the airport Charlie Steel returned. His face wore a wide grin and she knew that he had come up with an idea. He was clutching a supermarket carrier bag but she didn't have a clue what was inside.

"I want you to listen to what I have to say and don't interrupt until I've finished. Now as luck would have it Kenny needs something brought into the country. If we help him out he said he would pay for the wedding. Whatever you want, dresses, flowers, cars the whole works."

Zena couldn't believe her ears.

"What does he want brought in?"

Naively she imagined it was watches or something, at worst a few diamonds. When Charlie explained about the Ketamine her jaw dropped open.

"I couldn't do that! Charlie if I got caught it wouldn't only be my career in ruins but I could also end up going to prison."

"That's why we've got to make sure you don't get caught and it is only once. Look it's not as if he wants you to do it on a regular basis."

Seeing that he wasn't convincing her Charlie played his ace card.

102

"Well its either this or we have to put the wedding on hold until I've saved up enough money and that could take years."

Charlie instantly saw Zena's bottom lip begin to quiver. Walking round to where she sat he placed his arm around her shoulder.

"Will you do it?"

Zena Cartwright knew she had no choice. It was either carry out Charlie's wishes or she knew deep down that she would lose him forever.

"What do you want me to do?"

"I've got it all planned out. On your next trip you will do a dry run to see if you're going to come up against any problems. If all goes well it will happen the following week. Now you'd better get a move on or you're going to be late. Don't look so worried, like I said I aint ever let you down have I?"

The next two weeks were going to be a nightmare for her but Zena knew she didn't have any choice in the matter not if she wanted to become Mrs Charlie Steel.

CHAPTER TEN

Michelle Steel was up with the larks and already on her way round to Julie Sullivan's before anyone else in her house was awake. The pair were due to fly out to Marbella the following afternoon and there was still so much to do. In one hand she carried her Channel clutch bag and in the other a small mysterious looking box that she knew would intrigue Julie. Arriving at her friends she could see that the Sullivan house was in darkness and all the curtains were still drawn. Michelle let out a sigh of anger, she'd told Julie to be ready early and Shell hated to be kept waiting. Not wanting to wake Ruby as shed never really hit it off with Julies mum, Michelle picked up a handful of pea shingle that carpeted the front garden and tentatively threw it up at the bedroom window. With no reply she threw more only this time she did it with anger. Suddenly a face appeared from behind the curtains with the most unruly mop of ginger hair sticking out in all directions. Julie yawned as she peered down to see who had woken her. Realising she had overslept she mouthed the word sorry before once more disappearing behind the fabric. A few seconds later and Michelle could hear her friend puffing and panting as she made her way down the stairs to the front door.

"Sorry Shell me alarm didn't go off. Now don't make a lot of noise because me old lady's still a kip."

Michelle Steel hissed out her words as she spoke.
"Well if you'd got up in time we wouldn't have to be quiet in the first place."
Julie didn't argue, she was still half asleep and knew that as always her friend would get the better of her. As they made their way into Julies bedroom Michelle wrinkled her nose at the strange smell.
"Whatever's that stink Jules?"
"Yeh sorry it is a bit farty aint it. My mum did us sprouts last night and me arse has been going off like a bleeding machine gun ever since. Open the window a bit and let the smell out. I'll just have a quick wash and we can get off."
Michelle took a seat at the end of the bed and as she waited for her friend placed a hand over her mouth and nipped the bottom of her nose with her forefinger and thumb as the smell was making her gag. It must have been the quickest wash on record as within a couple of minutes Julie Sullivan was once more in the room. Pulling on a pair of leggings she rummaged about in the small wardrobe until she found a jumper that wasn't too creased. Placing her nose onto the wool she inhaled to make sure it hadn't absorbed to much of the sweat her body had omitted the last time she wore it. Happy that it could pass muster at least one more time she stretched it over her head. After running a brush through her hair and putting on her favourite black jelly shoes she was at last ready to go. It was now just past nine and although most

105

of the shops on Canning Town high Street were open it was still relatively quiet. Pushing open the door of Tan To Tan Michelle walked up to the counter and informed the shop assistant who was perched on a high stool filing her nails that they would both like a full body San Tropez spray tan. The assistants hair was dyed a bright platinum blond and she looked both girls up and down which annoyed Michelle and made Julie feel very uncomfortable. She extended her arm and with a long manicured talon pointed to a leather couch. "Take a seat over there and I'll tell Jordan you're here."

Within a few seconds a tall woman with ebony black hair appeared and showed Michelle to an empty cubicle. Handing her a robe she instructed Michelle to take off her clothes and put on a tiny paper thong. The small tented area still bore the remnants of the last tan carried out and Michelle stood in the middle careful not to stand on the sticky orange mess. The process only took a few minutes and before she dressed Michelle admired herself in the full length mirror. Jordan Polter had done a very good job and Michelle's skin now had a warm Mediterranean colour. It was Julies turn next and while Michelle waited she studied the girl sitting at the counter. Michelle Steel thought she looked rather elegant and on a whim decided that when she had finished college she would get Kenny to buy her a salon just like this one. Several minutes later her daydreaming was abruptly halted when Julie Sullivan emerged from the tanning area.

"OMG! Jules. You look like an Umpa Lumpa."

Her words were cruel and as Julie studied her reflection in the mirror she began to cry. Jordan Polter heard the commotion and was soon by her client's side.

"What's the matter babe, you don't like it?"

Through raking sobs and Michelle's nasty fit of giggles Julie shook her head.

"Right then you need to get it off as soon as possible. It won't go completely but it will fade significantly. You'll need some lemon juice, vinegar, an exfoliating glove and someone to rub you down all over."

Michelle had listened intently to everything being said and she now wore a look of horror.

"Don't look at me Jules; you'll have to get your mum to do it."

The girls paid for their treatments and rushed back to Julie Sullivan's home. When Ruby saw the state her daughter was in she gave Michelle a look of pure anger. Julie proceeded to tell her mother all that Jordan had told her and then looked at Ruby with pleading eyes.

"Right young lady get up those stairs and into the bath. I'll be up in five minutes and gawd help you Michelle Steel if this doesn't work."

Michelle stifled a giggle but she was starting to feel a little bit guilty, at least she thought it was guilt.

The realisation was starting to sink in that if Julie ended up being red raw she might not be able to go to Marbella and in all honesty that was Michelle's biggest concern. She also didn't like Julie's mum's insinuations but she knew better than to argue. It took Ruby Sullivan over half an hour of hard work but at last Julie reappeared in the front room and she didn't look to bad. Seeing the fear on her friends face she sat down and placed her arm around Michelle.

"Don't worry Shell; I'm as good as new again. I must have had a bad reaction that's all, anyway what's next on the to do list?"

Michelle removed the mysterious looking little box from her bag and handed it to Julie Sullivan.

"I got two do it yourself vajazzle kits off of ebay."

"OMG Shell! I've always wanted one of them come on lets go up to my room."

When Ruby Sullivan had finished scrubbing the orange dye from the floor of her bathtub she popped her head into her daughter's bedroom. She still wasn't happy about the trip to Spain and this little episode had proved to her that the pair of them couldn't be trusted.

"What are you up to now?"

Michelle and Julie had waited. They both knew Ruby would be keeping an eye on them and when she looked in they were both sitting on the bed flicking through magazines.

"Nothing mum. You going down the market this

morning?"

"Yeh I said I'd meet Silvia at the bus stop though after all your shenanigans I'll probably be late now." As soon as Ruby retreated from the room and the door was closed Michelle tipped the contents of the box onto the bed. It didn't contain much, just two tubes of glue and a couple of small bags holding the various sized crystals that they would need. Michelle had drawn a little picture of what she wanted but Julie was still making her mind up.

"Now you have shaved Jules?"

"Ughhh that's disgusting."

"Oh don't be so stupid. How are they going to stick if your minge is all hairy."

Suddenly Julie Sullivan burst into a fit of giggles and it wasn't long before Michelle joined in as well. Julie picked up a razor from her dressing table and disappeared into the bathroom. Seconds later Michelle heard a scream and then laughter but luckily for them both Ruby Sullivan had already gone shopping. Julie reappeared and when she opened her robe showed her friend the problem. Small squares of tissue paper were covering three or four razor nicks on Julies fat little mound.

"Oh don't worry about that it'll soon stop bleeding. How often do you change your razor?"

Julie Sullivan looked confused.

"I got this one last Christmas and it's been good until now."

"Sometimes I just can't believe you Jules! Anyway

109

I'm first and here's what I want you to create. Take your time and when it's finished I'll do you."
Surprisingly Julie did a very good job and the small crystal heart was neat and centralised. Next it was her turn. Julie lay on the bed with her legs akimbo and the sight of her friend's almost bald minge with just a few tufts of hair dotted about made Michelle grimace.

"So what do you want Jules?"

"A little flower or something? As long as it's pretty I don't mind. I'll leave it up to you."

"I think you'll need a whole bleeding bouquet to cover that lot!"

Michelle bent in close but pulled back sharply. Her friend's personal hygiene left a lot to be desired but even Michelle knew that to comment might just push Julie over the edge. What with all the Umpa Lumpa stuff and then the shaving, she'd been through enough today.

"You're going to have to hold your gut up Jules, I can hardly see where to stick them."

Ten minutes later and the task was complete but it was a sorry sight. Michelle had just stuck the jewels on wherever she felt like it and as Julie Sullivan stood to admire her decorated Minnie as she like to call it, her lip dropped. Not wanting to hurt her friend she told Michelle it was great even though Julie knew she would probably spend all night picking them off.

At twelve the following day Kenny drove his sister

over to collect her friend Julie. They both couldn't help laughing as Julie Sullivan emerged from the house wearing a massive sun hat and shades. She lugged her case as quickly as she could but it was large and so heavy that even Kenny remarked on the weight as he lifted it into the boot.

"Fuck me girl whatever you got in here?"

Julie just smiled; she didn't want to admit that on the insistence of her mother she had half of the local chemist shop inside her case. Climbing into the back she grabbed Michelle's shoulder and squeezed.

"Excited Shell?"

"I can't wait Jules. How's your vajazzle doing?"

"I picked a few off in the night and there was a couple more in me bed this morning but other than that it aint too bad but it does look a bit like I've got a Dalmatian puppy down me knickers. How's yours?"

"Perfect. Shush, Kenny's now getting in."

"Right ladies are we all set?"

The drive over to Gatwick took just under an hour and in that time the girls chatted away almost nonstop. Michelle noticed that her brother was a little on the quiet side but put it down to the fact that she was going away. For once nothing was further from the truth. Today was Zena Cartwright's dry run and Kenny Steel was on tender hooks. As flight EZY8602 to Malaga took off with two excited young girls on board flight BA256

111

touched down at Heathrow airport. Zena
Cartwright carried out her duties to the letter and
when all the passengers had disembarked she
collected her flight bag and joined the other cabin
crew staff ready to enter through passport control.
Marvin Lennon had worked in terminal five for the
last three years and from the day he had first set
eyes on Zena he'd been smitten. Now an official
customs officer he tried to be on duty whenever one
of her flights came in. He didn't hide the fact that
he was keen on her and it had been the butt of many
jokes when the crew were air bound. Allowing two
of her colleges to pass first Zena then walked slowly
but with her head held high through the body
scanner. Lifting her bag from the rollers as it had
passed through x-ray Zena thought she was all clear
until she felt Marvin's hand on her shoulder.
"Hi there Zena, mind if I take a look in your bag?"
Zena tried to control her breathing and not let her
nerves show.
"Of course not, how are you Marvin?"
"Oh you know not too bad considering. My
mother's legs are bad with the ulcers bless her and I
have to take her shopping once a week but on the
whole I suppose I shouldn't moan."
The image made Zena feel sick but she smiled as
sweetly as she could. Lifting the small trolley case
on to the table she proceeded to unzip it. Glancing
round Zena noticed that she wasn't the only one to

112

be stopped and that made her relax a little. Marvin removed a few personal items along with teabags and a bag of sugar.

"Like your tea do you?"

"Nah it's for the pilots they like me to get them PG. The buggers never give me any money though."

"Typical! Well there you go love all ship shape. Perhaps I'll see you next week then?"

Zena didn't reply and placing her bag on the floor walked out of the airport as quickly as she could without raising suspicion. Charlie was already at the flat when she walked in and on seeing him Zena burst into tears.

"Whatever's the matter babe, no problems were there?"

"No nothing like that it's just relief I suppose."

Zena told Charlie all about being stopped and also about Marvin. She had kept his interest a secret up until now but was just glad that he'd been on duty today. Deep down she hoped that Charlie would get jealous but he showed no interest and her heart sank.

"Well if it all goes the same next week then we've got nothing to worry about. Now how about you go and rustle up something for me to eat I'm bleeding starving."

Charlie didn't care that she had just finished a fourteen hour shift and that after being stopped by customs she was emotionally drained. As usual all Charlie Steel thought about was himself.

After watching Zena walk into the kitchen he scrolled down his phone to call his brother. Kenny, with a heavy heart had just waved goodbye to Shell. He wasn't looking forward to a week without her but the sound of his brothers voice cheered him up a bit.

"How's it going?"

"Fine she's just got back and there weren't any problems. This time next week Bro well all be millionaires."

"Don't even go there Charlie I don't want a fucking jinx put on things."

"Kenny you worry too much. Just chill man everything's going to be pukka."

Without another word Kenny Steel hung up. Tonight was party night and he just hoped that Tommy Bex had done a good job and selected a fresh batch of girls. Chrissie was getting a bit stale and after the good news he had received today he felt like seeing a little pain inflicted.

CHAPTER ELEVEN

After a messy divorce Max Bishop had moved to Puerto Banus in nineteen ninety six. Previously he had run a successful Bentley franchise close to Chigwell in Essex. After paying off his wife he was still left with a considerable amount of money. Deciding to move abroad his only concern had been that he wouldn't see much of his three year old son Leon. It was the main factor in why he'd chosen Spain and not somewhere further afield. Originally Max had been involved in the time share business but had quickly moved into sourcing and supplying high quality holiday accommodation. His client list rapidly expanded and he was now enjoying the fruits of his labours. When his son reached fourteen he became a troublesome teenager and after one particularly heated argument with his mother, Leon decided he wanted to live with his father. Shirley Bishop was relieved and thought it was about time Max took on some parental responsibility. If she got six months peace before her son came back with his tail between his legs it would at least be something. Much to her surprise that hadn't happened and for the last six years things had ran smoothly. Max had a small office above the Irish bar at the marina. As most of his work was carried out over the phone he was able to spend his days down at the beach or mixing with his expat friends in the Irish bar below. Lately things had become tense between Max and his son. Now that the boy had left school Max expected Leon to find work but his son had out rightly refused. He wanted his father to support him regarding the party lifestyle he had become accustomed to. Leon Bishop was only average in height but he did have a face and body to die for. On the downside he was slimy and sneaky and although they were pleasant to him, none of his father's friends were really very keen on the boy. Michelle and Julie landed on time and after taking a taxi from the airport arrived at the marina late in the afternoon. Michelle hadn't bothered to book a hotel after deciding that she wanted to have a look around before choosing one. The girls ended up sitting at a table outside Fubar, a place Michelle had heard about on Towie but the girls didn't have a clue what to do next. As Leon Bishop walked by he winked at Michelle and she smiled back. Never one to miss an opportunity he pulled up a chair and sat down.

"Mind if I join you two ladies?"

Michelle and Julie giggled but no words passed between the three. Leon ordered a bottle of Cristal champagne and Michelle Steels eyes opened wide. Little did she know that the cash he had used to pay for it was the weekly shopping money his father had handed over earlier that morning. As he'd been walking by on his way to the supermarket Leon had quickly scanned the two and noticed that Michelle's clothes were expensive as were her luggage, handbag and accessories. He liked a gamble and she looked a bit dim, making him think that over the next few days he could possibly scam a few hundred Euros out of her. Leaving the girls alone he excused himself and headed to the toilet.

"OMG Jules! What a hunk and Cristal, he's actually bought us a bottle of Cristal champagne. Watch out he's on his way back."

"So lady's what brings you to Puerto Banus?"

Michelle went on to explain that they had come for a week's holiday but as yet had nowhere to stay.

"Well it must be fate that we've met then. My dad runs a business down on the marina. He finds accommodation for holiday makers but I have to warn you it aint cheap."

Michelle Steel waved her hand in the air.

"Moneys not a problem."

Julie Sullivan's mouth dropped open. True Shell could have most things she wanted and Kenny had actually given her a credit card before they left England but even Julie knew you didn't bandy that fact around in front of strangers.

"So would you like me to take you both down and introduce you to him?"

Michelle nodded her head vigorously and after a five minute walk the three arrived outside the Irish bar. Max Bishop was sitting on the veranda talking to a couple of his drinking buddies. Like him Joey and Stevie Norris were expats but whereas Max had moved to Spain to get over his divorce, these two had arrived after finishing a lengthy prison term for armed robbery the loot from which had never been recovered by the law. When Max saw his son approach with the two girls he stood up and removed his wallet from his pocket. Pulling out a ten euro note he handed it to Leon.

"Here you go Son! Get yourself and the ladies a drink?"

"Thanks Dad but we aint here for that. These two lovelies have got a bit of a problem."

Leon explained the girl's predicament and his father smiled. Max was a nice man and would try and help anyone. Unlike his son he didn't judge a person by what they wore and only saw two young girls that could possibly end up in trouble as the night wore on if he didn't help them out.

"Take the ladies over to the Benabola hotel. I've got a room on hold there but as it happens I've just had a call saying it won't be needed. Must be your lucky day girls."

"Aint you got anything a bit more upmarket Dad?"

Max was pleased that his son was trying to earn him money but he couldn't see the point in wasting the girl's cash on some room in a swanky five star that they would hardly spend any time in.

"Leon money doesn't grow on trees and I'm sure your friends would rather save their cash for partying, am I right girls?"

Michelle and Julie both nodded their heads which pissed Leon off big time. By the time Michelle and

118

Julie were settled in it was already six o'clock and Leon had arranged to collect them and show them the sights at seven thirty.

"Come on Jules get a move on."

"I'm tired Shell, maybe you should go on your own?"

Michelle Steel feigned disappointment but really she was as pleased as punch to be having Leon all to herself. Not trying to talk her friend round she was out of the room and waiting in reception by seven fifteen. The night was like a dream as he took her to all the posh clubs and bars, which were all paid for on Kenny's credit card. Finishing up at Lineker's bar Michelle thought she had died and gone to heaven when she spied Joey Essex on the dance floor or at least she thought it was him but then again in Puerto Banus everyone looked like Joey Essex. After walking her back to the hotel Leon took Michelle in his arms and kissed her passionately. Due to Kenny always watching her like a hawk Michelle had never had a boyfriend but right there on the steps of the Benabola she fell in love. They agreed to meet at ten the next day outside the hotel. Michelle had told him how she dreamed of going to one of the champagne spray parties at the Ocean Club, the place that all the stars attended. Leon Bishop was only too happy to oblige and he even said he would pay for the day. Julie was snoring loudly when she entered the bedroom but for once it didn't bother Michelle, nothing could dampen her spirits as shed just experienced the best night of her life.

Waking early the next day she nudged Julie Sullivan.

"Come on Jules wake up!"

It was already hot outside and Michelle was eager to get going but her friend still remained in bed with the covers over her head.

"Oh please Jules, we're missing the best part of the day and I've got something special planned for us."

Julie sat up and after wiping the dribble from her chin began to pick the sleep from the corner of her eyes.

"Wos that then?"

"Only a spray party at the Ocean Club!"

It didn't really mean anything to Julie Sullivan but she could see the look of excitement on her friends face and didn't want to upset her.

"What are we going to do there?"

"OMG Jules, don't tell me you aint heard of it. The Ocean Club is known worldwide for its spray parties. You just chill round a pool listening to great tunes and watching for celebs, at least I think that's what you do."

Fifteen minutes later and the girls were standing outside the Benabola waiting for Leon. Michelle wore a beautiful couture bikini covered by an expensive sheer crepe beach dress. The outfit was topped off with a pair of designer sunglasses and a rodeo hat like the one shed seen a picture of Lauren out of Towie wearing. For once Julie Sullivan hadn't tried to copy her friend. After watching Shell get dressed she had known it would be a useless exercise. Today Julie wore a pair of tight denim cut offs, a Minnie mouse t-shirt and bright yellow sun hat. Her outfit was topped off with her favourite jellies and a pair of star shaped sunglasses which shed purchased at the airport just before their flight out. While they waited Michelle relayed every detail of her date the previous evening.

"Sounds like you had a good night, I'm well jel." Michelle smiled at her friend. She knew Jules was doing her best to get into the Towie scene but somehow the phrases never sounded that good when they emerged from her chubby little mouth. As Leon approached he gave Michelle the once over and even he had to admit she looked good. Moving his gaze to Julie he groaned heavily. As the three walked towards the marina Julie lagged behind slightly and Leon pulled Michelle close.

"I aint being funny babe but she aint going to get in looking like that. I've got to go and see me old man for a minute so that'll give you time to get rid."

Michelle felt mean but not mean enough to say no. Taking Julie by the hand she led her to a small table outside one of the many cafes.

"Wos up Shell?"

"Oh Jules I don't know how to say this but Leon reckons you aint going to get in looking like that."

"Do you want me to go back and get changed then?"

121

This was turning out to be more difficult than she had hoped and Michelle Steel decided that in this case honesty was the best policy.

"Look babe I aint being nasty but I don't think you'll get in the Ocean Club period!"

Julie Sullivan's lip dropped and she could feel tears begin to well up which she quickly wiped away.

"It's ok Shell I understand. You go and have fun and I'll meet you back at the hotel later."

Julie wanted her friend to say no way we will always stick together but nothing was said and Michelle was out of her seat in seconds. The Ocean Club was vast and due to Max Bishop sending so many of his clients to the place Leon had a couple of free passes. A massive swimming pool was surrounded by crisp white padded sun beds and even at this early hour there were a couple of hundred people milling about. They were all thin and beautiful and by their accents and the clothes that they wore Michelle could tell that the majority of them had money. This was all so far away from Canning Town but it was a life she knew she wanted. Michelle didn't give her family a second thought, whatever it took she would do it as long as she didn't have to go back to dreary old London. As she stared up at the VIP area the look on her face told Leon it was where she really wanted to be.

"Looks good don't it? Trouble is you have to buy a bed and champagne for the day and its over three hundred nicker each."

Michelle pulled Kenny's credit card from her bag and waved it in the air. Leon Bishop liked this girl and grabbing her hand they laughed and ran to the roped off exclusive area. Julie Sullivan mooched round the high end shops and boutiques for a couple of hours but as she had very little money window shopping soon became boring. Settling herself down on the beach she looked over to the private roped off deck area and sighed. She couldn't see her friend but from the sound of the music and the laughing and shrieking it looked like they were all having a brilliant time. As the heat became more intense Julie Sullivan stripped down to her bathing costume. The one piece was electric blue in colour and had a small frilly skirt around the bottom. Ruby had purchased it for her daughter on one of her trips to the market but it did nothing to flatter Julies figure and it was very uncomfortable due to the fact that it was two sizes too small. After sitting in the sun for three hours she decided to return to the hotel. Her skin felt tight and her ankles had swelled to an unbelievable size. In the privacy of her room Julie Sullivan stripped off her clothes and gasped as she looked at herself in the mirror. Every bit of skin that had been exposed to the sun was now red raw and had begun to blister. For once Julie was glad that she'd done as her mother had asked and packed the vast selection of medical supplies. Covering herself in after sun and TCP she lay on the bed and waited patiently for her friend to return. Her whole body hurt and she consumed four large bottles of water as she tried to cool herself down. Nothing seemed to work but after shed thrown up from sunstroke for the third time, Julie did at last manage to drift off to sleep. It was the early hours of the morning before Michelle showed her face again and Julie had long since been in the land of dreams. The following day Michelle showed little concern for her friend's pain and was only interested in telling Julie every little detail of what she had got up to at the spray party. The rest of the holiday followed the same pattern and Julie Sullivan spent the days and nights holed up alone in her room. After getting so badly sunburnt she didn't venture out much and Shell didn't seem interested in doing anything at all with her friend. Julie couldn't wait for Saturday to come and wished with all her heart that she'd never stepped foot on Spanish soil. The morning of their departure saw Julie Sullivan up with the larks. Shell was still out cold and as she packed Julie decided to let her friend sleep a little longer. When she was dressed and her oversized case was forced shut and strapped down Julie patted Michelle on the shoulder.

"Come on sleepy head you need to get a move on." Michelle yawned and turned over in the bed.

"I aint going home."

"Don't be daft. We've got college next week and your Kenny's going to be at the airport waiting for us."

"I don't care Jules, I aint going back. I love Leon and he loves me and I'm staying here with him."

Julie began to panic but she knew that when Shell made up her mind there was no changing it. She also knew that Kenny Steel would go mad and that she was the one who would have to relay the bad news to him. A further hour of arguing took place but at the end of it Julie Sullivan was no further forward. Finally accepting defeat she hauled her case to the bus stop as unlike on her arrival there was no taxi waiting. Julie had never travelled alone, still she knew she had no choice and after a few hiccups and an hour's drive she at long last made it to the airport.

As Julie boarded her plane Michelle was packed and heading over to the Los Granados urbanisation. She was nervous and praying that she had made the right decision. As far as Leon was concerned they had said their goodbyes last night. When her taxi pulled up outside the villa, Michelle was pleased with its appearance and as she made her way around to the back of the property let out a shriek of excitement when she saw that it had a large swimming pool. The noise woke Leon Bishop and as he peered out of the window was shocked to see her standing there. Quickly dressing he ran down the marble staircase and out onto the sun terrace.

"Shell?"

Michelle Steel flung her arms around the young

man that she had known for only a week and covered him in kisses.

"I couldn't go Leon, I just couldn't leave you."

Leon Bishop hastily ran over in his mind all the different scenarios that could be the outcome of his week of romance. On the plus side she wasn't bad looking and had money or so it seemed and after all, he hadn't had a shag in a long while. On the down side he couldn't see his father agreeing to let her stay. Leon dismissed the second scenario as trivial, he had always been able to twist his dad round his little finger. This might turn out to be better than he could have hoped for. Deciding to let her stay for a while at least he invited Michelle inside.

"I don't know what me old man is going to say but we can worry about that later. Now how do you fancy having a look at my room?"

Leon slapped her hard on the backside and Michelle began to giggle. Eagerly she ran up the staircase and knew that she was about to lose her virginity. It didn't bother her; in fact it was something she welcomed. For a second but only that she thought of Kenny and knew that he would go ballistic but then she reasoned, he was hundreds of miles away and what he didn't know couldn't hurt him or at least that's what she hoped.

CHAPTER TWELVE

The previous two days had been a nightmare for
Zena Cartwright. After landing in Delhi she was
now supposed to be enjoying a two day rest, instead
she had to venture into the city to meet Joginder
Choudhary. Zena didn't like India, as far as she was
concerned it was a dirty smelly place and far too
hot. While her colleagues basked in the sun around
a fabulous swimming pool she was making her way
to the address Charlie Steel had given her. Stepping
from the taxi she glanced around at the poor excuse
for a street. It was dusty, strewn with litter, stank
strongly of sewage and was very run down. The
many men who were milling around looked at her
in a menacing way and she began to get scared. As
two men started to approach her she was desperate
to be let in and rapped hard on the metal door with
her fist. Luckily, just as one put out his hand to
touch Zena Joginder opened the door. Seeing the
fear on her face he shouted something at the men in
Hindi and they turned and walked away.
"Thank you, thank you so much."
"You are welcome but this really isn't a safe place
for a European lady to be out on the street alone.
When Mr Steel told me he would send someone to
collect his purchase I didn't think for one moment
that it would be a woman. Now please come in
before you raise any further suspicion."
Joginder Choudhary led her through the factory to

the same small office Kenny Steel had stood in a couple of weeks earlier. Opening a filing cabinet that was situated in the corner he removed two clear polythene bags containing a white powder and placed them onto the desk.

"For your safety I will drive you back to your hotel but please inform Mr Steel that in future he will have to make other arrangements."

The words future arrangements filled Zena with dread. Was she being taken for a fool, Charlie had told her this was to help with the wedding and nothing more. If she got the stuff back to England without getting caught then Zena made up her mind she would have it out with him once and for all. Back in her hotel room she slowly emptied two bags of sugar down the toilet and began to refilled them with the Ketamine. As she poured she realised there was a problem, there wasn't enough room. No one had bothered to work out the volumes and she now had too much powder to get into the sugar bags. Not daring to dispose of the excess she emptied her makeup into the bottom of her trolley and proceeded to stuff the plastic bag containing the remainder of the drug inside. Zena just hoped that her clothes wouldn't end up with mascara and eye shadow all over them. The only other alternative would be to throw the cosmetics away but the Dior and Channel items had cost her a fortune so she decided to take the chance. Zipping up her trolley case she placed it back into the small wardrobe and went down to the pool to join her work mates. There would be questions regarding her absence but hopefully her lie would be convincing enough when she explained that it had been a case of the Delhi belly and that she had needed to take a trip to the chemists. Zena Cartwright willed the next twenty four hours to pass as quickly as possible.

Kenny Steel had parked up at Gatwick airport and was waiting with anticipation in the arrivals area. He had really missed his sister and couldn't wait for her return. It was also the first day of his special deliveries and he prayed that Zena Cartwright could pull it off. Looking at his watch Kenny knew that if the plane coming in from Delhi hadn't yet landed at Heathrow then it would in the next few minutes. He kept glancing at his phone in the hope that Charlie would call but in all honesty that wouldn't happen for at least another hour. Charlie Steel had arranged, providing there were no problems, to meet his girlfriend at the Dartford tunnel entrance. For once he was on time and pulling over into the lay-by got out of his car to smoke a cigarette. As far as he knew no one was aware that he smoked but just lately the habit was taking hold and it was getting more and more difficult to go even a couple of hours without one. He kidded himself that it was due to the stress he was under but deep down he knew it was an addiction pure and simple.

Just like the last time Zena's plane landed on schedule and she let a couple of the other cabin crew go ahead of her through passport control. Marvin was again on duty and she prayed he wouldn't call her over but her prayer wasn't answered.

"Can I have a look in your bag Zena love?"

She felt a lump in her throat as she turned and smiled. Inside she was shaking like a leaf but as Marvin stared into her eyes he didn't notice anything strange. Dutifully she unzipped her bag and waited with baited breath. Once again he had a look at the contents but after quickly surveying her personal items and running a hand seductively across the packet of tea and two bags of sugar he smiled and waved her on. As the automatic door slid open Zena Cartwright felt the acid taste of vomit as it began to rise in her mouth. Walking towards the car she could visibly see her hand shaking and she promised herself that if she got away with it this time then there would never be a repeat performance. Placing her car key into the lock she knew she couldn't hold onto the contents of her stomach any longer. Bending over Zena retched and retched until there was nothing left inside and she felt faint. Grabbing hold of the wing mirror she steadied herself and swallowing hard tried desperately to pull herself together. Right at this moment Zena didn't know how she was going to make the sixty mile drive to meet her fiancé but she had no alternative and slowly she pulled out of the car park and began her journey.

Charlie stubbed out the cigarette when he saw her car approaching. He quickly removed a breath freshener from his pocket and hoped that she wouldn't smell the tobacco on his clothes. A row would draw attention to them and it was the last thing he needed with two kilos of ketamine in his possession. Expecting her to run into his arms he was shocked when she remained seated in her car. Reluctantly he walked over and got inside the Corsa.

"Hi babe!"

Leaning towards her Charlie tried to kiss her on the cheek but she turned away from him. Zena Cartwright felt that she had been abused and deep down she was disgusted and angry with herself.

"Oh come on darling it aint that bad, we got away with it didn't we and just think about the wedding and how good it's going to be."

"Think about the wedding! Do you realise what I've just done? No Charlie I don't suppose you do!"

This wasn't how it was supposed to be and for a moment Charlie thought he may have lost his touch. The idea worried him a lot, not because of Zena but purely down to the fact that he could end up letting his brother down. Charlie was well aware that Kenny wanted another delivery and right at this moment it looked as though Zena wasn't about to play ball. Reaching over into the

131

back seat she grabbed a carrier bag containing the two bags of ketamine that were disguised as sugar. Half way through her journey from the airport to Dartford she had felt the need to pull over and remove them from her trolley case. The thought of the drugs inside her work bag was more than she could bear. All that she had worked for, her career, her standard of living, had all been jeopardised for the love of a man that deep down she wasn't even sure cared for her. Charlie Steel realised he had to act and act fast if he was to salvage anything of the so called relationship and safeguard any future trips.

"Look babe I know you didn't want to do this and I didn't want you to either but it's the only way we can achieve what we want."

Zena turned to face him and her look was one of stone, a look he had never seen before and which said tread very carefully or this will all go tits up.

"Do you love me Charlie?"

"You soppy mare of course I do I....."

Zena cut him off mid sentence.

"Don't fill me full of bull shit Charlie. I've heard the same line every other Saturday night for the past year. I've done this favour for your brother and don't try and tell me it's for our wedding because that's a lie. Now I'll ask you again, do you love me?"

Charlie breathed in deeply and acting as though his life depended on it he spoke.

"With all my heart. Now can we just put this all behind us and focus on what really matters?"
Zena was still angry but she now felt a little better about the situation. Once again Charlie had smoothed things over but they both knew he would have to work very hard, at least for the next few days, to make things right between the two of them. Getting out of the car he told Zena he would meet up with her back at the flat. Removing his phone he called Kenny and informed him that everything had gone exactly to plan.

Still in the arrival area Kenny Steel wore a grin that stretched from ear to ear. Julie Sullivan on the other hand was anything but happy. For some reason all the passengers had been left sitting on the plane for thirty minutes after landing. Her suitcase was the last to come onto the carousel and when it did it had burst at the seams. Large flowery knickers and a massive double F cup bra sailed round the carousel. Hauling her huge case to the floor she snatched up, for want of a better word her smalls, to the sniggers of the other passengers standing by.

Rummaging about in the case she managed to find a couple of belts and after securing her bag walked through the area that signalled nothing to declare. Scanning the entrance Julie soon spotted Kenny and reluctantly made her way over. Kenny stood up and for a moment wore a confused look.

"Where's Shell?"
Julie started to cry and ran off at the mouth at such

speed that he didn't have a clue what she was
saying.

"I'm so sorry but she wouldn't come, I begged and
begged but you know Shell. Oh Mr Steel I'm sorry
but I......"

Kenny grabbed Julie by the shoulders and shook
her roughly.

"Stop! Now take your time and tell me what
happened."

"We met this bloke on our first day and he..."

"Bloke! What bloke?"

"His names Leon and oh Mr Steel I didn't like him
but Shell well she was crazy on him and he got her
spending loads of money and I'm really worried Mr
Steel."

Julie Sullivan relayed all the events of her sad week
in Spain but Kenny felt no pity. She could see that
he was full of rage and as he turned and walked
away Julie called out to him.

"But what about me Mr Steel?"

Kenny pointed to a large sign that had the words
Bus Terminal emblazed in big black letters.

"You can find your own fucking way home!"

Kenny Steel walked back to his car and all the time
visions of some little toe rag with his hands all over
Michelle invaded his mind. Seated in the Range
Rover he knew he had to put a stop to it and now.
Phoning her mobile he didn't think for a second that
she would answer and when he heard her voice he
sighed with relief.

134

"Shell its Kenny, what the hell do you think you're playing at?"

Michelle had been expecting the call. She knew that Kenny wouldn't let her stay there, well not without a fight but if it was a fight he wanted then she would give it to him, she'd made her mind up about that.

"I take it you've spoken to Jules?"

"Fucking spoke to Jules! Who the fucks this Leon geezer and what does he want from you?"

Michelle Steel pulled the phone from her ear. Looking at Leon she rolled her eyes upwards as she argued with her brother.

"Look I aint coming home and that's an end to it."

"Well let's just see how you manage without any cash because I'm cancelling the credit card as from now."

Michelle Steel pressed the call end button on her phone. She had heard the pain in her brother's voice but it didn't worry her, well not as much as the loss of her meal ticket. She didn't know what it was like not to have money and turning to Leon she relayed Kenny's message.

"What! Now how are we going to live?"

They weren't the words she wanted to hear and for a fleeting moment doubt about what she'd done crossed her mind.

"Look let's just have a little holiday and if we can't manage we can go back to London. Me mums got room and I'm sure she wouldn't mind."

After just a few hours Leon was seriously starting to get fed up with her. She always seemed to be whining and was so needy that he was now beginning to feel suffocated.

Kenny stared down at his phone in dismay. He couldn't believe that she had hung up on him but at the same time knew that phoning her again would be futile. After driving back to Canning Town he slammed his mother's front door as he entered the house. Sandra was in the kitchen sharing a cup of tea with Vic and they both looked up in surprise when Kenny walked in.

"Fuck me boy! After the way you closed that I bet there aint no glass left in me bloody front door?"

"Sorry Mum but you aint never going to believe what that leery little cow has gone and done?"

"I take it the leery little cow you're referring to is your sister and yes when it comes down to our Shell I can believe just about anything. Now sit your arse down and I'll get you some tea. Refill Vic?"

"I think I'd better mum."

Kenny relayed Julie Sullivan's version of events and waited to see what his mother and brother would say.

"Look son, she's over eighteen and you have to let her go sometime. You can't make her come back but knowing Shell when the money runs out she will be home with her tail between her legs and twisting you round her little finger again as usual."

His mother's words made Kenny feel slightly more

136

at ease but he had already made his mind up that if she wasn't home by the end of the month then he would go and get her. Right at this moment he had bigger fish to fry than worrying about his spoilt little sister.

"Any news from Charlie yet?"

"Yeah Vic, everything's pukka. I'm going to pay Bethnal Green Barry another visit tomorrow regarding where we go from here with you know what."

Sandra Steel let out a laugh.

"If you think talking in bleeding riddles is going to stop me knowing what you're on about you can think again."

They both looked at their mother but weren't sure if she was just winding them up. Kenny didn't continue the conversation just in case she did have an inkling of what was going on as somehow he couldn't see his mother approving of the deal he had just carried out or worse still how he had involved Zena Cartwright.

Just like on his previous visit to Pentonville Prison and after going through all the security checks, Kenny once more sat waiting for Barry in the visitor's room. As his old friend approached the table Kenny couldn't be off noticing the purple shiner that Barry's right eye was now sporting.

"Fuck me that's a beauty Barry."

"You should see the other bloke!"

The two men laughed but no more conversation

about Barry's injury took place. Kenny Steel was here for one thing and one thing only.

"Everything go ok?"

"Sweet as a nut. Why you ended up here when all that was on offer I'll never fucking know."

"I told you, I only ever did small amounts. I didn't mind moving the tabs but I wasn't really into all the other malarkey and to be honest Choudhary pissed me off. Smarmy lot them fucking Indians. Anyway you'll be wanting a contact number no doubt."

Kenny only nodded. He was sick of being here already and wanted to get back out into the fresh air as soon as possible. That said he wouldn't be rude to Barry as the bloke had helped him out big time and he wasn't about to forget it.

"Mickey Sandish over in Hoxton is who you need to see. Big black geezer, nice with it though but watch him he can be a right slippery bastard. Turn your back for a second and he will cut the gear with anything he can lay his hands on and I do mean anything.   You can usually find him in the Stags Head around teatime. By all accounts he's a bit of an early doors drinker."

Kenny thanked his friend and once more stepped outside the gates of Pentonville Prison. He hoped it was for the last time because the place unnerved him. Glancing at his watch and seeing that it was almost four he decided to go and meet this Mickey Sandish straight away. Hoxton was close and it would only take him a few minutes to reach his

138

destination. Driving along Kingsland Road Kenny then turned left into Oarsman Road and the Stags Head was situated on the left hand side. The Victorian redbrick building looked much like any other pub in London town but Kenny Steel was still on his guard. He only ever felt comfortable in his own manor and being out of his comfort zone didn't make for a happy man. Pushing open the double doors Kenny surveyed his surroundings. Some nondescript tune played on the juke box but the volume was so low that he couldn't really make out what song it was. A couple of old geezers were huddled in the corner playing dominos and the landlord was behind the bar engrossed in one of the tabloids. A pool table was situated at the far end of the bar where two youths were half way through a match. Kenny spied a lone man who stood close by watching the game. He instantly knew that this was who he needed to see and slowly walked over.

"You Mickey Sandish?"

"Who wants to know?"

The man's tone was off hand and defensive and it wasn't a trait Kenny liked.

"Don't get uptight pal! Bethnal Green Barry recommended you."

Instantly Mickey's mood relaxed and he offered his hand. The men took a seat at one of the cast iron tables and Mickey shouted at the landlord to bring two pints of lager over. Kenny explained that he had a shipment of gear that needed to be cut and made into tabs. Mickey Sandish nodded and when a price was agreed the deal was struck. Kenny wasn't a fool and to begin with had asked for only a half kilo to be cut. He wanted to see for himself if the man could be trusted. Agreeing to meet the next day they shook hands and Kenny headed back home.

CHAPTER THIRTEEN

Kenny Steel now had three weeks to get the
Ketamine cut and sold on and for Zena to come
through with the second shipment. As for Michelle,
he hoped she would get her arse back to Canning
Town within the time that he'd set, that or he would
definitely go and get her and being so busy with
everything else that was going on, he wouldn't be
best pleased. He was only able to sort out getting
the K cut but the rest was up to others and that
didn't make him feel as if he was in control.
Agreeing to meet Charlie at the office he sat behind
the desk and didn't expect to be kept waiting. For
once Charlie was on time and removing the
Ketamine he placed it onto the desk.
"Told you I wouldn't let you down Kenny."
"You did well Charlie but how does the Cartwright
girl feel about the next shipment?"
"Well that's a bit of a problem at the moment. She
said that she's never doing it again."
"I fucking hope not Charlie! We've got a good thing
going here and you'll just have to work harder to
keep her on side. Now I need the next lot to be
collected in three weeks. You're always telling us
what a stud you are now fucking prove it!"
"I might be able to talk her round one more time but
then that really will be it I'm afraid."
"Really, that will be it? I don't Fuckin think so!"
Charlie Steel knew better than to argue or push the

matter any further when his brother was in a bad mood. He didn't want another back hander that would possibly mark his beautiful face. Deciding to leave it a few days before he tackled Zena further Charlie headed home to work out a plan. Kenny had arranged to meet Mickey Sandish outside the Stags Head at noon. He was really starting to feel that he was losing control of everything and the thought worried him. The half kilo of pure Ketamine was in the pocket of his coat and as he pulled up outside the pub he looked round in all directions. There had been nothing to worry about but still for some reason he felt anxious. Mickey had seen his newest customer approach and after getting out of his own car now stood on the edge of the kerb. Not giving Kenny the chance to step from the Range Rover, Mickey opened the passenger door and without an invitation got inside.

"Nice day for it Mr Steel?"

Kenny didn't reply. Since their initial meeting Mickey had carried out his own investigations to find out who he would be working for. When he'd received news that Kenny Steel wasn't to be messed with it hadn't scared him, in fact it had intrigued him. Mickey Sandish was always on the look out to make some easy money and he had a funny feeling that his new associate might just help him out in that department. He knew he had to be careful but as far as Mickey was concerned he'd dealt with bigger fish than Kenny Steel. Mickey gave the directions and they were soon pulling up outside a lockup on Dunloe Street. The unit was the second along in a row of five. They all backed onto the railway line and although they were now vacant had once been used for light industrial work. Mickey placed his key into the small door which was built into the roller shutter and the two men made their way inside. After Mickey switched on the fluorescent light Kenny was able to see that the place was almost empty. Scanning the room he noticed a long steel table that was situated horizontally across the room at the far end. The back wall had been kitted out with standard kitchen units upon which stood an array of glass tubes like the type found in a science lab. Kenny handed over the Ketamine and leant against the wall as Mickey set to work. Due to the fact that Kenny had purchased the Ketamine in powder form the process was relatively simple. Much to Mickey's happiness the pills would be easier to create as there was no cooking up to be done. Emptying the packet out onto the steel table he removed three large canisters from one of the units.

"What's that?"

"Well its Sodium bicarbonate, caffeine and ephedrine. Now you need to tell me how you want it."

"How I want it?"

Kenny didn't want to appear naive but when all was said and done that's exactly what he was. Selling pills through the clubs was one thing but this was a whole new ball game. Even when he'd been smuggling drugs in the army he hadn't had any dealings with the merchandise once it had landed on English soil. Mickey loved to show off his skills and rolling up his sleeves he picked up the bicarbonate.

"If you want it for snorting then this stuff isn't a good idea. On the other hand if you want it in tablet form then it is."

"What's the other two?"

"Caffeine and ephedrine. The first is self explanatory and the ephedrine is a natural amphetamine gives you a mild trippy speedy effect, so what's it to be then?"

Mickey Sandish waited for a reply.

"Look pal I just want tabs that's all."

"Fine, now do you want pill form or capsule. It's down to personal preference but I would recommend the pills as the caps sometimes split."

"Pills then, fuck me it aint fucking rocket science mate."

"Maybe it aint but could you fucking do it?"

Kenny couldn't argue and Mickey proceeded to weigh out the ketamine and then added equal measures of the bicarbonate, caffeine and ephedrine. When the four powders were piled on top of each other he picked up two blades that resembled meat cleavers with the handles removed. Vigorously he chopped and mixed, chopped and

144

mixed until the pile had totally blended. Moving along the table to an electric machine that had a large steel funnel attached Mickey poured in the powder and switched on the motor. The big wheel on the side began to turn and suddenly pills started to pop out of the bottom.

"Impressive!"

Mickey Sandish grinned.

"This my friend is a single punch double sided rotary tablet press. Before I got this little beauty I was doing it all by hand but now I can produce up to five thousand an hour. Thank god for internet auction sites is all I can say."

Within the hour the process was complete and after dropping Mickey back at the Stag Kenny made his way to the office. Vic was already there and handing his brother a small bag Kenny instructed him to give it to Mattie Singer at Chinnerys bar later that night. For Vic this instruction really went against the grain but he knew better than to argue. One way or another and no matter who protested, his brother always got what he wanted. It was now late afternoon and Kenny headed home to his mothers where he gave Charlie an identical bag to sell over at the clubs. Sandra had just finished preparing the evening meal and after pouring her eldest son a cup of tea she sat down with him at the kitchen table.

"You had any news from our Shell mum?"

"You're joking aint you. The only time we're going

145

to hear from that little mare is when she wants some cash."

"Well that might be sooner than you think as I've cancelled her credit card. Let's just see how independent she really is."

"Our Shell, independent? You've got to be bleeding joking son aint you?"

They all laughed but Kenny was starting to get concerned. This was the longest he'd ever gone without seeing his sister and he missed her terribly, though he didn't voice his feelings to his mother or brother.

Michelle Steel had now been living with her boyfriend in Marbella for a week but things were not the bed of roses she had dreamed of. She had quickly found out that Leon could be moody, nasty and downright rude towards her. His dad didn't seem to bad but neither of them were very forthcoming with money like her brother was. Still she was determined to make a go of things if only to prove Kenny wrong. It was noon and she decided to get up and spend an hour around the pool. Leon had gone out earlier and was now down at the Irish bar with Max and all his cronies. That morning Max had left a note inviting his son join him for lunch but to come alone. When he'd first asked his father if Michelle could stay it hadn't gone down too well but Max was always polite and had agreed in the short term. Expecting it to only be for a couple of days things were now starting to wear thin.

146

When every morning he had come downstairs to clothes and underwear strew around his immaculate lounge he was starting to get angry with the setup and it didn't help matters that the girl was bone idle to boot. She never made a cup of tea, cooked a meal or attempted to tidy the house and Max had finally had enough. As his son approached the bar he was all geared up for a row but Leon's first sentence surprised him.

"I know what you're going to say Dad and I'm sorry I've put you in this situation."

"What the hell possessed you to invite her to stay, bloody hell boy you've only known her a week."

"That's just the problem, I didn't. I thought she'd got on the plane and then she turns up declaring her undying love for me. What was I supposed to do?" Max Bishop shook his head.

"You aint been scamming the girl have you?"

Leon put his head down. There was no point in lying to his father as Max could always see right through him.

"Fuck me boy when on earth are you going to learn? So how much is it this time?"

"All told about five grand."

"So what are you doing about it?"

"She said if it didn't work out here then we could go and stay at her mums. I think I might take her home and then after a couple of weeks tell her it aint working out and come back."

Max Bishop puffed out his cheeks. He didn't like

people getting hurt but just maybe this would teach his son a lesson.

"So when are the pair of you going?"

"Tomorrow hopefully but I aint got any money for tickets and her brothers cancelled her credit card." Once again Max would have to bail his son out and he hoped it would be for the last time but he wasn't holding his breath. Back at the villa Michelle was now bored of being on her own. Making her way into the kitchen she opened the fridge in the hope of finding something to eat but apart from two lemons and a bottle of ketchup it was bare. It wasn't like this at home, her mother's fridge and cupboards were always well stocked up with food and suddenly she missed Sandra more than ever. When she heard the front door open she ran into the hall. Leon didn't look happy and she knew he was in one of his moods, something that was becoming a daily occurrence and she didn't like it.

"Hi babe!"

Leon walked straight past her and into the kitchen. Opening the cupboard he helped himself to a bottle of Stella and placing the bottle neck into his mouth pulled off the top with his teeth. At the meeting with his father he had banked on Max telling him everything was alright and that he would help them out financially. When that hadn't happened he realised that for once and all because of the stupid bitch standing in front of him, he would have to stand on his own two feet.

"Start packing we're going to pay your mum a visit."
"But I don't want to go home yet I like it here and...."
Michelle Steel didn't get to finish her sentence as
Leon's fist landed hard on the top of her arm and
she was knocked to the floor. She screamed out in
pain as his foot made contact with her ribs. Leon
Bishop wasn't stupid and made sure that he didn't
mark her anywhere that would be visible. A few
seconds later he pulled her to her feet.
"Now look what you've made me do. Why do you
always have to argue? Honestly Shell it's because I
love you so much that you make me go into these
rages. Now do as I ask and go and get packed."
No one in her entire life had ever laid a hand on her
so for some insane reason she believed him,
stupidly believed that he was madly in love with
her. The couple spent the next day hanging around
the villa as Max wasn't able to get flights for them
until the following day. Finally when it was time to
leave he dropped them at the airport and slipped a
hundred Euros into his son's hand. Leon needed to
stand on his own two feet but he couldn't allow his
boy to arrive at a stranger's home penniless. The
flight was taken in silence. Leon didn't want to be
there and Shell was in terrible pain. Her ribs felt as
though they had been hit with a hammer and she
couldn't get comfortable in her seat no matter how
hard she tried. An inbuilt alarm told her not to
complain as shed quickly come to realise that the
slightest thing could tip her boyfriend over the

149

edge. Unlike her outward journey from Gatwick the couple arrived via Luton airport and now had to find their own way to the capital. Leon didn't want to spend much money so after boarding the national express and a journey that took an hour and a half, they were finally arrived in London and were dropped off in Bethnal Green.

"How much further?"

"We need to get another bus. I suppose it's going to take about another half an hour."

"Fuck me Shell I'm knackered!"

"I know babe but it aint much further and me mums going to make you really welcome. You aint never tasted food like hers and....."

"Shell!"

"Sorry Leon. I know I run on sometimes but I'll try harder I promise."

By the time Michelle Steel opened the front gate it was almost seven o'clock. The pair had been travelling for most of the day and she could sense that Leon was starting to get in a mood. Foolishly she thought that he would snap out of it once they were inside. Sandra was just removing one of her famous shepherd's pies from the oven and the aroma which filled the house was mouth watering. Kenny and Charlie were already seated at the table and as she entered the kitchen Kenny's face beamed when he saw his sister. The smile instantly disappeared when he noticed that she wasn't alone. Sandra shook her head but smiled as she did so.

"Look what the bleeding cats dragged in."

"Nice to see you as well mum. Everyone I'd like to introduce me fella. Kenny, Charlie, this is Leon." Charlie reached over the table and offered his hand but Kenny just nodded. Sandra gave a warm smile as she looked him up and down.

"Well take a seat the pair of you before it gets cold." Soon they were all tucking in and Michelle was running off at the mouth at how wonderful Marbella was. When Leon couldn't take anymore he grabbed her hand and squeezed it hard which made her wince. Within seconds Kenny was on his feet and leaning over the table.

"Get your fucking hands off her you cunt!"

"No Kenny! It's alright honest. I just run on sometimes and Leon lets me know when I should stop, don't you babe?"

Kenny Steel couldn't stand to see his sister fawning over another man and violently pushing his chair from the table made his way to the door.

"You coming Charlie?"

Charlie Steel looked in his mother's direction and shrugged his shoulders.

"See you later Mum."

Sandra wasn't happy, her daughter had been home for less than an hour and already there was aggro in the family. Still it was nice to have her baby back. As for Leon, he realised quickly that as long as he could control Michelle he would have a hold over her eldest brother as well. Stretching his arms out

151

he yawned.

"I don't mean to sound rude Mrs Steel but we've been travelling all day and I'm really tired, would you mind if I turned in?"

"Of course not son. Shell show Leon up to the spare room will you?"

The couple looked at each other in surprise.

"Mum, me and Leon will be in my room."

Sandra didn't protest, after all Michelle was eighteen and if her mother kept treating her like a child then Shell might leave again.

"Ok love, whatever makes you happy."

Leon walked out into the hall and as Michelle went to follow him her mother gently touched her arm.

"Take it slow with our Kenny Shell. You know he don't take too well to strangers especially where you're concerned."

Waiting for the usual outburst Sandra was shocked when her daughter only gave a weak smile. She knew her girl, knew her too well and something was very wrong. Deciding to sleep on it, Sandra Steel was adamant that come hell or high water she would get to the bottom of things once and for all in the morning.

CHAPTER FOURTEEN

Normally a good sleeper, Sandra Steel had tossed and turned for the entire night. By six o'clock she couldn't stand it any longer and quietly made her way down into the kitchen. As she opened the door and switched on the light she was shocked to see her daughter who had been sitting alone at the table in the dark. Making her way across the kitchen she tenderly placed her hand onto her youngest child's shoulder. They didn't usually have a tactile relationship and normally her daughter would have shrugged away any attempt at physical contact but not today.

"You alright darling?"

"I'm fine mum I just couldn't sleep that's all."

As she put the kettle on to boil Sandra studied the face of her only girl. There were dark circles under her eyes and her normally beautiful face seemed to have lost its glow. Taking two mugs from the overhead unit she filled them with coffee and milk and poured over boiling water. Placing them onto the table Sandra sat down and reaching over took her daughters hand in hers.

"You would tell me if anything was troubling you wouldn't you Shell?"

"Mum I'm fine honest. Leon snores and fidgets and I couldn't get to sleep that's all."

Throughout the hours of darkness when sleep had evaded her Sandra had tried to work out what to say to her girl, how to ask what was going on but now in the cold light of day she knew there was no point. She wasn't daft and it was obvious that there was far more to this but just like her eldest Shell couldn't be pushed. When the time was right she would open up to her mother but until then Sandra knew she would just have to wait.

"So what plans do you have, I mean you and Leon?"

"I aint sure really. I suppose I should go back to college, maybe I'll think about it in a few days time."

Michelle Steel quickly changed the subject which was totally out of character as she normally only wanted to talk about herself.

"You heard anything from Jules Mum?"

Sandra took a mouthful of coffee and then placed her cup back down.

"No, only from her old lady and she was none too happy I can tell you. Ruby Sullivan can have a right spiteful tongue when she sets her mind to it. She came round here all guns blazing and gave Kenny a real ear bashing; he ended up slamming the front door in her face. Shell I don't think you treated that girl very nicely I mean Julie has been a good friend to you for years and you all but abandoned her."

"I know I did mum and it's been playing on my mind for the last couple of days. Once we're settled I'll call round and see her. Perhaps I'll get her some chocolates, they normally do the trick."

"I think you probably need to let things die down a bit first or you won't get a bleeding foot inside the

Sullivan house let alone set eyes on Julie. Well not if Ruby's got anything to do with it you won't."

"Oh mum why does being in love have to be so painful?"

The conversation had now suddenly switched back to being all about Michelle and Sandra laughed. Deep down she wondered if her daughter meant more than the emotional feelings of a young girl and she hoped and prayed that it really was all Michelle was asking about.

"Love is always painful darling but you'll get used to it. Now what say I do us some breakfast?"

"Thanks mum but I aint that hungry. I'll go and see what Leon would like though."

The previous night Kenny couldn't face returning to his mothers and totally breaking his routine had slept at the house midweek. There was no Tommy Bex, no young girls to abuse and no Mrs Brooks to tend to his every need. Strangely it didn't bother him and he found that the solitude actually helped to calm him as he recalled the events that happened last night round at his mothers. Knowing he would have to apologise really went against the grain but Kenny would do anything not to upset his sister. He had just finished off his second cup of freshly ground coffee when his mobile burst into life.

"Hi Kenny, its Mattie Singer."

"Morning Matt, no trouble last night was there?"

"No no, it aint nothing like that. I just wanted to let you know that the Special K sold like a storm.

There's always a good market at Chinnerys but last night it went mental. The punters reckon they aint never had fucking gear like it. They were actually phoning their friends to come down and try some and if it carries on like this demands going to outstrip supply."

"Well that's a nice start to me day, thanks for ringing Matt."

Kenny punched the air with euphoria. This was going to make the Steels far richer than they could ever have imagined and once again it was all down to him. Dialling both his brothers he told Vic to meet him at the office in an hour and Charlie, well as usual Charlie was still fast asleep so he left an abrupt voicemail telling him to move his arse. The ringing had woken Charlie Steel but he hadn't bothered to answer it. He knew who the caller would be and if he spoke to his brother in person then he would have to get up. Zena was still asleep and as she nuzzled his chest he didn't want to wake her. Usually he would have roughly pushed her away but for the next week at least he had to play the perfect boyfriend. Slowly he inched out of bed and had soon returned with a tray of coffee and croissants. Opening her eyes Zena couldn't believe what she was seeing. In a whole year there wasn't one time when she could ever recall Charlie even making her a cup of tea let alone bringing her breakfast in bed.

"Morning darling, you sleep well?"

156

Zena Cartwright smiled as she stretched out her arms. Her whole body ached from their antics last night but it was an enjoyable discomfort. Kenny had told his brother to act the stud and Charlie had given it his all in an Oscar winning performance. Zena had climaxed time and time again and for the first time she actually thought that Charlie cared about pleasing her and whether or not she was satisfied.

"Like a dream thanks. Where you going babe?"

"Just off to work. Some of us have to turn out every day you know, we don't all have a brilliant job that allows us to stay in bed."

Zena giggled and sitting up took hold of one of the mugs.

"Will you be back later?"

Charlie Steel was now dressed and couldn't wait to get out of the flat though his body language gave nothing away. Bending down he placed a kiss on her forehead.

"You try stopping me."

When she heard the front door close Zena laid her head back down onto the pillow. The last few days had been a nightmare but at last she felt as though things were going well, so well in fact that she decided to pay her parents a visit and tell them that she and Charlie were going to get married.

Entering the office Kenny's mobile rang and as he pressed the accept button he held up his hand to acknowledge Vic who was seated at the desk.

"Its Tommy. Fuck me mate wherever did you get that gear? I popped into Mayhem and Element and moved a few but by the time I got over to Romford, well I was just about to step inside Liquid when my phone started ringing. The greedy cunts over in Southend only wanted more and I had to turn round and drive straight back again."

"Good work Tommy. Pop in to the office later and I'll give you a fresh supply."

With that Kenny hung up and turning towards his brother smiled from ear to ear.

"What's got you so fucking cheery?"

Kenny relayed both of the conversations he'd had with Tommy Bex and Mattie Singer. Not expecting a pat on the back he would have liked to hear the words well done but there was nothing. Vic Steel hated drugs. Whenever he saw the doormen doing deals at the pubs it turned his stomach but now his greedy brother had moved up a league and Vic was worried.

"Fuck me Vic you could at least act pleased. By the time I've replenished the boys I'm going to have to get the rest cut ready for the weekend that or we won't have any stock to sell. I tell you, if things carry on like this well soon be supplying the whole of the fucking smoke."

Vic shook his head, he didn't like what he was hearing but as usual there was absolutely nothing he could do about it. Twenty minutes later and Charlie appeared. Kenny once again relayed the calls and this time his younger brothers reaction was more to Kenny's liking.

"That's fucking blinding. We're going to have more money than we can poke a fucking stick at soon!"

"That's why we need to get the ball Rolling. You had any more luck with the girl?"

"No but I'm working on it. I've got a few days yet before she flies out to India again and I know I can get her on side, I just have to tread carefully and tell a few porkies. I think a bit of a sob story is in order as Zena's a sucker for the underdog."

Kenny didn't want to hear anymore. He had a busy day and Charlie, once you got him started could talk for England.

"I aint interested in how you do it Bro just as long as you do. Now I've got to go and smooth things over with Romford Ronnie this morning. The fat cunts threatening to jump ship and with things going as they are I can't afford to lose one of the clubs. Vic are you able to go and get the second cut done?"

As luck would have it little Vic had a doctor's appointment mid morning and when Vic made his excuses both Kenny and Charlie rolled their eyes upwards.

"Don't fucking give me that look the pair of you. My boy comes first no matter what. Charlie will just have to do it."

"Yeh I can do it Kenny, no probs."

Kenny walked over to the safe and removing the one and a half kilos of Ketamine, placed them onto the desk. He didn't say anything for a moment and only stared at his brother intently.

"If I give you a chance Charlie you better not let me fucking down. There's a lot of reddies rolling on this little lot."

"No problem! Don't worry so much I'll take care of it."

"And a word of warning! Watch the black bastard because he's a slippery cunt by all accounts."

Kenny placed the Ketamine into a carrier bag and handed it to Charlie. Picking up his mobile he dialled Mickey Sandish and explained that he would be sending over his brother. It was agreed that Charlie would go straight to the lock up and after Kenny had instructed him about exactly where to go, Charlie Steel set off. Due to the traffic the six and a half mile journey took nearly twenty minutes and when he pulled up outside felt the first rumblings of hunger. Looking round he spied a cafe at the end of the road and for a moment contemplated going in for breakfast. Knowing his brother wouldn't approve he rubbed his stomach then got out of the car. Tapping on the roller shutter he was soon let in by Mickey. The two men shook hands and walked to the far end of the unit.

"Got any grub in here mate I'm fucking starving?" Mickey laughed but he was already starting to see the onset of an opportunity.

"Nah sorry mate. I had a full English down the road before I got here, blinding it was. You should give it a go when we're all finished here."

The image of sausage and bacon entered Charlie's thoughts to such a degree that he could almost taste it. Mickey went over to the unit and began to remove the cutting agents only this time he did it slowly one canister at a time. Measuring out the Ketamine took ages and all the time Charlie's hunger pains were getting worse and worse. Walking over to the press Mickey fiddled with the wheel making it look like the machine was faulty in some way.

"Is this going to take long?"

"Shouldn't do but this bastards been playing up lately so I might have to change the washers. Probably be about an hour, shouldn't be anymore." Charlie Steel tried to weigh up if he could trust the man. The bloke seemed genuine enough and it wasn't the first time he'd done business with the Steels. He remembered his brother's words about Mickey being slippery but then Kenny thought everyone was slippery and not to be trusted.

"I think while I'm waiting I'll pop over that cafe and get something to eat."

Mickey Sandish had his head bent low inspecting the machine.

"Ok mate, you go fill your gut while I sort this little lot out."

As soon as Charlie stepped from the unit Mickey swept all of the Ketamine into a plastic tub and measured out three kilos of baking powder, one and

161

a half of caffeine and the same quantity of ephedrine. After putting the mixture into the machine he was soon turning out pill after pill. Bagging them up in manageable amounts, the machine was just pumping out the last few when Charlie returned.

"Fuck me mate you was right that place does a real choice fry up."

Seeing that everything was in order made Charlie happy and after placing all the packets of pills into the carrier bag and paying Mickey for his work he said his farewell and left. Mickey Sandish knew he had to move fast and once again poured the Ketamine onto the table. Adding the other ingredients he worked at record speed and within thirty minutes had produced thousands of Special K pills. Knowing the going rate he worked out that he was set to make well over a million. He would have to go into hiding for a while after he got rid of them but it would soon be followed by hello Jamaica and goodbye to cold old London town.

Returning to the office Charlie Steel placed the K tablets into the safe and then went home. At Boreham Avenue Kenny was seated at the kitchen table with Michelle. In the past whenever the two of them were together the room had always been filled with laughter. Today there was hardly a word being spoken and it was a relief to both of them when Charlie came through the door.

"Everything go alright?"

"Yep. I like that geezer Mickey he's a diamond bloke."

"Aint no room for fucking friendships in our game Charlie and you'd be wise to remember that."

Charlie pulled a can from the fridge and rolled his eyes at his brother's words.

"Where's mum?"

"Took Shells new friend down the shops."

Her brother's referral to Leon as a new friend angered Michelle but she knew better than to argue. For some reason Kenny seemed in a funny mood and she didn't want another blow up today. Charlie gulped down the drink then lazily put the empty can onto the kitchen table.

"Right I'm off!"

"Not so fast sunshine. Seems our Shell here, wants me to give her friend a job. So you might as well take him along with you tonight."

"Not tonight Kenny, I'm taking Zena out for a slap up meal. I'll call into the clubs later but I aint driving all the way back here to pick up Lord Leon."

Charlie winked at his brother, which meant the plan was in action regarding Zena and for once he didn't have a go at Charlie.

"Fair dues. Sorry Shell it will have to wait until tomorrow."

Within seconds both of her brothers had disappeared and Michelle Steel was left alone. Deciding to tidy up a bit for her mother she had just placed Charlie's can into the bin and was standing

163

at the sink when she heard the front door open. Thinking that one of the boys had forgotten something she was a little surprised when Leon walked into the kitchen.

"Hi babe had a good time?"

Leon glared at her which told her the answer was a definite no.

"Where's my mum?"

"Gone round to Irene's whoever the fuck that is. She's done my fucking head in with her nonstop talking; I can see where you get it from now."

His words cut Michelle. Her mother was a kind woman who always talked a lot of sense and she didn't like to hear her being bad mouthed.

"I've got some good news Leon."

"Oh yeh and what's that?"

"Well I've been talking to Kenny and he says you can have a job."

Searing pain rushed through her when she felt the full force of his fist strike her stomach.

Grasping the handle of the fridge Michelle doubled over in pain.

"And who the fuck gave you the right to get me a job. If I want to work then I'll find something myself you dozy bitch!"

Leon grabbed a handful of her hair and yanked her head back. His eyes were cold and hard and Michelle began to shake with fear. He quickly released her when he heard Sandra call out from the hall.

164

"Hiya! I'm back. Irene wasn't there I reckon she's round at her Sharon's."
Sandra could feel the tension as she entered the kitchen but she acted as if there was nothing wrong.
"I've just bumped into our Kenny. He's says you're starting work tomorrow night Leon aint that brilliant news?"
Sandra now busied herself putting the shopping away and she had her back to him so couldn't see him sneer in Michelle's direction.
"That's fantastic Mrs Steel, just brilliant."

CHAPTER FIFTEEN

Charlie had booked a table at the two Michelin star Midsummer House restaurant in Cambridge. It was a drive of nearly an hour and a half but if he achieved the end result he was after it would all be worth it. Charlie had told Zena that they were going somewhere really upmarket and to make sure she dressed for the occasion. He wasn't disappointed and couldn't deny that she looked amazing. Her hair was piled high on top of her head and the sapphire blue silk dress fitted where it touched. Zena had never been the stereo typical Essex girl but still he couldn't bear embarrassment and had warned her in advance. As she walked out of her front door the one thing that Charlie wasn't happy about was the fact that her mother and father were with her. She smiled weakly knowing he would be pissed off but not having the heart to refuse her parents request to join the happy couple, she had smiled and told them that of course they could come along. Earlier that day Zena had been so excited when shed relayed the happy news about her wedding and the look on her mother's face was a picture. Her dad wasn't as thrilled with the announcement but she was sure he'd come round eventually. Charlie Steel now sat in the back of Stan Cartwright's Vauxhall Vectra and he wasn't best pleased. He'd had visions of turning up at the restaurant in his Porsche and being treated like royalty but that definitely wouldn't be happening now. There was little conversation on the drive over, just the odd remarks from Linda to her daughter about having to make wedding plans. When they reached Cambridge Charlie Steel did his best to hide his disappointed. For a start they had to park a few streets away on a pay and display car park and the restaurant itself resembled any other detached Victorian house with the addition of a large conservatory. He had expected some kind of grand stately home not a house that looked like so many others back in London. Once inside it was a different matter. The place was decorated in high end chic and the staff were all overly attentive. Charlie basked in all the attention but Stan and Linda felt uncomfortable. Until tonight, fine dining to them meant an eight ounce fillet down at the local steak house. Zena on the other hand felt like a princess and she knew this night would be etched in her memory forever. After studying the menu Charlie soon realised that with wine, he wouldn't get much change out of a grand and that was only if they stuck to the taster menu. He would make damn sure Kenny reimbursed him the next day or there was going to be a right row. There were ten courses in all and although they were small by the end of the meal all four of them were stuffed. Suddenly Charlie stood up and taking hold of Zena's hand he knelt down on one knee.

"I never done this properly in the first place so Zena

Marie Cartwright will you do me the honour of becoming me wife?"

Zena and her mother both squealed with delight causing the other diners to look over.

"Yes Charlie oh yes please."

Charlie Steel removed a crimson velvet box from his pocket. Inside sat what appeared to be a huge diamond ring and Zena's eyes opened wide when she saw it.

"Let's have a look love."

Before Charlie had chance to put it on her finger Stan snatched the box away.

"Stan!!!"

Linda wasn't pleased with her husband's action but he totally ignored her. Removing the ring he scrutinized it from every angle and when he saw the eighteen carat gold stamp inside he had to admit that it was a beauty. What he didn't know was the fact that earlier that same day Charlie had met up with Joey Taylor a notorious local fence who lived on the manor. It was the oldest trick in the book to put a cubic zirconia into a ring shank that bore a high carat hallmark and hey presto everyone would think you'd spent a shed load of money. Charlie knew that if he did get found out it would probably take several weeks and by then Zena would have served her purpose and he would be long gone. Stan Cartwright passed the box back to his daughter and then held out his hand.

"I think I might have got you all wrong son,

168

welcome to the family."

Linda started to cry and right at this moment she was so proud of her daughter and husband. A bottle of champagne was sent to the table courtesy of the restaurant and much to Charlie's relief. The evening had so far gone to plan; now all he needed to do was get Zena back to the flat for a heart to heart chat. Sitting silently for a few moments he began to rub gently on his forehead.

"You alright babe?"

"Bit of a headache that's all."

Zena looked in her mother's direction and Linda Cartwright could tell that her daughter was concerned.

"Stan it's time we we're leaving Charlie's got a bad head."

"You need to get that checked out boy. A pal of mine kept having headaches and the next thing we knew he'd dropped down dead."

"Stan!"

"Well I was only saying what happened."

"Well don't! Just go and get the car will you. Sorry about that Charlie he always puts his mouth into action before his bloody brain is in gear."

Stan and Linda Cartwright dropped the happy couple back at Zena's flat before going home. As Zena opened the front door she could see Charlie was in real pain. Up until the last couple of days he hadn't realised he was so good at acting and for a second he wanted to laugh.

169

"Come on babe sit down and I'll get you a couple of aspirin."

"It'll take more than a few pills to make this one go away."

"Whatever's brought it on; I mean we were all having such a lovely time."

As Zena handed him the tablets and a glass of water he held onto her wrist.

"I need to talk to you and I really don't know how to go about it. That's probably the reason for the migraine. God you're going to hate me after this I just know it."

Suddenly Zena felt afraid, afraid that for some reason he was going to call the engagement off but that didn't make sense after the wonderful evening they'd just shared.

"Whatever it is you can tell me."

Charlie put his head in his hands as he spoke.

"I'm in debt babe."

"Is that all! Tell me how much and I'll see if my dad will lend it too..."

"You don't understand your dad aint got that kind of money."

"But none of this makes any sense; you've just given me this very beautiful and very expensive ring. Well there's nothing for it, we'll just have to porn it. I really don't mind Charlie; you're all that matters to me."

"Sweetheart, that wouldn't even make a dent in what I owe."

"Well how much are you talking about?"

"Two hundred grand."

"What! But how Charlie, how can you owe that much?"

"Gambling and if I don't pay it they're going to break my legs."

Zena sat down beside him and wrapped her arms around the man she loved more than anything in the world.

"Oh Charlie whatever are we going to do?"

With his head resting on her chest he grinned.

"I spoke to Kenny and he came up with an answer but I said I couldn't do it."

"What, what did he say?"

"I can't Zee I really can't ask you."

Zena Cartwright was scared and had tears in her eyes. Grabbing Charlie's hand in hers her face was pleading as she spoke.

"Please tell me babe I'll do anything."

Charlie Steel looked into her eyes and when he saw the tears begin to form he momentarily felt guilty but sadly not guilty enough.

"He said that if you do another Ketamine run that it would clear the debt."

For a moment Zena was silent as she took in the enormity of what he was asking. Her life or the life she knew would be put on the line for a second time. Then again his life was all that mattered and through her tears she smiled.

"I'll do it."

"But Zee I couldn't ask..."

Gently she placed her index finger onto his lips. There and then Charlie Steel knew that he'd accomplished what he'd set out to do and he wrapped his arms around her. Zena took the action as a show of gratitude and it probably was but not for the reasons she thought.

Kenny had spent the evening round at his mums and after watching Shell and her boyfriend cuddling on the sofa for the best part of an hour he'd had just about as much as he could take. Sandra had been oblivious to their kissing and giggling, she was too engrossed in River Cottage to bother about what her daughter was doing. Kenny walked into the kitchen and pulled a beer from the fridge. Sitting at the table he felt helpless and it wasn't something he could discuss with anyone. Deep down all he wanted to do was go into the sitting room and yank the intruder to his feet and punch his lights out. Suddenly the door opened and his mother appeared.

"You alright boy?"

Kenny forced a smile but she knew him better than anyone.

"What's the matter son? I know you aint keen on him and I can't say that I've taken to the lad but there aint much we can do about it. If it's meant to be then they will find a way and if not, then we're all here for her when it goes tits up. I know you have a special bond with our Shell."

His mother's words came like a bolt out of the blue. For all these years he'd tried so hard to hide his feelings and here she was stating the obvious. "What do you mean?"
"You know fine well what I'm on about so we don't need to go into the finer details. My darling you need to make a life for yourself and not wish for something that can never happen. Michelle is your sister and that's all she will ever be."
Kenny loved his mother, adored her in fact but what she was saying was all wrong. Oh she wasn't wrong in her thinking but actually coming right out with it was just too much to hear especially from her.
"I don't know what you're on about and I don't want to discuss it any further. I'm going to bed."
As he disappeared from the room Sandra Steel could only shake her head. She hated to see her boy in pain but there was nothing she could do to help him. Kenny had to let go of his sister, she had her own life to live and Sandra wished with all her heart that her eldest could find a woman of his own. Deciding to go to bed herself Sandra said goodnight to the young love birds and climbed the stairs to her room. She couldn't have known from their earlier actions that her daughter was scared to be alone with Leon Bishop. Her frail little body ached from the bruises and she was certain that he would soon inflict more. It sounded ridiculous when she thought about it but Michelle Steel was beginning to

realise that her boyfriend actually enjoyed hurting her. As soon as the front room door closed he nipped her arm so hard that she could do nothing but cry out. Leon was clever when it came down to knowing just how far he could go when he hurt her. Her cry wasn't loud enough to bring her mother running back in and Michelle was at least grateful for that. She knew that if that had happened there would have been murders in the house. Leon Bishop was skating on thin ice but as yet he didn't realise just how thin that ice was.

The next few days passed uneventfully. Leon had gone to work with Charlie each night and although he would never admit it to Shell, was actually enjoying himself. There were so many gorgeous birds in the clubs and being part of the security firm somehow gave him a kind of kudos he'd never known before. He wouldn't say they were falling at his feet to get laid but it was pretty close. Not wanting to play away in front of Charlie he had sneakily taken them round to the back of the clubs. After a quick shag he would straighten his clothes and re-enter the venue wearing a broad smile. Leon thought that so far he had got away with things but nothing went unnoticed by the team and it was soon brought to Charlie's attention. Not wanting any aggro he hadn't said anything but on the following Saturday night tensions were running high. Zena was due to fly out to India the next day and Charlie was on tender hooks, he'd also just

taken a call from Tommy Bex to say that there was a
possible problem with the latest batch of tablets he
was selling. Tommy had only shifted a few but he
was already getting complaints that there was no
effect and the punters wanted their money back. Of
course he'd told them to sling their hook but he
could plainly see that they were all as sober as
judges. Charlie started to panic and as he made his
way into the clubs office noticed Leon on one of the
security cameras that covered the rear yard. Some
dirty slag was up against the wall with her knickers
round her ankles and Leon was going at it like a
rabbit. Not one to usually bother about his sisters
feelings Charlie would normally have continued to
turn a blind eye but he was stressed out and
something about the image of this little tosser taking
the piss out of them really riled him up. Marching
outside he grabbed the neck of Leon's shirt collar
while he was still engrossed with the girl. She
didn't recognise Charlie Steel in the dim light and
wasn't best pleased at being stopped before she had
climaxed.
"Oi! What the fuck are you doing you cunt!"
One look at Charlie Steels menacing face was
enough to stop any further argument.
"Oh sorry Charlie I didn't know it was you."
Without any concern for Leon she bent down,
pulled up her underwear and walked towards the
back door. By now Charlie had roughly pushed his
sister's boyfriend up against the wall.

175

"Do you think we're fucking mugs?"

Leon Bishop tried to placate Charlie and reached out to touch him on the shoulder but Charlie swiftly moved sideways.

"Of course I don't but come on man; it's like a fucking sweet shop in there. I've seen you have a taster more than once."

Charlie leaned in so close that Leon could feel his breath as he spoke.

"That may be so but I aint Michelle Steels boyfriend am I? I think you should fuck off back to me mum's Leon before I change my mind and call our Kenny. You want to thank your lucky stars that it's me out here and not him because if it was you'd be fucking dead, now sling your hook."

Reluctantly Leon Bishop did as he was told and now faced with a hefty cab fear he was in a dark and brooding mood. The next forty eight hours would turn out to be explosive for everyone.

CHAPTER SIXTEEN

Just as Charlie went back inside the club his mobile began to ring. Looking down at the screen he saw it was Mattie Singer over at Chinnerys and was about to ignore it when he had second thoughts. If there was some kind of trouble and Kenny found out he hadn't taken the call then he would be in deep shit. Just lately he didn't seem to be able to please his brother no matter how hard he tried, Kenny always seemed to make fun of him and treat him as if he was a waster.

"Yeh?"

"Hi Charlie its Mattie. We've got a real problem over here with the special K."

Charlie shook his head, this was all he needed.

"Problem what problem?"

"All the tabs are duff."

Charlie instantly went into panic mode. Kenny would blame him and he would now have to admit that he had left Mickey Sandish alone with the Ketamine.

"All or just some?"

"Well we've shifted over a hundred tonight and most of the punters are up in arms. They're all demanding a refund, what do you want me to do?"

"Tell them to fuck off!"

"I can't do that Charlie; I'm surrounded by about fifty of them as we speak."

Charlie Steel now knew he was in deep trouble and

didn't want two bashed up doormen to add to his woes.

"Ok give them their fucking money back and for fucks sake don't sell anymore."

With that Charlie hung up and started to pace up and down desperately trying to think about what to do next. He didn't have to try too hard as within the hour the matter would be taken out of his hands.

With it being a Saturday Kenny was once more at the house for one of his party's. In the middle of watching a couple of girls being screwed by another wearing an extra large strap on dildo he was disturbed when Tommy Bex's mobile started to ring. Kenny didn't say a word but the look he gave Tommy spoke volumes. Slipping out of the bedroom Tommy answered his phone but his tone was curt and angry sounding.

"Whoever the fuck you are you'd better have a damn good reason for ringing me!"

"Tommy its Jock Denman can I speak to Mr Steel?"

"No you Fucking cant you knob head."

"Please Tommy! I'm over at Brannigans in Romford and there's a problem with the K."

Tommy was starting to become irate.

"Well what's the problem Jock? Fuck me cant you sort it out yourself?"

"No I can't Tom they're all fake."

"What's all fucking fake? You aint making any sense."

"The tabs are fake. I don't know what they've got in them but there certainly aint any K. They all want their reddies back and its starting to get a bit out of hand. To be honest its really out of fucking hand! Me and Davey Hinchson are holed up in the office and the cunts are trying to bust down the door. I wouldn't mind but there must be at least thirty of them, we don't stand a chance."

Tommy told Jock to stay on the line as he thought for a moment. Finally he made a decision.

"Give back the money and then get over to the office as quick as you can. Oh and give Mattie Singer a call and see if he's had any trouble. If he has tell him to get over to Poplar as well."

Tommy was worried that he may have done the wrong thing but he had no other choice. Quietly he entered the bedroom and made his way over to the back of the room where Kenny stood totally engrossed and totally naked.

"Sorry boss but I need to have a word and I mean like yesterday!"

Kenny Steel knew that his old buddy would never interrupt him unless it was really serious.

"Get rid of the slags and meet me in the study."

A few minutes later after he'd called a cab and had almost forced the girls from the house, Tommy Bex knocked on the study door and entered.

"This had better be fucking serious Tom?"

Tommy relayed the conversation he'd had with Jock and as he did so could visibly see the colour drain from Kenny Steels face. Before he had finished talking Kenny was already on the phone to Charlie. When Charlie saw who was calling the words fuck it! escaped from his mouth. Kenny asked if there'd been a problem at his end and when his brother told him there had he instructed Charlie to get back to Canning Town sharpish. For a moment Charlie had wondered if he might get away with not being found out but knew deep down that it wouldn't be the case. Getting into his Porsche he kept to the speed limit for once, not doing as he'd been told wasn't an option but he still tried to drag out his return. As he entered the office his feet momentarily left the floor as he was hurled against the wall. Kenny Steel used his forearm to hold his youngest brother in place and as he shouted rather than spoke fine spittle escaped from his mouth.

"I'm going to ask you once and fucking gawd help you if you fucking lie to me. Did you leave Mickey Sandish alone with my drugs?"

Charlie knew it was futile not to tell the truth and slowly he nodded his head.

"You cunt! I told you to fucking watch him. Do you realise if we don't get it back we've lost close on two million quid."

Charlie Steel was scared, he'd never seen his brother this angry but he didn't utter another word. Sorry would only wind Kenny up further and when it came down to it there really was no one to blame but himself. If Kenny beat the crap out of him, then as far as Charlie was concerned he'd gotten off lightly. Tommy Bex sat in the office but didn't add anything to the conversation and only spoke to acknowledge Vic when he entered. A few seconds later Mattie Singer and Jock Denman came in and the search party was complete.

"Right you lot we're going to find that cunt if it's the last thing we do. As for you Charlie, right at this minute I can't stand to fucking look at you so you can travel with Mattie and Jock."

No other words were spoken and the two cars set of for Hoxton and the Stags Head. It was almost two am when they screeched to a halt outside and the pub was in darkness. Originally from Oxford, John Gathercole had been the tenant at the Stags Head for the last five years. The pub would never earn him a fortune but it provided an adequate living and he liked all the locals. As Kenny Steel kicked in the front door, John Gathercole sat bolt upright in his bed. Whoever it was if they were after the takings they were in for a shock. For a Saturday night it had been really quiet and he didn't think there was much more than a couple of hundred quid in the safe. Getting out of bed he pulled on his trousers and a jumper just as his bedroom door flew open. The six men, well apart from Charlie, all looked menacing and John was starting to think that maybe wasn't a robbery after all. Backing up against the wall John Gathercole stretched out his hands with his palms facing towards his intruders.

"Whatever you want just take it but I warn you there isn't much."

Kenny Steel didn't know the man and he had no malice towards him. That said he was here for one thing and one thing only to get information and he didn't care what it took to obtain it.

"I want to talk to one of your regulars and I need to find him."

John Gathercole breathed out a sigh of relief.

"Is that all! If you'd have knocked on the door like any sane person we could have discussed this without the need to burst in here mob handed."

Kenny instantly took a step forward and the landlord a step back. Maybe he had overstepped the mark with his words and he was once again worried.

"Who is it you're after?"

"A cunt by the name of Mickey Sandish!"

John smiled but it wasn't a smile of ridicule more one of now completely understanding what was going on. He liked Mickey always had but he wouldn't trust him as far as he could thrown him. From the first day he'd taken over the pub John had known that sooner or later

Mickey Sandish would get into serious bother but it had never crossed his mind that he would ever be involved.

"He's got a flat above the butchers on the high Street. Entrance is round the back but be careful as they reckon he booby traps the staircase every night

182

I don't know how true it is but well you know just in case."

So far this was going good and as the six men turned to leave Kenny had a final word of warning for the landlord.

"Don't be fucking clever and phone ahead to warn the slag or think about shouting your mouth off to anyone or I'll be back and it won't be a friendly visit."

John Gathercole nodded his head and was soon alone again in his bedroom. As the adrenalin died down he could feel his body begin to shake. He was now fearful for Mickey Sandish but at the same time he was about as involved as he ever wanted to get. John would keep his mouth shut and as far as he was concerned the intrusion never happened. Whatever the outcome he was sure it would be all round the manor by daybreak.

The flat was just as John had described and easy to find. Kenny removed a large torch from the boot of his car and shone it on the metal staircase but there was nothing out of the ordinary. As quietly as they could the men climbed the stairs and were soon standing outside Mickey's front door. Kenny knew that his luck was in when he saw that it was the only occupied flat. The others were boarded up and if they did happen to be inhabited by squatters then they would probably all be out of their heads on smack. Having to deal with a nosey neighbour would have caused more trouble and he wasn't in a frame of mind to be nice. After a couple of hard kicks the door flew open with relative ease. Mickey had heard them a few seconds earlier and as they entered his home he hid behind the bedroom door clutching a pickaxe handle. He had upset a few people in the past and the nicely weighted timber was now a compulsory item that he always kept at the side of his bed. He was scared like a cornered animal and that fact alone made him dangerous. He knew who it was and just wished that it could have been a few hours later when he would have already been on a plane to Jamaica. Shifting the drugs had taken longer than he'd first thought, in fact he'd only gotten rid of the last batch a couple of hours earlier. As Kenny entered the room Mickey swung the pickaxe handle as hard as he could but his aim was off and the tip only skimmed Kenny's shoulder. Seeing that his visitor had come mob handed he realised that he now had a fight on his hands and it was one that he couldn't possibly win. Adamant that whatever happened he wasn't going to return the cash, Mickey Sandish braced himself for a beating. Tommy, Mattie, Jock and Charlie bundled Mickey to the floor. Charlie knew he had to show willing but Vic could only look on in horror. It was one thing to have a rumpus at one of the pubs or clubs but this, this was so wrong. Vic Steel watched as blow after blow was rained down on the man and it sickened him. Turning from the sight he walked out of the flat and waited by the cars.

Kenny stood up signalling for them all to stop. Staring down at the bloody mess on the floor he spoke.

"Right cunt! Where are my drugs?"

Mickey knew he had misjudged the situation and he wasn't getting out of this alive, so in defiance and with a gritty determination he stared up at Kenny Steel and spat blood from his mouth.

"Go fuck yourself."

Kenny kicked out at Mickey's head and a cracking sound was heard. His left eye split open and the force made it sink back into its socket. Kenny straddled Mickey's body in a mounted position and forcibly gripped Mickey's throat with one hand.

"Last chance Mickey."

Once again Mickey spat a mixture of blood and phlegm into Kenny's face.

"Fuck you!"

Kenny started to squeeze Mickey's neck with a vice like grip. The room was silent apart from a low throaty choking sound that emanated from the mouth of Mickey Sandish. Surprisingly it took quite some time for the choking sound to subside but finally Mickey took his last breath. Kenny was physically drained from the exertion and as he stood up and wiped his face with the back of his hand his men were staring at him but not one of them dared to breath a word. As he led the way out there was total silence until they reached the cars and even then it was just hushed words of 'catch

You later'. Vic had expected an ear bashing from his elder brother for bottling out but it didn't happen. It was now three am and Kenny Steel was mentally in a dark place. He didn't want to talk and after driving back to the office closed the door and locked it. The rest of the crew had all squeezed into one car and made their way back to Poplar High Street. Mattie, Jock and Tommy Bex dropped off Vic and Charlie then went home. The brothers were left standing in the street and could only stare at one another, both in shock at what had occurred. Vic hated this kind of violence and was worried about any repercussions. Charlie on the other hand was only worried about himself and what his brother was going to do to him.

"Now what?"

"I think you'd better come back to mine Charlie. With the mood he's in he could end up fucking killing you as well. Well leave it a few hours and hopefully he will have calmed down a bit."

"If you think that's best but I won't stay at yours thanks. I'm going to get back to Southend, Zena's flight lands in a few hours and I want to be at the flat when she gets there."

Vic nodded and rubbed his baby brother's head before getting into his car and driving off. When he met up with Kenny again he would suggest a meeting to talk things over. It was starting to get out of hand; for god's sake a man had lost his life and all for the sake of a few drugs. Vic didn't know if Kenny was losing the plot but one way or another things had to be sorted out. Charlie drove back to Southend and as he entered the flat looked down at his hands and saw they still had the blood of Mickey Sandish on them. Running to the bathroom he only just made it to the toilet as he violently threw up. He knew it wasn't over yet and he prayed that Zena would come through for him, that or he was facing punishment from his brother and after what he'd seen earlier he didn't fancy his chances.

Kenny sat alone in the dark and ran through everything that had happened in his mind. True he hadn't lost much in the way of cash. He'd actually made a substantial sum from the original sample batch and he had after all bought the Ketamine so cheaply. What he had lost was face and somehow for Kenny Steel that was far harder to handle. When the next shipment arrived he wasn't going to let it out of his sight and he swore to himself that being ripped off would never happen again.

CHAPTER SEVENTEEN

Sandra Steel had left Michelle and Leon in bed when she set off for the shops. They were bickering away until the early hours and it had kept her awake for most of the night. All was now quiet but she knew she would have to have a talk with her girl when she got back from the supermarket. When Sandra called for her friend Irene who lived a few doors down the street she was shocked when the woman commented on her appearance.

"You had a heavy night love?"

Sandra's face wore a puzzled expression.

"Why do you say that?"

"Well the bags under your bleeding eyes for one thing. It's not like you Sandra is something bothering you love?"

About to reveal her concerns she then thought better of it. Irene was a good friend but Sandra would never take the chance that her family business could end up being bandied about the manor."

"Everything's fine just a bad night's sleep that's all. You know how it is at our age if you get a straight two hours shut eye you're bleeding lucky. I tell you Irene what with the constant sweats my top sheet was on and off more times than a whores drawers last night."

Accepting the explanation from her friend the two women set off to do their weekly shop but Sandra had a bad feeling in her gut. What angered her most was that she didn't know which of her children it concerned. Deciding not to beat herself up over it she linked arms with her friend as they walked along.

Kenny had stayed at the office for the remainder of the previous night and had managed to get at least some sleep. Now as the traffic began to build up outside he stretched out his arms and yawned. His mouth tasted like a Turkish wrestlers jock strap and he could smell the onset of body odour. About to go back to his mothers for a wash he was stopped when Vic walked in.

"Fuck me Kenny you don't half look rough."

Kenny steel walked over to the small kitchen area and placing the kettle onto boil looked at his reflection in the mirror that hung above the sink.

"Well aint you the fucking observant one! Where's that little wanker Charlie?"

"Went back to Southend to wait for the Cartwright girl I think. Kenny ease up on him a bit will you?"

Kenny Steel walked back to the desk with his coffee but didn't offer his brother a drink. He studied Vic for a few seconds which made his brother feel uncomfortable.

"What?"

"You never cease to fucking amaze me Vic. Go easy on the cunt? Do you know what his cock up has fucking cost this firm?"

Not expecting a comeback Kenny was slightly

surprised when his brother spoke.

"I don't know what the fucks got into you lately but it aint the firm who has lost out is it, it's you. I never fucking wanted a part of dealing in the first place but like usual Kenny no one else gets to voice an opinion. Why does it always have to be your way or the fucking highway? The security side of things was doing fine without all this shit. Tell me are you ever going to have enough money or is it about something else?"

"Leave it out will you and I don't know where you get off being all fucking high and mighty but if it weren't for me Vic you'd still be driving for the fucking Standard."

"Maybe I would but at least my conscience would be clear. You don't give a fuck about the poor little sods you're getting hooked on K now do you?"

"No not in the least. They pay their money and take their chances no one's fucking forcing them!"

Vic Steel knew his brother well and there was no point in arguing the toss any further. When Kenny was in a mood it was best to keep your head down until it blew over. Deciding to leave before there was another row he headed home ever hopeful that Deidre had already gone out.

Sandra Steel had been wrong in her assumption and Michelle hadn't got a wink of sleep. Leon was as spiteful as ever and when he'd finally had enough of arguing he had physically forced her out of bed. Michelle had spent the whole night on the floor like

190

a dog but she knew better than to leave the room. Now he was awake and she could feel his eyes boring down on her. He leant out of bed to touch her head and she flinched in fear.

"What the fucks up with you?"

"Nothing, I just thought you was going to hit me that's all."

Leon Bishop didn't think of himself as a bully but sometimes she wound him up like a top and he just had to release the frustration somehow. If she would only learn to keep her trap shut then things would be alright. Her voice always seemed to grate on him and if the truth was told he was getting fed up with the grey skies of London and wanted to go home to Spain.

"Leon?"

"What?"

"Do you love me? Only when you came home last night I could smell cheap perfume. I couldn't stand it if you cheated on me Leon and Kenny would go mad."

This was all he needed. Why the fuck she couldn't just keep quiet god only knew. Suddenly he could feel his whole body tense up and a red mist seemed to envelop him. Jumping out of bed he almost ran to where she was now cowering on the floor.

"You bitch! Right I've had about as much of you and your fucking family as I can take. I think its about time you was taught a lesson once and for all."

Leon Bishop began to kick her, slowly at first but his inner demons took hold and soon his actions became more ferocious. Michelle Steel screamed out but there was no one to hear her cries. Desperately she clawed at his leg in an attempt to make him stop but it did no good. Michelle knew at least two of her front teeth were now loose and as if things were happening in slow motion that above all else was playing on her mind. Kenny had always commented on what a nice set of gnasher's she had, god she wished he was here with her now. Michelle's face was soon swollen beyond recognition and when he kicked her in the stomach she let out a piercing scream that shocked even Leon. Her whole body shook and she began to tremble. The pain was excruciating and shed never felt anything like it in her life. Now scared that he'd taken things too far, Leon grabbed his bag from the top of the wardrobe and stuffed his clothes inside. He could hear her throwing up on the carpet but didn't bother to see if she was alright. The only thing he could think of was getting as far away from this godforsaken place as quickly as he could. Michelle heard the front door slam as he left but she was in too much pain to move. Leon Bishop ran down the road and jumped aboard the first bus that came along. Aware that his breath stank he kept his head low and didn't make eye contact with anyone. As the bus made its way along the high street he didn't see Sandra Steel as she came out of the pound

192

shop. For a moment she stopped but the bus passed so quickly that she couldn't be a hundred percent sure that it was Leon on it. Irene touched her arm.

"You alright love?"

"Yeh! I thought I saw our Shells fella on that bus but it couldn't have been. I just had the weirdest sensation Irene, like someone walked over me grave and its right shook me up. I think I'm going to go home now."

"You want me to come with you? Only I just need to pop into Smiff's and get me lottery."

"Nah you're alright girl I'll be fine."

Sandra kissed her old friend on the cheek and then headed in the direction of Boreham Avenue as fast as she could. Quickly opening the front door, she stopped for a moment to listen but everywhere was silent. Sandra chastised herself for being silly they were both probably still in the land of nod after their shenanigans last night. Placing the kettle onto boil she began to put the shopping away and was starting to feel a little better when a loud thud was heard from upstairs. Popping her head into the hallway she called out.

"Shell? Shell you alright love?"

There was no answer and Sandra returned to the kitchen but not for long. As hard as she tried something was nagging away at her and five minutes later she tiptoed up the stairs. Her daughter's bedroom door was slightly ajar but she didn't like to intrude and again she asked.

"Shell you alright?"

When there was still no reply Sandra slowly pushed the door open a little wider. Apart from the bed being empty she didn't notice anything out of the ordinary and was about to go back downstairs again when she heard the faintest groan. Marching into the room she scanned the floor and when her eyes settled on the bloody mess that was her baby she screamed out. Michelle was barely conscious but she still managed to reach out her hand to her mother. Sandra screamed out, her beautiful girl was unrecognisable. Michelle's eyes were shut and swollen like a bull frogs. Blood was smeared around her mouth from where she'd lost her teeth and her beautiful hair was a tangled mess and stuck to the floor by congealed blood. Dropping to her knees Sandra called out for Leon but as soon as his name left her lips she realised that he wouldn't appear as he was almost certainly the culprit. Bending over she tried to take her daughter in her arms but when Michelle screamed out in pain Sandra gently let go and laid her back down. Suddenly all of her maternal instincts kicked in and she was up on her feet in seconds.

"I'm just going to call an ambulance darling then mummy's coming right back."

By now Michelle Steel was so far gone that she didn't even hear her mother. Sandra ran down the stairs and grabbed the phone. Strangely she remained calm as she relayed the state that her

daughter was in. The operator confirmed that a
paramedic would be there within ten minutes but
that in the meantime Sandra needed to make sure
that Michelle's airways were clear. As if on auto
pilot she ran back upstairs. Carrying out his
instructions to the letter Sandra then placed her
daughter's body into the recovery position.
"It'll be alright darling the ambulance is on its way."
The emergency services let themselves in and when
she heard them Sandra Steel called down.
"We're up here oh please hurry."
Looking down at her baby who right at this moment
was fighting for her life she could feel the first
stirrings of tears as they began to build in the
corners of her eyes. Just as Sandra had done so
many times before with her children, she reminded
herself that she was a Steel and sniffing loudly she
didn't allow the tears to fall.
"How's she doing Mr?"
"It's too early to tell but we need to get her to
hospital as soon as possible."
A brace was placed onto Michelle's neck and after
the two paramedics lifted her onto a stretcher
oxygen was administered.
"Where are you taking her to? I need to let me boys
know where well be."
"Mile End Hospital."
"Mile End! But that's nearly five mile away what's
wrong with Newham General?"
"Mrs Steel as much as time is of the essence your

daughter really needs a good critical care unit and the Mile End has one of the best in the area."

As the paramedics carried Michelle from her room Sandra spied her daughter's mobile phone on the dressing table. Picking it up she scanned the contacts for Kenny's number and dialled.

"Hi babe what you up to?"

"Son this aint Shell its Mum. Oh god Kenny she's in a right fucking mess and I don't even know if she's...."

Sandra began to sob and Kenny couldn't believe what he was hearing. His tone was tender as he tried to calm her down.

"Mum darling you aint making any sense. Now take a deep breath and tell me what is wrong sweetheart."

"It's our Shell she's been beaten to a pulp. They're now taking her to the Mile End Hospital, oh Kenny I'm so scared for her I think she might die."

Kenny Steel was pacing up and down as he spoke to his mother. He was full of rage but also fear, an emotion that was alien to him. His fist was clenched tight and he was desperate to ask who had done this to his beautiful sister. He also knew that if he pushed his mother now she might just break down again and he couldn't handle that.

"You go with her and I'll phone Vic and Charlie. Now try not to worry Mum, remember she's a Steel and made of stronger stuff."

His words were more of a comfort than he could

ever have known and ending the call she followed the stretcher down the stairs and into the back of the ambulance. The distance was only four and a half miles but even with the sirens blearing it would take fifteen minutes. The traffic was heavy and people weren't in a hurry to pull over even if it was for an ambulance. After a couple of minutes Michelle Steel went into cardiac arrest and the monitors started to bleep loudly making Sandra panic.

"What's wrong? What's happening, oh please god no not my baby please!!!!!"

The paramedic didn't have time to calm her down and gently but firmly he used his arm to push her away from Michelle so that he could use the defibrillator. When he was sure she wouldn't grab hold of her daughter again he set the dials and shouted clear. Michelle's body, for a second lifted up off the stretcher like something from a horror film. Luckily it only took the one shock before her heart was beating again.

"Can I touch her now?"

The paramedic smiled and nodded.

"It could happen again Mrs Steel so just be ready to move away quickly if I tell you to ok?"

God must have been looking down on them and when they pulled up outside the emergency department a team were ready and waiting to take over. Sandra argued that she wanted to stay with her daughter but the paramedic who had saved

Michelle on the journey over placed his arm on Sandra's shoulder and told her that it would be better for her girl if she waited in the relative's room.

"Is there anyone I can call to be with you?"

"Thanks love but I'll be alright. My boys will be here in a bit and they'll take care of everything I need."

The relative's room was small and claustrophobic. The hospital had tried to make it welcoming but somewhere along the line had failed dismally. Standing all alone in the room Sandra desperately willed Kenny to get here. Knowing her eldest as well as she did she was only too aware that he would be in a rage but right at this minute that was the least of her worries, Michelle staying alive was all that mattered.

CHAPTER EIGHTEEN

The three o'clock flight from Delhi into Heathrow
arrived on time and onboard Zena Cartwright
carried out her final duties as usual. The trip had
gone smoothly and Joginder Choudhary had been a
complete gentleman. After arranging to meet at her
hotel the pair had dined together and before he left
he gave her a wrapped gift. Back in her room Zena
opened the parcel and once more carried out the
task of swapping the sugar for Ketamine and just as
before there was a larger volume of K than sugar.
This time she had thought ahead and brought along
a spare makeup bag. When everything was carried
out to her satisfaction Zena washed her hands and
then placed the bags into her trolley case. For some
reason she felt more relaxed on this trip but was
adamant that once shed paid off Charlie's debt that
would definitely be it as far as she and drug
smuggling was concerned. After checking the cabin
one last time for any lost property Zena left the
plane with Sarah Morrison a fellow cabin crew
member. As the women walked through the exit
tunnel they chatted away about nothing in
particular and Zena felt calm. Entering passport
control she stopped dead in her tracks when she
saw a stranger sitting where Marvin Lennon usually
was. Panic started to set in and she didn't know
what to do. Not concentrating she dropped her
handbag and makeup and loose change scattered

across the floor. Sarah Morrison stooped down and began to pick up the items while Zena remained rooted to the spot. Staring up at her colleague Sarah saw the look of terror on Zena's face.

"Whatever's the mater Zena?"

Zena didn't reply and continued staring straight ahead at the stranger. Sarah gently touched her arm as she handed back the bag. The woman's touch startled Zena but it did at least bring her back to reality.

"Where's Marvin?"

"Who?"

"You know Marvin the bloke who is usually sitting at that desk."

"Oh that idiot! Thank your lucky stars he's off sick, he gives me the creeps. He's nothing but a perv Zena anyway come on lets go through I've got a hot date tonight with one of the pilots and I don't want to be late."

Zena had no option but to do as her friend asked and the two made idle chit chat as they passed by the desks. Almost at the exit Zena froze when a customs officer approached her.

"Excuse me Miss but I would like to have a look in your flight bag if that's alright."

It wasn't alright but Zena could hardly complain. Her only hope was that he would take a quick look just as Marvin had done and then let her go. Lifting her trolley onto the table she unzipped it and then stood with her hands behind her back and crossed her fingers.

"Alright Miss?"

Zena slowly nodded her head.

"We don't usually get stopped is there something wrong?"

"Not as far as I know but we've had word from above that we are not being thorough enough. Bloody pen pushers are always finding us more to do but I'll get through this as quickly as I can so that you can get on your way. Lovely weather for the time of year we're having. Now where have you flown in from?"

"India."

"India hey, I've always wanted to go there myself. Me and the Mrs love a ruby on a Saturday night." As he spoke David Dunstall probed and prodded around in Zena's trolley case. Just when she thought he was about to let her go he removed the teabags and then the two bags of sugar. Seeing that the tea hadn't been opened he placed it back into the case. Picking up a bag of sugar he examined it and then placed it beside the tea. Zena breathed a sigh of relief and as he lifted the second bag she waited for him to do the same but for some reason he studied it for a few seconds longer than she had hoped. Lifting it up and down he was trying to judge the weight and now all Zena could do was hold her breath as she waited. Pulling gently at the folded seal David Dunstall had soon opened the packet and was jabbing a finger inside.

201

He withdrew it when he realised the contents were definitely not sugar. His finger tip was coated in a fine white powder and he looked quizzically into Zena's eyes.

"Any idea what this might be Miss because I'm certain it's not sugar."

Zena's bottom lip began to tremble.

Did you pack the case yourself?"

For a moment she considered lying and saying that someone else had helped her pack but knew that it wouldn't take long for them to work out the truth. Zena was in panic mode but after a few seconds quickly accepted that she had no alternative but to admit her wrongdoing. Her voice was timid as she spoke.

"Yes I did."

"Then Miss, I'll need you to accompany me to the interview room."

Leading her away from the main area Zena Cartwright hung her head low but could still feel the eyes of her colleagues following her every move. Sarah Morrison was having everything taken out of her bag as it was assumed she was in on the crime. She wasn't pleased with her friend but at the same time knowing Zena had nothing to hide, Sarah couldn't help but feel sorry for Zena. The area Zena was taken to was a far different from anything she had seen before. The holding room resembled a prison cell and she was scared beyond belief. Left alone for over an hour she didn't know if they had forgotten about her or if it was common practice. She sat at the table and placed her hands onto the surface, Charlie would be worried sick and she wished she had a way to contact him. Suddenly the door opened and David Dunstall entered but he wasn't alone. Two female customs officers were with him and they both wore latex gloves. Zena knew the drill or at least she thought she did and even though she was aware of what they were about to ask she still felt petrified.

"Right Miss Cartwright, these officers are here to do a strip search. I know it isn't nice but the sooner we get on with things the sooner this will all be over." Zena quickly stood up and the chair on which she had been sitting flew away from her and hit the wall.

"Please! You have the drugs, there isn't any more I promise."

David Dunstall wasn't merciless, he felt for the young woman but he had a job to do and a duty to carry it out to the letter especially if they were to secure a conviction.

"I appreciate what you're telling me Miss Cartwright but we do have to follow procedure. Now I will leave you with Jean and Grace who will carry out the necessary examination.

Believe me it will go in your favour if you are cooperative."

Jean Thomas had been with customs and excise for over ten years. She loved her job and loved

203

searching females even more. Her large butch appearance frightened most of the women she searched but she was oblivious to that fact. Women whatever their shape or form appealed to her and although her colleague was far from gay, would go along with anything Jean asked. Grace Hampton was a hard working single mother. She hated her job but it paid the bills and even though she had seen Jean do things that went way beyond the realms of a body search, she wasn't about to complain. Feeding her kids was far more important than a complaint from some bitch who wanted to go down the illegal route to earn a few extra pounds and besides anything else she hated drugs and the people who smuggled them with a vengeance. David Dunstall nodded his head in her direction before leaving the room. The two women now seemed, if only to Zena, to close in on her. She knew it was futile to refuse or kick up a fuss and with a pleading look asked them what they wanted her to do.

"Firstly Miss Cartwright we cannot force you to do this but I might add it will go against you in a court of law if you refuse."

Zena just wanted whatever was in store, to be over with as soon as possible.

"Look I know I've done wrong so can we just get on with it?"

Jean Thomas was an old hand at body searching. She didn't judge people but being a lesbian she wouldn't deny that all the same she enjoyed the searches.

"Right! This is purely a visible search and we are not allowed to touch you in anyway, is that understood?"

Zena nodded her head.

"I would like you to remove all and I do mean all of your clothing and then bend over and touch your toes."

Zena Cartwright did as she was asked. When she removed her knickers and bra she had never felt so vulnerable in her whole life. Bending over she screwed up her eyes and prayed that the examination wouldn't take long. It didn't and a few seconds later she was told to put her clothes back on.

"What happens now?"

"You will shortly be interviewed."

"Doesn't a solicitor have to be present?"

Jean Thomas sighed, this would take even longer now but she knew better than to deny the girl her rights.

"If you want one but it could delay things for hours."

"I don't care and yes I would like one please."

By the time a duty solicitor had been contacted it was late evening. Food had been brought to Zena Cartwright but she had no appetite at all and only pushed the meagre offering around her plate. When Steve Morgan entered the room and introduced himself as the duty solicitor the look of relief was evident on her face.

"Am I going to get out of here Mr Morgan?"

"Not tonight I'm afraid. You will be in court in the morning and we will do our best to secure bail but you must be aware that there's a good chance it will be denied and you will be remanded in custody. When I've made some notes I'll have a better idea of your chances. Now has anyone been contacted regarding your arrest?"

"No but I really need to let either my parents or my fiancé know where I am."

"Let's get the interview over with first and then I can contact one of them on your behalf. You do know you are looking at a very serious charge here Miss Cartwright. Did you say anything to the officer who arrested you?"

Zena was ashamed and hung her head low as she spoke.

"No but I didn't need to they caught me red handed. Mr Morgan I'm not going to plead my innocence there wouldn't be any point."

With that the door opened and two plain clothed detectives entered the room. Zena was questioned for over two hours but her answers were always the same. She had only done this once, she was desperately trying to get the money together for her wedding and no one else was involved. Zena would see hell freeze over before she named Charlie in any of this even if it did mean she would receive a lengthier sentence. The one thing she hoped, hoped with all her heart, was that after it was all over he would be waiting for her. When the officers were certain that she wouldn't change her story and that further questioning would be futile she was charged. Her solicitor informed Zena that due to the late hour she would be held in one of the airport cells until the morning. From there she would be transferred to Hounslow magistrate's court. Steve Morgan continued to inform her that it would just be a basic hearing and that even though she had pleaded guilty; her case would definitely be recommended for crown court. By now Zena was so tired that she couldn't think straight. As her solicitor left she passed him a piece of paper containing her parent's phone number. She also asked him to tell her father to let Charlie know what had happened. Steve Morgan waited until he was back in his car before telephoning. He hated this part of his job but it had to be done so after carefully reading the number he dialled. Oblivious to the bombshell that would soon be dropped on them Stan and Linda had already turned in for the night. Linda was snoring softly but Stan for some reason was having difficulty getting asleep. It was so bad that he was just contemplating getting up to make a cup of tea when the bedside phone burst into life. Not wanting to wake his wife he snatched up the receiver.

"Hello?"

"Is that Mr Cartwright?"

"It is. Who is that?"

"Mr Cartwright my name is Steven Morgan and I
work for Bridge Bridge and Lambert."

"Look mate if you're trying to sell me something
you've got a bloody cheek calling so late at...."

"Mr Cartwright if you will just let me explain. I
work for a legal firm and we are representing your
daughter Miss Zena Cartwright."

The mention of her name had Stan sitting bolt
upright in a second and the jolt he made woke
Linda.

"Stan whatever's the matter, who is it?"

Stan Cartwright shook his head in an agitated
manner which instantly told his wife to be quiet
because whatever was being said was important.

"Zena? Whatever are you on about?"

Steve Morgan sighed heavily, he knew that what he
was about to reveal would turn the Cartwright's
world upside down and that their life would never
be the same again.

"I'm sorry to be the bearer of bad news but your
daughter has been arrested and charged with drug
smuggling. I can't go into any details at the
moment, only to tell you that she will be appearing
at Hounslow magistrate's court in the morning.
Your daughter did ask for you to inform someone
called Charlie."

With that Steve Morgan said goodnight and the line
was silent. Stan relayed what he had been told to

Linda who immediately started to cry. Pulling her to him he felt in shock and helpless but just as his daughter had asked he proceeded to dial Charlie Steels number. The call only rang a couple of times before it was answered.

"Charlie its Stan."

"Hello there Stan how are you?"

"Charlie, Zena's been arrested."

There was no answer and suddenly the line went dead.

"Charlie? Charlie are you there?"

There was still no reply and Stand Cartwright suddenly had a bad feeling, a feeling that his daughter could be in deep deep trouble.

"What did he say Stan?"

"The bastards just hung up on me!"

CHAPTER NINETEEN

Within an hour of Zena Cartwright being arrested, Kenny, Vic and Charlie were arriving at Mile End hospital. Reluctantly Vic had left his son with a neighbour as Deidre was already too out of her head on wine to risk leaving the child with her. In a time of crisis he should have been able to call on his sister-in-law or mother in law but as usual they had been drinking from early in the morning with his wife so were in no fit state either. After receiving the call from Kenny Vic now had a bad feeling, a feeling that everything was starting to fall apart and he didn't know what to do about it. Charlie's phone had rung while he slept on the couch at Zena's flat and his mouth hung open as Kenny revealed what had happened to Michelle. For a second he had been torn as to what to do but in all honesty there really was no choice. Oblivious to what Zena was going through he had wanted to be waiting for her when she got back but his sister had to take priority. It was the Steels way and you never let a family member down when they were in trouble no matter what else was going on in your life. At the hospital Kenny marched into the accident and emergency department and even though there were three or four people standing at the counter he pushed his way to the front. The receptionist was about to inform him that they had a queuing system but one glare from Kenny Steel told her not to waste her breath. After being given directions to the intensive care unit Kenny was the first to enter the relative's room and when his mother saw him she ran into his arms. The circles under her eyes were dark and if he hadn't have known any different Kenny would have sworn that she was smaller and somehow more fragile looking than he had ever seen her before. Sandra sobbed into his chest and the sight tore at Kenny's heart making him want to take on the world, take on anyone if it would ease her pain. Tenderly he stroked her hair and held her close.

"It's ok mum we're all here now."

Slowly he led her over to the couch, a couch that in the past must have been witness to more heartache than any of them could have imagined.

"Has the doctor been in yet?"

Sandra Steel could only shake her head through continuous rounds of sobbing. Vic stood in the doorway and didn't know what to do. He was a deep thinker but never knew what to say when there was a crisis. It had been the same ever since he was a small child and right at this moment he was happy for Kenny or anyone else to take charge. Before the brothers could question their mother further the door opened and the emergency doctor walked in. Heading straight towards Sandra he stopped right in front of her.

"Mrs Steel we have managed to stabilise your daughter but she has suffered some severe internal injuries, so the next twenty four hours will be

211

crucial. We have also carried out blood and urine tests and I am sorry to tell you that despite my team's best efforts she has lost the baby."

Instantly Kenny was on his feet and staring at the doctor in a menacing way.

"Fucking baby! What baby? What the fuck are you on about?"

The doctor looked towards Sandra for an explanation as to who the man was but all Sandra could do was wave her hand as she managed to say He's my son. The doctor didn't look in Kenny's direction and carried on talking to the mother of his patient.

"I'm sorry Mrs Steel but your daughter was only just pregnant, possibly two or three weeks. We can't be sure exactly on the date but the stomach trauma she has suffered meant the foetus didn't have a chance of survival."

Kenny wanted to scream, he didn't think it was possible to ever feel this way but right at this moment it felt as though his heart had been ripped from his chest. Slowly he came back down to reality and nodding his head told the doctor he understood. Taking a seat back on the sofa he gently took his mothers hands in his and stared deep into her eyes.

"I know you're upset but you have to give me some answers. Who did this mum?"

Sandra knew she had to be strong if only for the sake of her beautiful daughter. She also knew that the answer she would give could turn out to be a death sentence for whoever had done this terrible thing to Michelle.

"I aint a hundred percent sure son but when I found her Leon was nowhere to be seen. I called out for him but when he didn't answer I realised that it must have been him."

Strangely it was Charlie who spoke next.

"The cunt! I thought after last night, he would tame it down a bit."

Instantly Kenny was again on his feet and nodding in Vic's direction which told him to take care of their mother, he frogmarched Charlie out into the corridor.

"What the fuck are you on about?"

Charlie knew he was in deep shit but to hold back now would be more than his life was worth.

"Look Kenny it's not my fault alright? I didn't want to say anything but he's a right little wanker. Seems he's been shagging anything he could get his hands on and all behind our Shells back. Last night I saw him on the CCTV fucking some slapper round the back of the club. I'd had enough so I pulled him up about it and told him to fuck off home. I reckon he must have had a right barney with Shell and then this happened."

Kenny grabbed his brother by the throat and pushed him up against the wall. Charlie knew that just like a cat his lives were running out fast, at least as far as his brother was concerned. His words were like a red rag to a bull and Kenny began to squeeze harder.

"Why the fuck didn't you tell me?"

Charlie Steel started to choke and as his eyes bulged and watered Kenny slightly lessened his grip. Gasping for breath Charlie's voice was husky as he spoke.

"Look I thought I could handle it ok but it seems that cunt was more slippery than any of us could have imagined."

Kenny released his grip and Charlie slowly slid down the wall.

"This is all your fault you toe rag!"

Charlie Steel still held his throat and even though he was having difficulty in speaking knew that he had to say something, had to say sorry if he was ever to get back in his brothers good books.

"I know, I know and I'm sorry! Look I will do whatever you want to make it up to you and the family. Please Kenny I really really am sorry."

When the doctor appeared Kenny didn't wait to hear anymore of his brothers whining. They had all spent hours in the relative's room and now there was finally some news. Sandra was informed that they could go into the intensive care for a few minutes and she almost ran to the door. When they all entered the only noise that could be heard was the pumping sound of the ventilator. Kenny instantly went to Michelle's side and gently taking her hand kissed it.

214

"My poor poor baby!"

As before Vic stood motionless just inside the door. As much as he loved his sister even he could see that his brothers concern wasn't natural. Sandra Steel stood on the other side of the bed and bending low placed a kiss on her daughter's forehead. Michael Farrow the intensive care doctor, stood at the end of the bed and watched as the family tended to their nearest and dearest. It was something he saw on a regular basis but somehow the younger the patient the harder it was to stomach.

"Now please don't be alarmed but we've put Michelle on a ventilator as she is so heavily sedated. I can assure you this is standard practice and it just helps to take the strain and work load temporarily from Michelle's lungs. By decreasing the work it takes to breath and giving extra oxygen the patient is able to reserve what little energy they have for healing. There is a built in alarm system that will detect any problems and notify us straight away. Hopefully by the morning she will be well enough to breathe on her own and we will be able to remove the tube. All we can hope for is that this time tomorrow there will be better news."

Michael Farrow quietly made his way from the room as he didn't know what else to say. If the girl made it through the night then she would be lucky and his team would have done a good job. For now it was in the hands of god, someone he hadn't believed in for a long time but all the same he still offered up a silent prayer. Kenny began to talk to his sister in low soft tones that he hoped she could hear.

"It's ok honey. You're going to be just fine and I'm going to kill the cunt that's done this to you."

Just then Charlie's mobile burst into life and if looks could kill then Charlie would have been dead ten times over. Kenny snarled his lip back as he spoke.

"Not in fucking here you tosser!"

Once more making his way into the corridor Charlie pressed the accept button on his phone only to realise it was Stan Cartwright on the other end. When he heard the one sentence he was dreading Charlie Steel hung up and went back into the room. Sandra said nothing; her body was draped over her daughter while she slowly sobbed her heart out. The sight of his mother hit Charlie hard and he now felt worse than ever, quietly he muttered words of revenge under his breath. After each of the family had kissed Michelle and said their goodnights the Steels made their way from the hospital. Sandra and Kenny were both struggling mentally and leaving Michelle alone in the Mile End weighed heavily on their consciences. The only place left to go; the only place in the world that any of them wanted to be when there was a crisis was back in the family home on Boreham Avenue. Slowly Sandra turned the key but as she entered the hallway her house seemed cold. Remembering being here just a few hours earlier and what had

occurred caused a shiver to run down her spine.
Just like shed done so many times before, Sandra
did her best to shrug off the feeling as she walked
into the kitchen. Placing the kettle on to boil she
smiled when she saw her three boys take a seat at
the table. Removing a bottle from the top cupboard
she added a liberal measure of rum to each of the
four mugs. Coffee and Rum was always good and
especially when you'd had a shock and that was
something they had all experienced today. Silently
they all sipped at the hot drinks and it was Vic who
was the first to break the silence.
"So Kenny what you got planned?"
Kenny Steel placed his cup onto the table and
looked from his mother to Charlie and then Vic.
"I want to annihilate the cunt fucking tear him limb
from limb for what he's done. I want you both to
pack because tomorrow we head for Spain."
Charlie Steel knew that he had to speak up now,
had no alternative but to tell them what had
happened to Zena. Turning to his mother he smiled
warmly.
"Why don't you have an early night mum you look
done in?"
Sandra was about to protest when she saw her
youngest slightly tilt his head to one side. It was
something he'd done since he was a toddler and it
told her he was pleading. Tenderly she kissed each
of her boys on the forehead before disappearing
from the kitchen. As soon as he was sure she

wouldn't return Charlie turned to face Kenny.
"Something's happened bro and you aint going to like it."
Kenny was still angry with his brother and it took every ounce of effort he could muster just to look at Charlie.
"Fuck me! Now what are you running on about?"
"You know when my phone went off at the hospital, well it was Stan Cartwright."
Kenny looked quizzically at Charlie as much as to say who?
"Stan! You know Zena's old man?"
"And?"
"She's been arrested."
Vic couldn't believe what he was hearing and slammed his mug onto the table.
"Fuck me! That poor little cows going to do time now and its all down to us. Well I hope you're both fucking proud of yourselves. I told you we shouldn't get mixed up in fucking drug smuggling and now look what's happened."
Kenny didn't like what Vic was saying but for once he didn't make comment on his brother's choice of words. He wouldn't admit it to anyone but Vic was right. Kenny didn't have any feelings towards the Cartwright girl but he was concerned that it could come back to his door and right at the moment he knew his mother couldn't take much more. Sandra Steel had always put on a brave face which told the world and his wife that no one should mess with

218

her family but tonight at the hospital Kenny had seen a different side to her and he was worried.

"You two are going to have to go to Spain on your own and sort that cunt out. Because of the girls cock up I need to be here in case the Old Bill come knocking. Either of you got a problem with that?" Charlie wasn't happy about the situation but at the same time knew to keep his mouth shut. Vic on the other hand had no reason to stay quiet.

"What! Look as much as I'd like to get me hands on the wanker and knock seven bells of shit out of him, he aint exactly my main priority. In case you've forgot Kenny I have a son to care for and a wife whose on the bottle more than she's off it."

Kenny Steel stood up and towering above his brother hissed his reply.

"I don't give a fuck! The kid won't come to any harm and we can't be seen to be letting the boy get away with this, besides we need revenge for our Shell. Now get packed and over to Heathrow tonight. Take the first plane out no matter what the cost. I aint asking the pair of you I'm fucking telling you!"

With that Kenny marched from the room and out of the house. He felt an overpowering need to return to the hospital and be with his sister. Back in the kitchen Charlie looked in his brother's direction.

"Now what do we do?"

Vic slowly shook his head.

"Exactly what we always do Charlie and that's

whatever Kenny wants. Get packed then we can call at mine to sort things out with Deidre and god help her if she aint sobered up by now."

CHAPTER TWENTY

Charlie and Vic entered the maisonette and walked up the flight of stairs. Deidre was out cold on the sofa and without a word Vic made his way over and dragged her up by her hair. His actions didn't shock Charlie, not that he had ever seen his brother behave like that before but simply because it was well over due. The pain brought Deidre to her senses and she started to scream and kick out. Vic ignored the sound and her resistance and grabbing her by the arm he pulled her into the kitchen. Throwing her onto the chair and without a second glance he proceeded to plug in the electric kettle. After forcing Deidre to drink five full cups of strong coffee and she protested all the way, he at last thought she was sober enough to hear what he was saying.

"Right you bitch! Now our Michelle's been hurt and is in the hospital. I have to go away for a couple of days and you for once are going to take care of our son. If he has so much as a scratch on him when I get back I swear I'll fucking kill you."

Even in her hazy state Deidre Steel had never seen her husband so angry, not even when he had been beating the crap out of her the other Sunday. Knowing that for her own self preservation she would do as he asked she couldn't help but form a sly grin on her face as she thought of Michelle lying in the hospital. As if he was reading her thoughts

221

Vic lashed out and the palm of his hand forcibly made contact with her cheek pushing her head violently backwards.

"What?"

"You fucking know what! Now first thing in the morning get your arse round to Dale and Susie's and collect little Vic. When I get back I don't want to hear a whisper that your skanky mother or sister have been here."

Deidre turned her face away and Vic roughly grabbed her cheeks with his hand and turned her back to face him.

"Do you hear me?"

Deidre Steel nodded her head and with that Vic made his way to the bedroom and quickly packed a bag. Charlie was standing in the kitchen door way leaning up against the frame and when his sister-in-law looked in his direction he smirked.

"What the fuck are you grinning at you twat?"

"Deidre love it's nice to see my brother actually getting some balls for once and gawd help you if you get pissed while he's away is all I can say."

Before they set off for the airport Vic and Charlie had one last place to visit. Pulling up outside Julie Sullivan's house they both got out of the car and Charlie rapped loudly on the front door. The place was in darkness and he guessed that she had turned in for the night. Not one to be put off he hammered on the door even harder and a couple of minutes later the hall light went on and he could see the

shape of Ruby Sullivan appear behind the glass.
"Who is it?"

"Its Charlie Steel Mrs Sullivan Shells brother. I need to have a world with Julie."

"Do you know what bleeding time it is? Can't you come back in the morning lad?"

Charlie looked at Vic and they both shook their heads.

"I'm sorry Mrs Sullivan but it's really important that we speak to her now!"

Ruby didn't reply but her form could be seen climbing the stairs again. Charlie wrapped his arms around himself and patted to keep warm. It was late and the night was starting to turn really chilly. After five minutes the door was unlocked and Julie stood in front of them in a baby pink onesie. Even Vic had to stifle a laugh but when Ruby reappeared things got serious.

"So what's all this about boys only we both need to get our beauty sleep you know."

Charlie stepped into the hallway and put his arm around Julie Sullivan's shoulder.

"I know you do but Jules if you value your friendship with me sister you'll help us out. Now I want you to think really hard love and tell me all you can about that tosser Leon Bishop."

Julie was about to protest that she knew no more than they did but Charlie put his hand up to stop her.

"Look Julie he's hurt our Shell real bad and she's in

the hospital. We think he's scarpered back to Spain and that's what I need to know about. Now do you know what his address is?"

After letting out a loud gasp Julie proceeded to explain that they never went to Leon's house but she did tell him about the Irish bar and that he sometimes worked for his dad who ran some kind of holiday accommodation. The information she had given wasn't much but at least it was something to go on. Vic and Charlie said their goodbyes and headed for Heathrow airport but neither of them was looking forward to the journey ahead.

Kenny spent an hour at his sister's bedside holding her hand. The pain and emotion he felt as he looked at her tore away at his insides and his anger was steadily building. He wished with all his heart that he could have gone to Spain with his brothers. When the nurse came in and persuaded him to go home as they weren't expecting any change for several hours, he reluctantly kissed his sister goodnight. There was no one to see him and Kenny's lips lingered on Michelle's mouth longer than was natural. His tears fell onto her cheek and he tenderly wiped them away. After composing himself and when he was sure that no one could see he had been crying he set off to do the nightly checks on a few of the pubs and clubs. The drive over to Southend did him good and with each mile he slowly put everything into perspective. Finally reaching Chinnerys he wearily climbed out of the

Range Rover and made his way inside. As usual Mattie Singer was on duty alongside Aaron Paige and when they spotted their boss they both made a bee line in his direction.

"Evening Mr Steel."

"Mattie, Aaron. Everything quiet tonight?"

"Sure is, aint had a spot of bother here since the K problem. Is everything on that score alright now?"

Kenny nodded. He wasn't about to let anyone know his business. True Mattie was loyal and had been more than helpful when they had gone mob handed after Mickey Sandish but as far as any other details went it was strictly on a need to know basis only. Mattie and Aaron walked outside with their boss and the three were about to say their goodnights when a man who was shouting loudly began to approach the pub.

Stan Cartwright was out on the war path. Since his phone call from Zena's solicitor he hadn't been able to sleep a wink. Linda had begged him not to go out but Stan was adamant that he was going to track down his daughter's scumbag fiancé and see what he had to say for himself. After two hours of trawling the clubs and without a single sighting of Charlie Steel he was about to admit defeat and go home when he spied Kenny Steel coming out of Chinnerys pub.

"Steel you cunt! My girls locked up because of you and that fucking brother of yours."

Kenny shook his head, this was all he needed.

225

He could see the man's anguish and smell the whisky on his breath. Deciding his best option was to try and calm Stan Cartwright down he spoke in a low gentle voice.

"Look I'm sorry about it all but I've only just heard the news myself. What say we go inside and talk about it over a pint?"

Kenny in a friendly manner went to touch Stan on the arm but the man wasn't having any of it and shrugged Kenny's hand away.

"You're all a bunch of gutless wankers. You let a young woman do your fucking dirty work for you because there aint one of you that's got any real balls!"

People passing by were starting to stare and Kenny wasn't happy with the man's outburst. From out of nowhere he saw red, whether it was the hurt he was feeling regarding Michelle or purely down to the fact that Stan's behaviour was wearing thin, either way Kenny now snapped.

"Why don't you just shut the fuck up and go home you stupid old cunt!"

His words were like a red rag to a bull and Stan started to shout at the top of his voice that the Steels were all drug dealers.

"Right I've had enough of this. Mattie, take him round the back and shut him up. Give him a fucking slap if you have to then get back inside. I've just about had a gutful today I can tell you"

Kenny Steel walked towards his car and didn't look

back but he could hear the ensuing scuffle as Mattie and Aaron grabbed Stan Cartwright and started to carry him down the side of the building. Mattie had Stan in a bear hug around his shoulders and Aaron grabbed him by the legs. To them it was as easy as carrying a rolled up carpet but all the time Stan continued to scream out obscenities and vows of revenge for his only child. Reaching the rear car park Aaron dropped Stan's legs to the ground but Mattie continued to grip him tightly. Aaron punched Stan Cartwright hard in the face and a cracking sound was heard. He screamed, surprisingly not because of the pain, there was very little but at the sound that seemed to echo throughout his head. Blood spurted out and his nose spread across his face. As his head went backwards from the force of the blow he butted Mattie squarely in the face.

"You cunt!"

Mattie rammed Stan Cartwright's face into the wall and as bone and skin made contact with the bricks he let go of his victim. Stan's body slid to the ground but that wasn't enough for Mattie Singer. Annoyed at being caught off guard he began to stamp on Stan's head and face. After his boot had made contact a couple of times and he'd kicked out at the man's ribs just for good measure Aaron pulled Mattie away from Stan.

"Leave it out Mat for fucks sake! Kenny said slap him not fucking kill him."

Mattie Singer knew that his rage had taken over and he'd possibly gone too far. Breathing in deeply he stepped back and surveyed the damage.

"Serves the wanker right. Come on let's get back inside."

Aaron wasn't shocked at the level of violence, after all it wasn't something that he hadn't seen most Saturday nights after closing but that didn't stop him being concerned for the old boy.

"You can't just leave him there Mat."

"Can't I? You just fucking watch me."

The two doormen walked back to the front of Chinnerys with no more thought for the state that Stan Cartwright was in. It would be a further hour before he was found by a couple who had made their way round the back for a drunken session of sex. The couple had been almost in the throes of passion when they heard a low groaning sound. The man, far older than his conquest, would have been happy to ignore the noise but the girl thankfully had a conscience. Pulling down her skirt Louise Adams walked over to the crumpled mess that was Zena Cartwright's father and when she saw the state of his face let out a scream.

"Liam! Liam get over here quick!"

Kneeling down Louise tried to cradle Stan in her arms but there was so much blood on his face and clothes and it was the first time she had worn her white lace dress. It had cost well over a week's wages from the cafe where she worked and as much

228

as she wanted to help the poor man, sadly her dress meant more.

"It's alright love well soon get you sorted. For fucks sake Liam put your cock away and get over here and call an ambulance will you?"

Liam Hilton did as he was asked and then left the scene as quickly as he could. His wife would be expecting him home and the last thing he needed was to be caught up with the Old Bill if they arrived. Louise watched in dismay as he walked away. She was under no illusion regarding his marital status but she still couldn't get over just how heartless he was. Biting the bullet she muttered under her breath Oh fuck it! as she tenderly took Stan Cartwright's head into her lap.

"Hold on in there sweetheart helps going to be here soon I promise."

As luck would have it, for the doormen at least, Southend was really busy so no police attended the scene. It seemed like an age before the ambulance arrived but when it did it was with all sirens blaring. At first due to the blood that she had on her, the paramedic thought it was Louise who was injured but she soon put them straight. The paramedic helped her to her feet and told her what a Good Samaritan she was before whisking Stan into the ambulance and leaving her alone in the alley. As Louise Adams watched the flashing lights disappear out of sight she was alone and suddenly scared. Making her way to the main road she just hoped she could get home safely. There was blood on her dress which didn't look good, so she doubted that anyone would come to her aid if she needed them.

At the University hospital and after Stan had been examined, it was determined that his injuries were not life threatening so he was moved up to a ward. He had been able to give them his home number and Linda's name before passing out and when the bedside phone began to ring his wife was awake in a second. Reaching over to grab the receiver Linda Cartwright mouthed the words God help us now what? When she heard her husband's name and the word hospital mentioned Linda began to cry. Within a few hours it seemed as if her whole world had fallen apart. Informing the nurse that she would be there as soon as she could Linda dressed quickly and then phoned for a taxi. Anxiously waiting she realised just how vulnerable and helpless she was. Stan always did the driving and now when he needed her most she couldn't even get to him without having to rely heavily on others. Swearing that once all this was over she was going to take lessons Linda Cartwright made her way to the hospital. Once there she began to panic when she realised that she didn't know where to look for her husband. Several fraught minutes were spent walking about in all directions before she was finally taken up to the correct ward. The porter who had been so helpful when she first arrived pointed in the direction of Stan's bed and Linda let out a gasp when she saw him. His face was battered and bruised and there was dried blood covering both his hands.

"Oh my darling whatever have they done to you?" Stan just managed to clasp her hand in his and in an almost inaudible whisper said.

"Zena's who we need to worry about love; our Zena is all that matters now."

CHAPTER TWENTY ONE

The cell Zena was being held in was stark and cold but even if that hadn't have been the case her mind was working in overdrive. All through the night she had constantly thought of her mum, dad and Charlie. So much so that she hadn't slept a wink. With the first light now coming through the glass brick window high above her head she began to think about what was going to happen to her. Zena had never felt so alone in her entire life and not being able to speak to her parents and reassure them played heavily on her mind. At ten that morning Zena Cartwright made an appearance at Hounslow Magistrates Court. Steve Morgan was waiting for her in the holding room below the court and even though they hardly knew each other she felt like crying when she saw him. Just to recognise someone among the numerous strangers that now followed her every move brought a small amount of relief.

"Morning Miss Cartwright. Did you manage to get any sleep last night?"

Steve Morgan had dealt with many such cases in the past and already knew the answer to his question. He also knew from experience that asking such a normal thing would help her to relax.

"No not really. Were you able to get in contact with my family?"

"I spoke to your father and as you can imagine he

was shocked to say the least but he did say he would contact the young man named Charlie. Now before we go in Zena are you sure there is nothing more you wish to tell me?"

Zena had thought about nothing else all night but she hadn't changed her mind. Charlie Steel was the love of her life and she would keep him out of this no matter what.

"There's nothing more than I've already told you."

"In that case I need to run through what will happen when we go up to the court room."

Steve Morgan explained that in a few minutes time she would be led upstairs and made to stand before the Magistrates. He also explained that this was just the first stage of a lengthy procedure which would definitely end up being transferred to the Crown Court for sentencing. As she had pleaded guilty it would help her case somewhat but she would still be looking at a hefty prison term.

"The only thing I'm hoping to achieve today is to get you bail. If I succeed then you will be able to walk out of here for a while at least. Please don't build your hopes up Zena as I've seen stronger reasons than yours refused bail before. It will all depend on how badly the prosecution want you remanded. Now keep your chin up and I will see you in a little while."

With that he was gone and Zena was left alone in the room to wait. Just as shed been told by Steve Morgan a few minutes later two police officers came in and led her up to the courtroom. Apart from watching numerous dramas on television this was the first experience that Zena had ever had of a court and she could feel her legs shaking as she was led into the dock. The bench was made up of three magistrates, two men and the senior member a woman by the name of Felicity Haversham. They all wore spectacles on the tips of their noses which made Zena feel as if she was in some kind of Dickensian time warp. Felicity Haversham studied Zena and was pleased to see that the young woman was smartly turned out unlike so many of the local criminals who appeared before her. Zena stood tall and upright and it was a trait Felicity liked in a young person.

"Do you understand the charges against you that have been read out in this courtroom?"

"Yes Madam."

"And how do you plead?"

"Guilty Madam."

"Very well. You may sit down now and I will hear arguments regarding a bail application."

Zena wasn't required to speak again and all she could do was listen as the strangers in front of her talked about her life and why or why not she should or shouldn't be allowed to remain at liberty. It was the first day in court for Peter Wardor and the first time for him to speak on behalf of the Crown Prosecution Service.

"Madam the CPS does not feel it would be in the

public's best interest if the defendant was granted bail."

Felicity Haversham was well known by the legal establishment for being a hard task mistress and along with that came the fact that she always seemed to favour women defendants. Steve Morgan had been overly pleased when he'd first seen her name on the court list of bench members. All decisions regarding a case were supposed to be made equally between the three Magistrates but they were all aware that Felicity Haversham always got her way. As the prosecution droned on but didn't really say anything of any substance Felicity started to get annoyed. Holding up the palm of her hand she momentarily stopped the proceeding.

"Mr Wardor I hope I do not need to remind you of Gault v UK 2007. I do not wish for this to end up in the Court of Human rights for any reason whatsoever, especially due to negligence on behalf of the CPS. Please show some respect and refrain from argument if you do not have any reasonable evidence to provide regarding an application to deny bail. Now are there any police reports?"

"Yes Madam."

"Well?"

Peter Wardor scoured through his paperwork and was becoming more and more flustered by the second.

"Young man I really am starting to lose my patience!"

Now fumbling about in his brief case he was desperate to locate his notes and he didn't dare look the magistrate in the face. Her tone made him nervous enough without seeing her frown down at him, which he knew would make him feel like a school boy. Finally he at last found the report he was looking for.

"The police and CPS feel that if the defendant is released on bail she will abscond or reoffend Madam."

"Is that it Mr Wardor?"

"Yes it is Madam."

As nothing else was offered, the panel retired to the inner chamber to discuss the reasoning that had been put before them. Zena was once again led downstairs where Steve Morgan was already waiting. Wringing her hands together she looked at him in a pleading way.

"So how do you think it went Mr Morgan?"

"I'm not a gambling man so I don't want to give you any odds or false hopes. Nor do I want to jinx matters by presuming anything but personally I think it went as well as it could have under the circumstances and you are lucky to have got Mrs Haversham. She's a tough old bird but strangely she doesn't always have a lot of time for the crown prosecution service. Madam Haversham usually doesn't believe in locking people up for the sake of it, so fingers crossed."

About to take a seat at the table even Steve Morgan

was shocked when they were asked to return to the court so soon. Everyone took their seats and the three Magistrates appeared from a door at the back of the panelled room. Felicity Haversham sat at the head of the bench and waited until there was silence before she began to speak.

"Right Mr Wardor. We have discussed the options and the reasoning put forward by the prosecution. We jointly feel that if certain conditions are adhered to then there is little chance of the defendant reoffending."

Turning to look at Zena Felicity Haversham spoke in a stern voice.

"Miss Cartwright you must agree to surrender your passport. Reside wholly at the address of your parents, which Mr Morgan assures me is acceptable to them. Finally you will be electronically tagged and be expected to stay indoors from six pm each night until eight am the following morning. If you fail to abide by any of these restrictions you will be brought back before this court and remanded. Do you understand everything I have said to you young lady?"

Zena's eyes were full of tears and she could only nod her head vigorously.

"I am referring this case to the Crown Court for sentencing at a date to be decided."

With that the court was dismissed and Zena Cartwright was left standing in the dock. It wasn't until Steve Morgan approached her that she finally took in everything that had been said.

"Miss Cartwright you are free to go home!"

Handing her a key Zena stared down at it long and hard.

"I'm sorry but they would only allow you to have your car key back. All of your other possessions are being held as evidence but at least you will be able to get home. Within the next few hours a Security Officer will call at you parents home to fit the tagging device. Please make sure you are there to greet them or you will automatically be in breach of your bail conditions."

Zena nodded her understanding and after Steve Morgan had dropped her back at the airport so that she could collect her car she set off for home with a very heavy heart. All the thinking she did on the hour and a half drive did nothing to lift her spirits. Her freedom was only temporary and Zena knew that before long she would probably be locked up for twenty three hours a day. As she pulled into the drive she noticed that her father's car was missing. If they were out somewhere then she wouldn't be able to get inside. Petrified that the man would be here to tag her before they got home she was relieved when her mother's face appeared from behind the net curtains. Instantly the front door opened and the two women fell into each other's arms crying. When the tears had at last subsided, Linda led her daughter into the house. Pouring them both a large measure of brandy they sat together on the bottom stair. It was a practice that had begun when Zena was small. Whenever something was troubling her she could be found sitting at the bottom of the stairs. Zena told her mother all that had happened and she didn't miss anything out. When she finished talking she was expecting her mother to say that Charlie had been to see them and that he was really worried about her. Linda then dropped the bombshell that her fiancé had hung up on Stan and Zena couldn't believe what she was hearing. Suddenly she realised that in the fifteen minutes or so that she'd been home she hadn't given a second thought to her father. Turning to look at her mother she asked in a quizzical way where he was. Lind Cartwright had been dreading this moment but she was also aware that there was no way of sugar coating things. Taking a deep breath she relayed all that had happened since they had received the telephone call from Steve Morgan.

"Are you telling me that the Steels beat my father to a pulp?"

Linda could only nod and Zena tried desperately to hold inside the anger that was trying to escape. Surprisingly she now accepted that Charlie had used her, accepted that her career had gone and that she was looking at a long stretch in prison. What she couldn't handle was the fact that her beautiful loyal dad had been beaten so badly in his attempt to stand up for her.

239

"I need to see him."

"Darling we have to wait for your tag to be put on and besides visiting is two until six."

Zena Cartwright retreated to her bedroom to wait. Sitting alone in the room she at last allowed herself to break down. Looking upwards she pleaded to god asking to know why this had all happened but just as she expected there was no answer. At just before two there was a knock at the door, a knock Linda had been dreading. As she watched the plastic tag being fitted onto her daughter's right ankle she began to sob. To Linda it was a shackle, a sign that she would soon be a prison visitor and that thought cut her deeply. When the Security Officer was happy that the technology was working as it should be he left. For a moment Zena and her mother stared down at the plastic tag in silence and then for some strange reason they both began to laugh at the absurdity of it all. Finally they composed themselves and were soon in Zena's car heading for the hospital. On Linda's advice her daughter had worn a pair of trousers and on arrival at the busy reception Zena was glad that for once she had done what her mother had asked. As they approached the ward Linda stopped and turning to her daughter grabbed her arm.

"Darling he's not in a good state."

"I didn't think he would be after coming up against the Steels. They are nothing but fucking animals Mum."

240

Linda Cartwright didn't comment on her daughter's choice of language but all the same she didn't like it. Deciding that tomorrow would be soon enough for reprimands she continued along the linoleum corridor.

"I know but I just wanted you to be prepared that's all."

Walking into the ward Zena didn't really know what to expect. When she laid eyes on her father she let out a gasp but was able to hold back any further emotions as she made her way over to his bedside. Stan Cartwright's eyes were so swollen they were almost closed. The bridge of his nose had a large cut above it and much to Linda's disgust; his hands hadn't been cleaned and were still full of dried blood. As Zena touched her father's arm he opened his eyes and even though he was in a lot of pain he managed a smile and a few words.

"Hello my darling you alright?"

From somewhere deep inside Zena found a strength that she had never known before.

"Hiya daddy. Yeh I'm fine and if your appearance is anything to go by I'm a lot better off than you are."

Stan Cartwright let out a tiny laugh which made his wife, daughter and the man in the next bed smile. The surroundings of the ward were so sombre that the other patients welcomed a few moments of light relief. Zena relayed all that had happened and how she now felt about Charlie Steel. His daughter's strength pleased Stan and he instantly grabbed her hand.

"Whatever happens we will get through this love and at the end of it me and your mum will be waiting and I don't want you to ever forget that."

"I won't dad I promise but I can't believe they did this to you."

"Sweetheart it takes all sorts and it's unfortunate that you got mixed up with the wrong sort but I know me and your mum will see you through it."

Zena grabbed her father's hand and smothered it with kisses. She wanted him to know, was desperate for him to know that she loved him with all of her heart. A plan was beginning to form deep inside but before she could put it into action she also needed to know that he loved her and believed in her.

"Now come on babe lets have no more tears. I will be out of here in a few days and then we can really get the ball rolling. Well show them Steels that the Cartwright's are made of stronger stuff, what you say?"

Zena had to swallow hard to contain her tears but she wouldn't show the hurt to her father no matter what. If he could be strong then so could she and she now knew that she would do whatever was necessary to get her revenge.

"Dad I was a fool to think that a man like Charlie Steel could ever love someone like me."

Stan Cartwright furrowed his brow and it caused

him pain but he couldn't believe what his daughter had just said.

"Darling you need to take a long hard look at yourself. Its him who was the lucky one. Any man that can bag a woman as beautiful as my girl needs to think himself lucky not the other way round. Now don't ever let me hear you talk like that again."

"Sorry Dad and I promise that from now on I will never let you down again."

Stan grabbed his daughters hand and squeezed it tightly.

"You never have my darling, you never have."

CHAPTER TWENTY TWO

At Heathrow airport Vic and Charlie had been put
on standby for the next available flight to Malaga.
After hours of hanging about without any sleep
they finally boarded a plane at seven thirty the next
morning. The Boeing seven three seven aircraft was
virtually full to capacity with holiday makers.
Charlie Steel was tired and in a bad mood when he
took his seat and much to Vic's amusement had an
unruly four year old seated behind him. As the
plane began to taxi along the runway the kicking
started in the back of his seat. At first it was just
once or twice but when it became more frequent
Charlie Steel turned round and glared at the child.
His annoyance only fuelled the fire and the boy
upped the speed and repetition of his kicks.
"Little wanker!"
Vic started to laugh which only wound his brother
up more.
"Right that's it!"
With that Charlie undid his seat belt and stood up.
Vic could see by the look on his face that his brother
was about to cause trouble.
"Leave it out Charlie he's only a kid."
"Maybe he is but his old man aint now is he?"
The air hostess, who was in the middle of her safety
routine, frowned at the disruption. Charlie lent
over the child until his face almost touched the
boy's father.

244

"Stop that little cunt from kicking my seat or I'll kick the shit out of you got it?"

The man instantly grabbed his son's legs and slapped them down making the boy cry. He'd been looking forward to his holiday all year and the last thing he wanted was to arrive in Marbella with two black eyes. He did contemplate calling a member of the cabin crew to complain but the vicious look in Charlie's eyes held him back. The rest of the journey passed without incident and the brothers even managed to get some sleep. Their plane touched down two hours later just as Zena Cartwright was led into court. Charlie was unaware of what was going on back home regarding her court appearance but even if he'd have known it wouldn't have made any difference. As far as he was concerned Zena was history and he was ready to move on to his next conquest, in fact he couldn't wait. With no transport arranged the brothers had to find their own way to the resort and after learning the cost of a taxi Vic moaned for the entire fifty minute journey. He was tired and the hot morning heat was starting to make him sweat which caused his shirt to stick to his body. Telling the taxi driver to drop them off at the marina so that they could get a feel for the place they then inquired about finding somewhere to stay. Carlos Abalos had been earning his living from the holiday trade for over twenty years and he hated foreigners with a passion. They were ignorant and rude but living in a holiday resort he had little choice but to do one of the few jobs on offer. That said if he could get one over on them it always made his day and he was now grinning from ear to ear as he recommended one of the most expensive hotels and further informed the brothers that it was so close it wasn't worth a taxi fare.

"The Melia Marbella is very good my friends. Turn left, right, left and then right again and you will find the hotel on the left. It is a very nice place my friends and very cheap."

Charlie and Vic began the walk, a walk that would take them over thirty minutes. By the time they arrived they were both drenched in sweat and totally knackered. The receptionist booked them in and handed over the door card.

"Aint you going to ask how much it is?"

"Fuck me Vic! You aint half a tight cunt."

Turning to the receptionist Charlie used his most alluring smile as he spoke.

"How much is the room going to cost us sweetheart?"

When they were informed that it was two hundred and eighty pounds a night and that didn't include breakfast Vic let out a groan.

"That fucking taxi driver has stitched us up good and proper and he could have dropped us here instead of making us walk for miles, the wanker!"

Charlie was already standing in the lift. He wasn't in the mood to argue and he definitely wasn't about to go looking for somewhere else to stay.

"Are you coming or what?"

Vic was still moaning as they entered the room but when he saw their accommodation even he had to admit it was a bit special. Everything was high class from the furniture down to the bedding and the view from the balcony was amazing. Vic Steel dropped his bag onto the floor and then collapsed onto the bed.

"Are we going to get out there and start looking for the boy then?"

"Charlie you can do what you like but I'm getting some shut eye. Tonight will be early enough and besides he probably don't even surface until after dark."

Charlie Steel walked over to the mini bar and peered inside. It was fully stocked and as he removed a beer, glanced in his brother's direction. "Don't fucking say a word alright? I'll pay for whatever drink I have so you aint got to worry."

Vic didn't reply and turning over was soon fast asleep. The brothers stayed in their room for the rest of the afternoon. Charlie woke around six and after sitting out on the balcony for an hour finally decided to wake Vic. After a quick shower they were soon walking along the marina and couldn't believe how alive the area was compared to earlier that day. Charlie laughed as he commented on the fact that the place had more Towie's than Essex. If he hadn't have been here for a reason then he would have had a whale of a time. He mentally made a note to return one day and by the selection of girls on offer it would be sooner rather than later. Calling in at Ristorante Italiano the brothers had dinner. Situated on the edge of the Marina they chose a table outside so that they could watch the passersby and get a proper feel for the place. The food was good and also far from cheap but after his earlier ranting, which had caused Charlie to get the hump, Vic didn't dare say a word. He had accepted that this trip was going to be expensive and as there weren't any fish and chip shops on the sea front he just had to go with the flow. After three courses Charlie was stuffed and in all honesty he just wanted to go back to the hotel and turn in for the night. Yawning out loud and stretching up his arms he looked at Vic.

"What say we continue tomorrow I'm fucking knackered!

"So am I but I don't plan on staying here any longer than I have to. At the rate we're spending I'm going to be fucking bankrupt before too long."

Charlie could only shake his head. He didn't know where his brother's tightness came from. It certainly wasn't the case with Kenny or their mum who could shop for England if she had a mind to. Then there was Shell, poor daft little Shell who was ten times worse than Sandra when it came to wasting money. The thought of his sister and all that she had gone through brought on a fresh anger in Charlie and throwing down his napkin he stood up.

"Come on then let's go and find that little cunt and give him a taste of his own medicine."

It was a warm night and the people milling about seemed to be in high spirits. All along the marina music pounded out making Charlie feel like enjoying himself. They called in at a few bars but when they reached one with the name IRISH BAR emblazed above the entrance, knew this was the place Julie Sullivan had told them about. Walking up to the bar they ordered two pints of Guinness and scanned the room. It was only just after nine and the barman told them that the place didn't really come to life until eleven. Vic again groaned, he wasn't one to stay out late unless it was for work. The thought that they would have to sit here for another two hours really grated on him. There were a couple of bar stools empty so the brothers took a seat. The barman, Jimmy MacKay, eyed them both suspiciously and he casually began to chat as he washed glasses. Charlie resembled many of the youngsters who frequented the place but to Jimmy it was obvious that Vic didn't look comfortable and definitely wasn't your average holiday maker.

"So lads, how long are you here for?"

Charlie scrutinised the man's face for any sign that Jimmy was being anything other than friendly. When he felt at ease he replied to the question.

"Just two or three days. We've both been working hard so felt we could do with a little break."

"And what better place to come to than good old Marbella. Whereabouts are you from only I recognise your accent. I know you're from London but I'm guessing East End?"

"Bang on Pal Canning Town to be precise how'd you know?"

Vic sharply dug his brother in the ribs as he felt he was offering too much information but Charlie ignored him.

"My mate lives in Stepney and I pay him a visit whenever I get the chance. You can't beat a good old East End knees up, not when you've had to put up with the snobby bastards that you get here all summer long. Where you staying?"

Vic was about to nudge his brother for a second time but it was too late.

"The Melia know it?"

"Very nice but a bit on the pricey side."

As soon as Vic heard Jimmy comment he couldn't help but join in the conversation.

"Tell me about it! The cunts want nearly three hundred nicker a night, greedy bastards!"

Vic Steel was now like a man on a mission as he went on and on about the price of things and Charlie could only roll his eyes upwards in frustration. Finally two hours and six pints later they were both a little the worse for wear and Charlie suggested they give up and start again in the morning.

By nine the next day they were both wide awake,

suffering with hangovers and feeling a little guilty. Charlie because he felt he had let Kenny down once again and Vic because he now knew he would have to stay at the hotel for another night. Deciding to call in at the Irish bar for breakfast they made their way to the marina. Jimmy MacKay was again on duty and he smiled when they entered. To the strangers it was a smile of friendship but as far as Jimmy was concerned nothing could be further from the truth. He had been witness to the same scenario many times over the years and he just wanted to find out who they were looking for. It was clear to him that they weren't the police but until he knew exactly who they were he would play his cards close to his chest.

"Morning lads and how are you both today or need I not ask?"

"My heads fucking pounding but I'm still famished Jimmy any chance of a breakfast?"

"Take a seat and I'll be with you in a couple of minutes."

Just as he spoke Joey and Stevie Norris walked in for their usual morning coffee. Looking at Jimmy they both frowned and he knew they wanted to know who the strangers were. Jimmy could only shrug his shoulders which told the men he wasn't sure yet. The Norris brothers sat at a table close to Charlie and Vic and each began to read one of the free newspapers that the bar provided. Jimmy came over and took all four of the breakfast orders then disappeared into the kitchen. When Vic started to speak to Charlie, Joey and Stevie both looked at each other over the top of their papers.

"I tell you what Charlie that little cunt is going to pay dearly when I get my fucking hands on him."

"That's if we find him?"

"We aint got no choice. If we go home without a result, Kenny will do his bleeding nut."

Jimmy MacKay soon appeared and was balancing four plates of full English on his arms. After laying them down at the two tables he was about to retreat behind the bar when Charlie called him back over.

"Here Jimmy! I wonder if you'd be able to help us out with a little problem?"

"I will if I can what's up?"

Vic was ravenous and tucked into his food while his brother spoke.

"We're trying to find a bloke but it's like looking for a needle in a fucking haystack round here. He goes by the name of Leon and he's about nineteen years old."

Jimmy scratched at the side of his neck as he pretended to think and Joey Norris once more glanced in his brother's direction.

"Can't say the name rings a bell. Mind me asking what you want him for."

Vic was about to kick his brother under the table but Charlie spoke before he got the chance.

"He's a friend of my sisters."

Joey and Stevie Norris both pricked up their ears.

"Well like I said the name doesn't ring any bells but I'll ask around. Why don't you come back around nine tonight, there's someone who comes in that just might be able to help."

Charlie Steel thanked the barman and then gave Vic a smug look that simply said See I do know how to handle things. Knowing his brother only too well he had already moved his legs sideways so Vic wouldn't be able to kick him. When Jimmy walked away Vic was about to read his young brother the riot act but changed his mind. If they ever wanted to get back home then maybe Charlie had done the right thing in asking. Joey and Stevie Norris quickly finished their food and after paying their bill they left. Their actions went unnoticed by the Steels who were too engrossed in conversation.

"Hopefully if that Jimmy bloke comes through we can get out of this shit hole by tomorrow."

Charlie shook his head; he would never understand his brother. Vic would rather have a wet weekend away in Clacton than be in a fantastic place like Marbella.

"Vic you never fucking cease to amaze me."

"What?"

"Never mind. Come on lets go back to the hotel and spend some time round the pool. As you're so fond of putting it this is costing us enough so we may as well get something out of it."

As they exited the bar Vic Steel rubbed the head of his baby brother.

"You're a cheeky little fucker!"
Jimmy MacKay watched the men leave. From past experience, he knew that there was trouble on the horizon.

CHAPTER TWENTY THREE

At nine o'clock the next day Kenny and Sandra Steel set off for the hospital. They had both spent a restless night of sleep worrying about Michelle and were desperate to get back to her. Turning onto Newham Way Kenny let out a loud groan when he saw the heavy build up of traffic. By the time they reached East India Dock Road his Range Rover had come to a complete standstill.

"Fuck it! We're going to be stuck here for bleeding ages now."

Sandra Steel smiled at her son. Right from a small child Kenny had never had any patience and she knew nothing was going to alter him now. That said she wouldn't change him for the world.

"It used to be a work house you know."

Kenny stared across at his mother with a quizzical look on his face.

"What did?"

"Mile End hospital."

"Get out of here?"

"Straight up. I can remember my granddad telling me that his father always worried about ending up in there. Of course that was years ago now but you know that old building at the front? Well that's the last bit of the work house still standing. It must have been horrendous for those poor people back then. All those little children growing up in a place like that."

Kenny thought about it for a minute and he didn't like the idea of his sister being in somewhere that was once a work house no matter how many years ago it had been. Suddenly the traffic began to move and he let out a sigh of relief. Five minutes later and they were turning into the car park. Kenny had been quiet since his mother's revelation about the hospital and she turned to face him as they entered the intensive care unit.

"You alright son?"

Kenny placed an arm lovingly around his mothers shoulder and hugged her tightly. He loved the fact that she could read him like a book and that she was the only person he could never hide anything from no matter how hard he tried.

"Yeah I suppose so but I still don't like our Shell being in a place like this."

"I don't want her here either Kenny but with all things considered we could have been coming to see her in the morgue."

"I know that but I don't mean the hospital side of things, though I do fucking hate that as well. What I mean is this place, you know after what you told me."

Sandra laughed and shook her head.

"Don't be so bleeding daft that was years and years ago."

"I know but it gives me the creeps."

"Silly sod!"

Entering the unit they both applied sterile foam to

their hands before walking over to the area where Michelle had been on their last visit. The bed was empty and Kenny could see the onset of panic in his mother's eyes. He grabbed her arm and together they headed in the direction of the nurses' station. Gemma Parker had worked on intensive care for the last five years and as they approached she looked up from her paperwork. Kenny explained that his sister had been in the bed last night and that now she was gone.

"I wasn't on duty yesterday but let me have a look at my paperwork and see what I can find out for you." Scanning her list she looked into Sandra's eyes and smiled.

"There's nothing to worry about my love. They took your daughter off of the ventilator at seven this morning. She came round really quickly and has been moved to the Jubilee ward. If you turn left at the end of this corridor and go up one flight of stairs you will find the ward situated on your right. Don't look so worried Mrs Steel; by all accounts your daughter is doing very well."

Following nurse Parkers directions Kenny led his mother out into the corridor and up the stairs. Sandra couldn't help but notice he now seemed to have a spring in his step. As he pushed on the double doors Kenny looked at his mother and could see that she was slightly out of breath.

"You alright mum?"

"I will be in a minute Son. Gawd walking with you

is like going on a bleeding route march."

Kenny laughed but he didn't slow up until he had Michelle's bed in his sights. Propped up by several pillows she smiled when she saw her brother. The tube from the ventilator had made her throat sore and as she tried to talk her voice made a husky sound. Kenny stroked her hand and told her not to speak. As Sandra reached the bed of her youngest child her eyes were full of tears. For the first time in her life Michelle returned the feeling and a tear rolled down her own cheek. The sight instantly made Sandra wipe her eyes and revert back to her maternal protective ways. Taking a seat on the edge of the bed she clasped Michelle's hand in hers.

"Now come on darling remember we don't do tears in the Steel family. We're all fighters and none more so than my baby girl. Has the doctor been round since you were moved up here?"

Michelle shook her head.

"Kenny love go see what you can find out will you?"

Dutifully he did as he was asked and when he reached the sluice room and saw a nurse inside he stopped in the doorway.

"Excuse me Miss but is there any chance of having a word with one of the doctors?"

Rita Oliver was in her final year before retirement and was old school when it came down to nursing. Unlike her counterpart down in Intensive care Rita was far from friendly. In her opinion friends and family shouldn't be allowed to just pop onto the

258

wards willy-nilly whenever they felt like it. Back in her day when Matrons ruled with an iron rod visiting times were followed to the rule without exception. Rita Oliver was a firm believer that there would be far less contamination on the wards if things were like they used to be. She was also in awe of the doctors and looked upon them as gods. As far as she was concerned interrupting their busy schedule was not an option.

"You will have to wait. Mr Framingham and Doctor Otis are far too busy to bother with relatives questions at this time of the day. Now if you will excuse me Sir, I have work to do after all this is a hospital you know!"

Her words incensed Kenny and he clenched his fists as he took a step closer to Rita Oliver. His body language was threatening and suddenly she felt scared.

"If you wouldn't mind stepping outside Sir as members of the public are not allowed in here." Again Kenny took a step closer and he was now almost touching Rita Oliver. Taking a step back she could feel the cold steel of the sluice dig into her back.

"If you do not leave now I will be forced to call security and have you removed from not only this ward but the entire hospital."

Suddenly Kenny raised his hand and clamped it firmly over Rita's mouth. Her eyes were wide with fear and she was petrified of what he was going to do next.

"Now you can shut the fuck up and listen to me do you understand?"

With wide eyes Rita could only nod her head.

"My baby sister almost died last night! She's been brought onto your ward though heaven fucking help her if she needs any further medical care if you're the best this dump has to offer. My mother and me only want to know what's going on and how our Shells doing. Now I want to speak to the organ grinder not the fucking monkey so if you wouldn't mind keeping your big trap shut and doing as I ask there won't be no need for any nastiness alright?"

At this point Rita Oliver only dared to nod her head. Removing his hand Kenny wiped it on the front of his shirt before walking out and returning to his sister's bedside. Alone in the sluice room Rita lifted up her hands and could visibly see them shaking. She knew she should report the matter but something about the man really scared her. If she complained he might come after her and as she lived all alone Rita decided to keep her mouth shut. Making her way to the doctor's office she lightly tapped on the door and went in. She informed Mr Framingham about the family's concerns and that they would like to have a word but she left out her altercation with Kenny. Ten minutes later and the consultant, accompanied by his second in command Doctor Otis, marched up to the end of Michelle

Steels bed. Kenny and Sandra who were seated on either side both leaned forward in anticipation as the men approached.

"Right Miss Steel how are you feeling today?"

With great difficulty Michelle struggled to talk and seeing her pain and anguish cut Kenny to the core.

"How the fuck do you think she's feeling? The poor cow has had the shit kicked out of her."

Mr Framingham raised his head and looked downwards at Kenny due to his glasses being perched on the tip of his nose. He wasn't shocked and it wasn't the first time he had been spoken to in this manner. For Doctor Otis it was and he started to stutter and stammer but was stopped when his superior put up his hand.

"Its fine Martin thank you but I'm quite capable of dealing with this. I take it you are a relative Sir?"

"I'm her brother."

"Then Mr Steel, I would thank you to not speak to either myself or my colleague in that tone. We are here to make your sister better and I would appreciate it if you had the decency to show myself and Doctor Otis some respect. Right Michelle, I see from your notes that you were taken off of the ventilator this morning and you are recovering remarkably well, considering what you have been through."

Kenny wasn't fazed in the least by the consultants reprimand and he again spoke without altering his tone.

"So when can she come home then?"

This time Mr Framingham didn't look in Kenny's direction and even though he answered the question his reply was spoken directly towards Michelle.

"Normally with injuries such as yours we would expect you to stay in hospital for a week or so. Now the internal bleeding has stopped, so young lady, the only thing to do is rest and recuperate."

Kenny stood up and he seemed to tower over the consultant as he spoke.

"We will be collecting my sister tomorrow and taking her home!"

"Mr Steel I would strongly advise against it. Michelle although on the mend has suffered serious injuries. If any complications should set in and she needs further treatment then the best place for her is here at the Mile End."

With that Mr Framingham marched out of the ward with Doctor Otis following in hot pursuit. Even though she was in pain Michelle still wore the slight glimmer of a smile as she looked at her brother but Sandra wasn't so proud of her son.

"Love you shouldn't have spoken to him like that and I for one happen to agree with him about Shell staying here until she's better."

Holding his sisters hand Kenny Steel stared for a few seconds in his mothers direction and she could see that no matter what she said he had made up his mind.

"There aint nothing they can do for her that we can't do at home aint that right Shell?"

Just as he finished speaking they were interrupted by Rita Oliver the nurse from the sluice room. She once more had her mojo back and pushed in between Sandra and the bed.

"Mind out of the way I have work to do."

Grabbing hold of the bed pillows she pushed Michelle forward. Her touch was overly rough and as Michelle winced in pain Sandra jumped to her feet.

"Get your fucking hands away from my girl. You were right Kenny we aint bleeding leaving her in this place!"

Sandra once more turned her gaze back to Nurse Oliver and as she spoke her words were full of venom.

"When we come back in the morning to collect her, make sure everything's sorted out and she's ready to go. Until then I don't want you coming anywhere near my daughter or I'll personally punch your fucking lights out. Do you understand me?"

Rita Oliver scurried away and Kenny laughed out loud.

"Nice one mum!"

"Well honestly have you ever seen anything bleeding like it! I thought it was supposed to be the caring profession. What a bitch!"

Kenny and Sandra left the hospital and were both in high spirits at the thought of Michelle coming home the next day but neither of them had bothered to ask her what she wanted. Alone in the ward she thought about all that had happened and when she recalled what the nurse had told her regarding the baby she began to cry. As the Range Rover pulled out of the hospital grounds Kenny was hyper and told his mother all that he had planned. He was going to go shopping later and get a new single bed and a wheelchair so that his sister had everything she needed.

"Fancy stopping off for a drink Mum to celebrate?"

"You know what son, I don't mind if I do."

The Bancroft Arms came into sight and Kenny Steel pulled into the curb. It wasn't somewhere he'd ever been before but from the outside it looked respectable and somewhere he felt comfortable to take his old mum into. Ordering a gin and tonic and a pint of lager they took a seat by the window.

"I wonder how those two wankers are getting on in Spain?"

Sandra Steel sipped at her drink and smiled. After all the upset of the last two days she finally felt that there was a light at the end of the tunnel.

"Why don't you give them a call?"

"You know what mum that aint a bad idea."

Removing his phone he decided to call Vic as Charlie would only lie or try and fill him full of bull shit. It only took a few seconds before his brother answered and he didn't sound very happy.

"Vic its Kenny's how's it going over there?"

"Not very good. The hotels costing a fucking fortune and we still aint seen neither hide nor hair of that toe rag yet. I don't know if we should just give up and come home."

Kenny's Steels happy mood instantly disappeared and he stood up from the table as he spoke in an overly loud voice. "Fucking come home you cunt! I don't want to set eyes on either of you until you find that little wanker and have beaten him to a pulp, do you hear me? By the way your sister is doing fine if you're bothered in any way."

"Don't be like that Kenny we...."

Kenny Steel cut his brother off before he could finish his sentence.

"I tell you what mum; my brothers are a couple of prize pricks! I knew I should have gone out there myself."

Sandra tenderly touched her sons arm as he sat back down again.

"Look I know you want revenge for our Shell and hopefully you'll get it but in the meantime let's just enjoy the fact that our baby is alive and getting better alright?"

Kenny took his mothers words on board but he was far from happy about the situation. If Vic and Charlie returned home without a result then heads were going to roll.

CHAPTER TWENTY FOUR

After Kenny had hung up on him Vic stared blankly down at his phone. Charlie who had been in the shower emerged from the bathroom with just a towel wrapped around his waist.

"Was that your phone I heard?"

"Yeh it was Kenny. I can't believe it the bastard just hung up on me."

"Now what have you done? Fuck me Vic you always seem to have a knack of pissing him off."

Vic Steel was rapidly growing tired of both his brothers and all the aggro that seemed to follow them around. Breaking his code of thriftiness he opened the mini bar and pulled out a beer.

"Charlie why do you always fucking assume it's me hey? He asked how it was going and I said we hadn't been able to find the tosser and were thinking of coming home. He just went mad and then hung up on me."

"Well that's it spelled out in a nutshell then. Let's just hope that Jimmy comes through with some information or we're looking at being here for the foreseeable. As much as I like the place even I'm starting to get a bit bored, I mean it aint like we're even on holiday and can enjoy ourselves. Having to share a room with you cramps my style big time. There was a real hot little bird down in the bar last night but with you snoring away in the next bed I aint got much chance of getting me leg over now

266

have I?"

This was exactly the kind of attitude Vic hated. There was the poor little Cartwright girl back in London and up to her neck in trouble and her so called boyfriend didn't give a toss. Vic Steel couldn't be bothered to argue with his brother. Pulling on his jacket he walked from the room hoping that a few hours apart would lessen the tension that was rapidly beginning to build. It was only just midday and they had hours before their scheduled return to the bar. Walking along the beach he admired the scantily clad beauties that passed him but deep down he didn't really have much interest. Vic missed his son and hoped that Kenny was keeping an eye on him because he didn't dare think about how Deidre was behaving. That said he couldn't have been any stronger with his warning and if any harm had come to his boy, well he didn't want to think about that at the moment. A few hundred yards ahead he saw a group of young people larking about at the water's edge and decided to sit for a while and watch them. Vic tried hard to remember when he had last been that happy and carefree but no matter how hard he wracked his brains he couldn't recall a time. Not even when he thought back to his childhood and his school days. Suddenly he spied Leon among the group and not wanting to be recognised he put his sunglasses on and pulled down his straw trilby hat. Leon Bishop didn't seem to have a care in the world and that fact alone riled Vic Steel. His poor sister had been left for dead only forty eight hours earlier and this bastard was out in the sun fooling around with a couple of girls. Vic slowly thought about what he should do. If he confronted Leon here on the beach he wasn't going to get anywhere, he'd be recognised and besides there were at least six of them. As tough as Vic was even he knew that he would undoubtedly come off worse. Standing up he brushed the sand from his trousers and made a hasty retreat back to the hotel. Poolside at the Melia Charlie was sitting on a sun lounger trying to chat up a young girl but he wasn't having much luck. Seeing his brother approach he let out a loud groan. Vic looked like a typical Brit with his sandals and white socks and Charlie thought he might as well have had a four knotted hankie on his head to top the look off. The girl in her tiny bikini sipped seductively at her cocktail and then sauntered back to her own sun bed.

"Well thanks a bunch mate!"

"Now what have I done?"

"Id nearly cracked it with that piece of skirt and then you turn up looking like Alf fucking Garnet on an away day to Clacton. I tell you what....."

"Stop fucking moaning and listen to what I've got to tell you. I've just seen Leon down at the beach."

Instantly Charlie Steel stood up from his lounger and Vic couldn't help but smile when he saw his brother was wearing the tiniest Speedos he'd ever seen.

"What the fuck are you wearing?"

"What you on about?"

"Them fucking budgie smugglers!"

Charlie chose to ignore his brother's remarks.

"Are you coming or what?"

"Where?"

"After that little tosser! Why the fuck you didn't sort him when you had the chance I don't know."

His words made Vic angry and it didn't go unnoticed by Charlie. Aware that he could have the odd jibe at his brother and get away with it he also knew that Vic in his own way could be just as nasty as Kenny if he put his mind to it and Charlie now felt he may have over stepped the mark.

"For your fucking information he wasn't alone. Now unless you want me banged up in some Spanish hellhole all because a bunch of kids witnessed me beat the crap out of him Id shut my fucking mouth if I were you!"

Charlie held his hands up and the rest of the afternoon was spent around the pool in silence. Vic tried to sleep while Charlie put on his sunglasses so that he could ogle all the women without being seen. At seven they finally went up to the room to get ready for the night ahead.

Joey and Stevie Norris had spent most of the day looking for Max Bishop. They had tried again and again to call him from their mobiles but for some reason he wasn't answering. Unaware of the brewing problem Max had been in Marbella for hours as he'd had five different holiday arrivals. All of them were mega rich and he had wanted to welcome his clients personally. Making it back to the villa at just before six he was hot and tired and definitely not in the mood for visitors. Pouring himself a beer he was about to sit outside to wind down when the Norris brothers pulled into the drive. Max sighed heavily as he went to greet his friends but never one to be rude he opened the door and welcomed them both with open arms.

"Hello lads nice to see you! Come on in."

Joey allowed Stevie to take the lead and when Max saw the serious look on his old friends face he knew this wasn't exactly a social call. Pouring two more beers Max led his friends out onto the terrace and when they were all seated he turned to face Stevie.

"So what's up mate?"

Stevie Norris explained in detail all that had happened earlier at the bar and that the two strangers would be calling back there at nine o'clock tonight.

"I don't know the real reason why they want your Leon. They said something about him knowing their sister but by the looks of them it aint a friendly visit."

Finishing up their beers the men arranged to meet up again later and Max Bishop went back inside the villa to wait for his son. It wasn't long before Leon appeared and after putting up his hand and

270

managing to say a swift Hi he began to climb the stairs to start getting ready for the night ahead. The little blonde he'd met on the beach was minted and Leon knew he was in for a free night with a shag at the end of it to round the evening off.

"Not so fast Leon I want a word."

Leon tutted loudly. If his dad was about to start again regarding him finding a job then he was going to give Max a right mouthful. As far as Leon was concerned life was for fun and his dad always seemed to try and cramp his style.

"What?"

"I've had a visit today from Joey and Stevie Norris. Seems there were a couple of blokes down at the marina who've been asking after you."

Max couldn't be off noticing the fear in his son's eyes and knew that whatever he'd done he had better own up now before things got out of hand. Leon shrugged his shoulders and his action really got his dads hackles up.

"Either you tell me what's going on or I'll tell the men where you are."

"You wouldn't?"

"Try me! I'm sick and tired of you sponging your way through life. Now I want the truth and don't even try and pull the wool over my eyes because I will know in a second if you're lying."

"Ok Ok! You remember Michelle?"

"Of course I remember her the girl stayed here for Christ's sake! What about her?"

"Well when we got back to her mother's she was always on at me you know nag nag nag!"
"And?"
"Well one day she just kept on and on. I tell you dad it really did my head in."
Max was starting to get worried about what his son was going to tell him but he knew that whatever it was he had to hear the truth.
"And?"
"Well I hit her."
"You did what! Fuck me boy where do you get off hitting a woman?"
Leon Bishop could see the disgust in his father's eyes and the look hurt him deeply. As much as his dad always seemed to be having a go at him Leon really did want to make him proud.
"I know I shouldn't have and I'm sorry ok?"
"When you say hit her exactly how far did you go Leon and I want the truth."
Leon was now starting to get angry. He hated being questioned and his dad was really giving him the third degree.
"I kicked her a bit alright! Look the bitch was asking for it and she just pushed me too far."
Max Bishop had never laid a hand on his son in his entire life but things were about to change. With one swift punch Leon landed on the floor and as he tried to get up his father hit him again. By the time Max finished Leon had the onset of a black eye and his nose was bleeding but in comparison to what

Michelle Steel had received it was nothing. Picking up his mobile phone Max dialled an old friend back in London and asked him to look into the Steels as soon as possible. The call was returned within a few minutes and as Max listened to what was being said the colour drained from his face.

"Well boy looks like you've finally done it this time. The family are real hard bastards and after what you've done I don't think they're going to walk away without their pound of flesh."

"What should I do dad?"

"I'll tell you what you're going to do absolutely nothing! I will sort this out but believe you me Leon it's the last time. As from tomorrow you will start toeing the line that or you can fuck off back to your mothers understood?"

Leon Bishop, who was still on the floor, now grabbed hold of his father's leg and looked at him pleadingly. It was a look that had always worked in the past but not this time. Max shook his leg hard like he was trying to get rid of something nasty.

"Please dad I'm sorry please!!!!"

"Leon it won't cut it this time. Do you know something boy? I'm ashamed of you and that's something I never thought I would say."

With that Max Bishop walked from the villa and after slamming the door as he left he then drove over to the Irish bar in the hope that this had all been over exaggerated but deep down he doubted that fact. As he entered the Norris brothers were already seated but they didn't acknowledge their friend. Making his way to the bar Max ordered a brandy and Jimmy winked in his direction as he poured a drink for one of the bars longest serving customers. A few minutes later Vic and Charlie walked in. They also headed in the direction of the bar and ordered two pints of Guinness from Jimmy Mackay. After a few seconds of silence Charlie Steel couldn't contain himself any longer and began to speak.

"So Jimmy got any news for us?"

"As it happens I have."

Gesturing with his hand he introduced Max.

"This is Max Bishop the father of the lad you've been asking about."

Instantly Vic knew that they had been stitched up like a couple of kippers and that the barman had known all along who they'd been asking about. Max smiled at the men but it wasn't a smile of welcome.

"So I hear you want a word with my boy. Can I ask why?"

Charlie who was always one to be free with the verbal launched into a tirade of four letter abuse and only stopped when Vic placed his hand on his brother's chest. His action stopped Charlie dead in his tracks but in all honesty he was running out of steam and glad of the interruption.

"Mr Bishop we have no beef with you but if you knew what that toe rag of a son did to my sister.

274

Well I think......."

Max cut Vic off mid sentence.

"I do know and while I'm disgusted with my boy he is still just that, my boy. I will deal with him in my own way and please believe me when I tell you that he will suffer."

"I'm sorry but that aint fucking good enough. The cunt needs punishing and we're here to carry out that task."

"Well then gentlemen we have a problem!"

Charlie as usual was all mouth.

"There aint no problem mate."

From behind them the brothers heard in unison one sentence from the Norris brothers.

"Oh yes there is."

Turning they saw both Joey and Stevie holding baseball bats and Vic heard Charlie say in a low voice Oh fuck. Max Bishop stood between both sets of brothers and began to speak.

"Now this aint fucking London lads its Marbella and we do things slightly differently here. As my friends and I see it you have two options. You either leave of your own free will and we will deal with this matter in our own way and be under no illusion that it will be dealt with, or you both return to Blighty in a box. Gentlemen the choice is yours."

There was a silent standoff for several seconds before Max again spoke.

"Well?"

Both Charlie and Vic knew they had Hobson's

choice in the matter and after holding up their hands in a show of surrender walked out of the bar as quickly as they could. Even suffering the wrath of Kenny was more appealing than what would happen to them if they stayed in Spain. It really went against the grain to walk away and it was something that never would have happened back home but what choice did they have. In London they would have returned mob handed, the bar would have been wrecked and the three men would now be dead or seriously injured. They were embarrassed that they had left the place like a couple of gutless wonders, just the type of men they both beat up regularly most Saturday nights at one of the pubs or clubs and all for being just a bit too mouthy.

The following morning they booked out of their hotel and made their way back to the airport. To make sure that the point had been clear enough to the Steels both Norris brothers were present to wave them off. Charlie complained for the entire return flight that Kenny was going to do his nut but Vic didn't comment. In all honesty he was glad to be going home and he couldn't care less what his elder brother said. As far as Vic Steel was concerned they had got off lightly and he couldn't wait to see his boy. As for Leon, he hoped he got what was coming to him but deep down he doubted that would happen. There was nothing stronger at least as far as Vic was concerned, than a love a father had for his son and he couldn't see that Max would hurt his boy no matter what he had done.

CHAPTER TWENTY FIVE

Zena and Linda Cartwright drove over to the University hospital to collect Stan at nine the next morning. They were unaware that Kenny was doing exactly the same thing for Michelle forty miles away at the Mile End hospital. Zena and her mother had talked long into the small hours but it hadn't made Zena feel any better. She felt as if she was in a deep dark abyss and there was no way out. Nothing her mother had said could lift her spirits but she didn't let Linda know that. As they drove along Linda watched her daughter out of the corner of her eye and she was worried. Her girl always seemed so happy and bubbly but now the spark had gone from her. Never one to share her feelings Zena thought she was doing well at hiding things but when she noticed her mother looking at her she realised that maybe she wasn't doing such a good job after all.

"Alright mum?"

"I'm fine darling but I don't know if I can say the same about you."

Zena knew that whatever happened from now on in she had to appear fine. Her mum and dad had been through a lot and the next few months would be even harder. If only she could turn the clock back but that was never going to happen so she would just have to deal with everything in the best way she could. Her parents had always been proud of her and the thought that they must now be so ashamed tore at her heart.

"I know I've let you both down mum and you will never know how sorry I am. I promise that I'm going to make everything alright."

"What do you mean?"

Zena had to be careful and not give anything away. The last thing she wanted was for anything or anyone to stop her putting her plan into action. Last night when she was at last alone in bed and after much soul searching she had come to the conclusion there really was only one way out. With just a chink of light shining through the curtains she had stared for what seemed like hours at the picture on her wall. It was an image of Jesus with his arms stretched open wide and she had felt as if he was talking to her and telling her what to do. What Zena Cartwright didn't understand was the fact that emotionally she was beginning to lose it. As she tried to convince herself that if she did what god wanted then everything would be good again a plan had begun to form in Zena's mind. Taking another quick sideways glance in her mother's direction she smiled.

"I mean that we will get through this just like dad said. Please don't look for something that's not there mum."

Linda placed her hand onto Zena's arm and gently squeezed.

"I'm sorry love but what with everything that's

happened in the last couple of days my nerves are in tatters."

"I know but for now we need to put on a brave face if only for dads sake."

Pulling into the car park Linda looked up at the hospital and a shiver ran down her spine. She didn't know why because today of all days she should have felt a little happiness at the thought of Stan coming home. Linking arms with her daughter they quickly made their way inside and up to Stan's ward. Ready and waiting Stan Cartwright sat in a wheelchair at the side of his bed. When he saw his daughter he smiled as best as he could but his face was badly swollen and it hurt like hell to show any expression. Zena had to fight to hold back her tears as she walked over to him. He wasn't old, well not really and yet today he seemed so frail and vulnerable. The image made her angry, angry at the Steels but most of all angry at herself. This was all her fault and she knew she could never forgive herself for putting the two people she loved most in the world through all this pain.

"Hi Dad how you feeling today?"

Stan took his daughters hand in his and gently squeezed it.

"Not too bad love but I'll be better when I get out of this place. The nurse said I can go now but I have to be wheeled out as its hospital policy. There aint bugger all wrong with me legs but it's best not to argue with her as she's a bit of a control freak and I don't want her turning round and telling me I have to stay another day just out of spite."

Zena laughed out loud but it was a hollow sound. Stan handed Linda a small paper bag containing pain killers and pleaded with his eyes for them to get going. Zena wheeled her father into the lift and within a few minutes they were finally on their way home. As the car turned into Burgess Terrace Stan had never in his life been so pleased to see his home. The house was his own little castle and he saw it as a place from where he could protect his wife and daughter. Linda led him into the front room while Zena put the kettle on to boil. She could hear her parents bickering and the sound made her smile. Linda and Stan Cartwright were not happy unless they were as her mother put it, having words and the sound of their voices was somehow comforting. The doctor had told Stan that he must rest and Linda was fighting to wrap a blanket around his legs as Zena entered with the tray of tea.

"Stanley Cartwright you are a stubborn old sod!"

"And you my love are a nag but I love you all the same."

Instantly the arguing stopped and as her father grabbed her mother's hand and kissed it tenderly Zena wanted to cry. Her sadness was purely for herself as she knew that she would never now experience a love as deep as her parents shared. After finishing her tea Linda once more put on her coat.

"Where are you going mum?"

"Sorry I forgot to say but Roy Painter from down the street lost his wife last week. The poor woman had been I'll for years but it was still a bit of a shock to everyone. Her old man used to say a creaking gate hangs on forever but in Audrey's case it finally fell off. It's the funeral today and I know I wasn't that friendly with them but I offered to sort out the tea and sandwiches for when they get back from the Crem. I shouldn't be more than a couple of hours." Kissing Stan and then her daughter she had soon disappeared from sight.

"You alright on your own for a bit Dad only I've got to sort one or two things out."

"Don't be daft of course I am I aint an invalid you know. I might take a little nap; those pain killers are making me feel really drowsy."

Zena gave her warmest smile and then went upstairs. In her old room she removed two rolls from behind the wardrobe; one was bubble wrap and the other brown paper. Linda always liked to have them on hand for parcels and things and today they would come in very handy. Entering her parent's room she made her way over to the bed and was careful not to tread on the squeaky boards that had caught her out so many times as a child. Opening up the bedside table she removed a small key that Stan kept taped under one of the drawers. Now as she crept across the room she prayed that she could remember where the rest of the creaky floorboards were. As she took one step forward and two across she thought she had made a mistake but luckily memories of her childhood still burned strong and the boards held up. Sliding the wardrobe door to one side she was able to open the gun cabinet that was hidden in the back. Zena hadn't seen the Purdey double barrel shotgun for years and the sight of it now strangely brought back happy memories. Memories from a long time ago, of her dad teaching her how to shoot when she was small. By the time she reached her teens it had become boring and she had stopped accompanying him when he took a few days off to go hunting or fishing. Removing the gun she caressed the wooden stock and it all came flooding back to her of how to load it, discharge the spent cartridges and reload. I fact Zena hadn't forgotten a thing it was just like riding a bike. Stooping down she picked up four cartridges before relocking the cabinet and once more sticking the key to the underside of the drawer. There was no reason for her parents to check but just in case they did she wanted everything to appear normal. Laying the Purdey on the bed she proceeded to roll it in bubble wrap again and again. By the time it was all covered in brown paper it no longer resembled a gun but merely a long narrow parcel of some sort. Tiptoeing down the stairs she carefully lifted the latch on the front door and made her way outside. Opening the boot to her car Zena placed the gun inside.

Checking in on Stan she smiled when she saw he was fast asleep and was now covered by the blanket, the one his wife had tried to put round him earlier and which he'd said he didn't need. Pulling on her coat Zena removed a pair of pliers from the kitchen drawer and placed them into her pocket. She had one more port of call to make before she could be properly on her way and heading out of Burgess Terrace she drove over to her flat. No one saw her as she slipped inside. The place was just as she'd left it a few days ago but it now felt as though she hadn't been here for months. Zena loved her little home and had always been so proud of it. The thought that she would never see it again brought a lump to her throat but she wouldn't allow herself to cry. In the bedroom she opened up a small leather jewellery case and removed a key that had a ring on saying Steel Security. Charlie had mislaid it weeks ago and had gotten another one cut much to the anger of his elder brother. For some reason when Zena had found the original down the side of the sofa she had placed it in the box and forgotten all about it until yesterday. Her eyes narrowed in anger and she gripped the key so hard that it almost cut into her skin. It was now time for payback and she just hoped she had the strength to see things through to the end.

Driving over to Romford Zena Cartwright parked her car in Dunton Road. It was a dead end and the Corsa would be less likely to be found. There was no reason to be in Romford but she thought it was as good a place as any and when they started to look for her it would she hoped, confuse and prolong the situation. Removing the pliers from her pocket she nipped away at her ankle tag. When it finally fell to the floor she breathed a sigh of relief. Removing the parcel from the boot she began the walk to the market and as she reached the hustle and bustle of the stalls and shoppers she discretely threw the ankle tag along with her mobile phone into a litter bin. The N15 bus for London was about to leave and after purchasing a ticket she climbed on board and took a seat right at the back. The journey would take roughly forty five minutes and for the whole time Zena was glancing in all directions. She was really nervous and felt that everyone was looking at her and knew what she was about to do but in reality she resembled any other shopper with a large parcel to post.   The bus at last pulled into All Saints bus station and after disembarking Zena slowly walked along Newby Place. It was a very long Road and the gun was becoming heavy and difficult for her to hold. Moving it from under one arm to the other she struggled on until she at last reached Poplar High Street. Never having been to the office before she stopped for a moment trying to remember exactly what Charlie had told her when he had described the Steel Security premises. Finally it came to her and she walked along looking for a kebab shop with a plain unaddressed door beside it. There were three or four takeaways but none fitted the description until she reached one that had Istanbul emblazed in red lettering above it. The door immediately after was painted in black gloss but there was no number or letterbox, in fact there was nothing to tell a person where it led to. Instinctively Zena knew this was the place and removing the key from her pocket she placed it into the lock and turned. As the door opened she glanced from left to right to see if anyone was watching. The road was surprisingly quiet and she slipped inside as quickly as she could. With the door now closed behind her she leant back against the cold paintwork and breathed out a sigh of relief. A thought suddenly entered her head and she froze with fear. Suppose there was already someone here then her plan would be brought to an abrupt halt before it had even got underway. Laying the parcel onto the lino she un-wrapped it with speed and removing two cartridges from her pocket Zena loaded the Purdey. Her hands were shaking and it took two attempts to carry out the task. Snapping the barrels shut she gathered up the wrapping material and made her way up the stairs. Her father had always told her that for safety reasons if the gun was loaded she must leave the barrels down but she couldn't take the chance that if there was someone already here they would be able to wrestle it from her as she tried to put the gun into its firing position. Clicking off the safety catch the Purdey was now ready to fire and carefully she opened the office door and stepped inside. Zena realised her fears were unfounded when she saw that the room was deserted. After clicking the safety back on she laid the gun up against wall and slowly walked around the office. The desk was in a tidy state and after looking through the drawers and finding nothing of interest she stared up at the large map on the wall. Red pins were stuck in numerous Essex locations and even though Charlie had told her the firm was doing well she could now see that he must have been somewhat economical with the truth. The bareness of the office gave away no indication of any wealth but by the amount of places they were doing business with Steel Security had to be coining it in. That realisation made it even harder for Zena to understand why they had branched out into the world of drugs. Last night when she had been alone in her bed she had thought long and hard about Charlie's story of being in debt. Zena now realised that it was all just a big fat lie to convince her to go along with their plan. They had used her in the worst way possible and were going to walk away scot free, well not if she had anything to do with it they wouldn't. Pulling one of the hard chairs into the centre of the room she picked up the gun and then sat down. Zena knew she would probably be in for a long wait and could have chosen a more comfortable seat but she needed to be alert and on her guard. Being uncomfortable would keep her awake and she needed to be ready to spring into action when the door opened. It was now starting to get dark outside and she felt cold and alone. Visions of her mother and father and all the happy memories they had shared began to invade her mind and this time she did allow herself to cry. Zena cried until she had no more tears left and at the end she felt slightly better about things. It was as if a heavy weight had been lifted from her shoulders and she now felt calm and more peaceful. Convincing herself that after she had carried out her deed everything would be alright she was now content to sit and wait.

Over in Southend her parents were beginning to worry. Linda had been back from the funeral tea for the past two hours and when she had dialled her daughter's mobile for the umpteenth time and after getting no reply had instinctively known that something was wrong. By the time Zena's curfew began Linda was pacing up and down and Stan sat with his head in his hands. Twenty minutes later and there was a knock at the door. Nervously opening up Linda wasn't surprised to see two police officers standing outside.

"We're sorry to bother you Mrs Cartwright but it appears your daughter has broken her bail conditions. Our electronic monitoring system is showing that your daughter is somewhere in Romford."

"Romford?"

Linda began to cry and the officers were not unsympathetic towards a respectable woman who was obviously going through a traumatic time at the moment.

"I'm sure there must be something wrong Officer! She wouldn't just go off like that our girl would never let us down."

"Don't worry Mrs Cartwright well find her but in the meantime if she does return home; ask her to contact the station immediately. If she doesn't go too much over time we may be able to smooth things over just this once."

Linda thanked them and closed the door.

She tried to put on a brave face for Stan's sake but deep down she knew that something was very very wrong.

CHAPTER TWENTY SIX

Getting Michelle Steel discharged from hospital turned out to be far more difficult than when Stan Cartwright had left hospital. Kenny had taken the brand new wheelchair up to the ward but as he tried to lift his sister out of bed she screamed out in pain. Two nurses came running on to the ward and asked in no uncertain terms what the hell he thought he was doing. Rita Oliver was no longer on duty and she had purposely ignored Kenny's request to have his sister ready to leave. When he explained the problem the two nurses gave each other a knowing look. Rita wasn't liked by anyone in the department and it was just like her to try and cause as much mayhem as possible. The most senior of the two Pam Whitmore, gently placed her hand onto Kenny's arm and he instantly laid Michelle back down onto the bed.

"I'm sorry about all of this Mr Steel but do you really think it's a good idea to be moving your sister so soon? It's only been a couple of days and she really isn't ready to be discharged."

Michelle held her stomach and just wished they would all go away. No one had bothered to ask her what she wanted and in all honesty she was more than happy to remain in hospital. It did cross her mind that it was more about what her family wanted than what was best for her but she didn't want to hurt her brother's feelings so sighing heavily, which caused a sharp pain in her side, she decided to remain silent.

"I know we can take good care, better care of her at home so don't try and stop me Miss?"

"My names Pam and I wouldn't dream of trying to stop you Sir. You will need to sign a release form, which states that you will take full responsibility for Michelle if anything should go wrong. Of course Mr Steel we are all forgetting the most important person in all of this and we haven't asked what she would like to do."

The nurse smiled at Michelle and asked if she really did want to leave. Michelle Steel looked into her brothers beautiful blue eyes and saw so much love for her that she couldn't refuse. Looking back at Pam Whitmore Shell slowly nodded her head.

"Fair enough if that's what you want. Now you rest for a while and I will have a word with the doctor regarding medication and discharge."

The process took a good thirty minutes but for once Kenny Steel kept calm. When nurse Whitmore finally returned she had everything they needed and placed a large paper bag onto the end of the bed.

"Now Michelle if you could just sign here."

It took all of her strength just to hold the pen but somehow Michelle managed to scribble her name.

"Mr Steel if you could sign here please."

Kenny did as he was asked and when all of the paperwork had been checked the nurse placed her clipboard onto the bed.

"Now Mr Steel if you would like to stand on that side of the bed I will show you the correct procedure and we will lift your sister into the chair together."

Gently Pam Whitmore helped Michelle to sit up in the bed and steered her legs round so that she was now facing Kenny.

"Right I want you to place one arm across your sister's back and under her other arm. Now place your other arm under her legs. I will do the same on this side and when I say, together we will lift her into the chair."

Kenny for once did exactly as he was asked and in seconds Michelle was in the wheelchair and pain free. This nurse unlike Rita Oliver, went against hospital guidelines and accompanied the Steels down to the car park. Once they had gotten Michelle into the Range Rover Pam Whitmore handed over the bag of medication and gave Kenny instructions as to what the doses were. After wishing them both well she quickly disappeared back into the hospital and hoped that she hadn't been seen. On the drive home Michelle was overly quiet and no matter how hard Kenny tried to make conversation she would only reply with a yes or a no. Even when he had told her that Charlie and Vic were out in Spain and about to sort out Leon she didn't bat an eyelid. This wasn't like her his sister who normally had more rabbit than Sainsbury's.

292

Kenny was worried, his sister always seemed to bounce back from anything but she now appeared empty and deflated. He consoled himself with the fact that once Michelle was back in the bosom of her family all would be well. As they pulled up outside the house on Boreham Avenue Kenny beeped the horn and his mother was outside in seconds. Just as he'd been shown Kenny instructed his mother on how to lift Michelle but it didn't turn out to be as successful as it had been at the hospital and Shell screamed out in pain several times. Not bothering with the wheelchair Kenny carried her inside and she nestled her head into his chest as they entered the front room. Seeing a bed had been set up she smiled as Kenny laid her down as carefully as he could. Michelle was finally able to get comfortable and it felt good to be home.

"There you go babe! I've even got you a brand spanking new bed."

Michelle smiled weakly but the pain she was feeling was clearly etched upon her beautiful face. Sandra had seen a lot of hurt people over the years and she really didn't like the look of her daughter. Michelle appeared washed out but it was the amount of pain that was worrying her mother.

"I'm not so sure she should be here son. Maybe it would have been better to have let her stay at the Mile End after all."

"Whatever are you talking about of course she should be here with us."

Sitting beside her Kenny stroked Michelle's brow and he could see she was hurting. He wouldn't admit it to his mother but he knew he may have made a mistake in bringing her home so early.

"She needs plenty of peace and quiet not to mention a good rest. Together well make sure she gets it mum Ok?"

Before his mother could reply they both heard the front door open and seconds later little Vic came bounding into the room. Kenny was fast and quickly scooped the boy up into his arms before he had chance to jump up onto the bed.

"Hello boy! Now what are you doing here?"

"I want aunty Shell."

"I know you do but she's a bit poorly so why don't you go into the kitchen with your Nan and see if she's got anything special for you."

Suddenly all concern for his aunt disappeared as little Vic's eyes rested on Sandra who was now seated in one of the armchairs. Kenny placed his nephew onto the floor and he ran over to Sandra and began to tug on her arm.

"Come on Nanny come on!"

Sandra laughed and even Michelle managed a slight smile. Little Vic was a nice child and very comical in his own little way. His Nan took hold of his hand and telling him about all the treats she had stashed away in her secret cupboard she led him from the room. When they reached the hall she spied Deidre out of the corner of her eye.

294

"Well now, look what the fucking cats dragged in. I wondered how long it would be before you showed your mug round here. Come to gloat have you?"
Deidre Steel ignored her mother-in-laws nasty comments and walked towards the sitting room door.
"I'm warning you Deidre if you go upsetting my girl you'll have me to deal with."
Little Vic seemed oblivious to the nasty words that were being spoken and again began to pull on Sandra's arm.
"Come on Nan!"
Not once did he look in his mother's direction and if he could have arrived at his Nan's house without his mother he would have been lot a happier.
Before she entered the sitting room Deidre couldn't resist a swipe at Sandra.
"And don't be giving him any of your homemade cakes because the last time you did he was throwing up all bleeding night and I aint in the mood to be clearing up a load of puke just because of you."
She didn't wait for a reply but knew her words would be enough to upset her mother-in-law.
Sandra prided herself on her cooking and to be told her cakes had made her grandson ill really hurt her.
Entering the room Deidre Steel was all smiles but Kenny's eyes narrowed when he saw her. She could be a right spiteful bitch if the mind took her and he wasn't about to have Michelle upset for anything.
Walking over to the bed Deidre placed a bag of

grapes beside her sister-in-law. Watching her every move Kenny was getting more uptight by the second as he didn't want this evil bitch anywhere near his sister.

"Fuck me Deidre you're pushing the boat out aint you?"

"If you must know I had a nice little touch on Foxy bingo this morning so you can cut the sarcasm right now Kenny Steel."

"Well there's a first me brother will be pleased to hear about that and anyway how come little Vic aint at school?"

"If you must know he overslept."

"He did or you did? You lazy cow."

Ignoring his remark Deidre lent in to give her sister-in-law a kiss. Michelle could smell the stale alcohol on her breath and it made her feel sick. Turning her head away Deidre's kiss only skimmed Michelle's cheek and the action angered Deidre.

"Well aint we Miss High and fucking mighty! I thought having the shit kicked out of you would have softened you a bit but I can see you're still the same stuck up cow as you always was. I tell you something Shell you're going to have to lower your standards now because you aint exactly god's gift anymore. Want me to get you a mirror sweetheart so you can see the damage?"

Michelle began to cry and the sight enraged Kenny. Grabbing hold of Deidre's arm he frog marched her to the front door.

"Get your fucking hands off me! I'm sick of this bastard family and all the double standards you live by! Did you hear me I said let go of me!"

Sandra came running out of the kitchen when she heard all the commotion. She quickly pulled the door closed so that little Vic didn't see what was going on but she wasn't quick enough and Deidre saw her son sitting at the table eating cakes.

"I told you not to feed him all that shit and tell your gorilla of a son to get off me before I call the Old Bill myself."

"Kenny let go of her Son she aint bleeding worth the aggro."

Kenny did as his mother asked but gave a hard push as he did so which made his sister-in-law fall onto the hall tiles. Landing in a heap on the floor her skirt was up round her waist and she did nothing to hide her modesty. For a moment she thought he was going to lash out at her and Deidre covered her head with her arms. Kenny only sneered at the poor excuse for a woman before disappearing back into the front room. As Deidre Steel struggled to get to her feet her mother-in-law offered no assistance. When she was once more standing she walked towards Sandra.

"And where the fuck do you think you're now going to?"

"To get my son! Now move out of the way you old cow because you aint going to stop me!"

"Aint I?"

Sandra launched herself in Deidre's direction and grabbing a large handful of hair yanked down hard. Deidre let out a howl but Sandra never once lessened her grip. Holding the hair with one hand she opened the front door with the other and with one hard pull she dragged Deidre out onto the front path. Only then did Sandra release her grip and she then proceeded to rub her hand down the front of her apron as if she'd touched something dirty.

Tears streamed down Deidre Steels face and her mascara was smudged in big black patches under her eyes.

"Now I suggest you get the fuck away from my door before I do you some real damage. It's been a long time coming and you can't say you aint fucking asked for it. I'll never understand you Deidre, you've got a beautiful boy and a good man, and you could have had it all."

Snot now hung from her nose but Deidre Steel did nothing to stop it. Her eyes were wild and bulging and Sandra thought she had finally lost the plot.

"Could have had it all? That's a fucking laugh for a start. I never stood a chance while that bitch in there has her paws all over him."

Suddenly Sandra understood why for so many years there had been so much animosity in her family and why it had always come from her daughter-in-law. She accepted Kenny's feelings for Michelle she always had but never once did she realise that Deidre wanted him.

298

"Kenny! Fuck me girl you never would have stood a chance with or without our Shell in the picture. My Vic loved you in the beginning why wasn't he enough for you?"

"Enough for me? Vic's a weak cunt and I can't stand to look at him. I only married him to get closer to his brother and as for you saying I never stood a chance? It aint stopped him coming round mine once or twice a week for a blow job while his brothers out now has it?"

With that Deidre Steel slammed the front gate shut and walked off up the Road. Sandra was stunned and normally she would have put it all down to sour grapes, nothing more than a pack of lies but there was just something about her daughter-in-laws revelation that rang true. Closing the door behind her she went into the kitchen and taking little Vic's hand led him into the front room.

"Now if you're nice and quiet, you can sit here with aunty Shell for a while. Can you do that for me darling?"

Her grandson smiled up at her and vigorously nodded his head. Winking in Michelle's direction she gently nudged little Vic forward.

"Kenny I want a word with you in the kitchen."

"In a bit mum, I...."

"Now!!!"

His mother didn't normally raise her voice to any of them especially him but Kenny could see by her face that she was really put out about something.

Silently he followed her from the room and when they were alone in the kitchen and the door had been closed his mother turned on him with a vengeance.

"Do you know what that little whore Deidre has just told me?"

Kenny shrugged his shoulders.

"That she gives you a blow job on a regular basis and don't try fucking denying it. I knew you was overly fond of your sister but I didn't let it worry me too much as I knew nothing would ever come of it but fucking your own brothers wife on a regular basis, how much lower can you get?"

"I have never fucked her and if she's said I have its a lie."

"So sucking your cock is ok is it? I tell you something Kenny and I never thought in a million years Id hear myself say it but I'm ashamed of you. Now get out of this house and don't come back!"

Kenny couldn't believe what he was hearing; his mother had turned against him and all because of a whore like Deidre Steel. He couldn't see that he had done any real harm and he was sure that Vic wouldn't have given a toss either way. Deidre had been a constant embarrassment to his brother, to the whole family if the truth be told. Still Sandra was mad and he thought it was best to let her calm down a bit before he returned. Deciding to check up on things and make a few phone calls he would go to the office until the dust settled.

300

CHAPTER TWENTY SEVEN

Kenny Steel was still seething as he drove over to the office and was in two minds whether to call in at Vic's flat on the way. He couldn't bear the thought of his mother loathing him and right at this moment he realised that was exactly how she was feeling towards him. Sandra had a special bond with her eldest son but Kenny knew that she also loved all her other children with a passion. If anyone ever interfered in her family she would act like a woman possessed but he had made things even more difficult for her as the betrayal had been committed within the family. God he felt like knocking Deidre into tomorrow. He knew it would make him feel a whole lot better but with things as they were with his family at the moment it would definitely make things a whole lot worse. Deciding to leave it for now he parked up his Range Rover and walked along Pimlico High Street in the direction of the office. By now the street was void of shoppers and the young crowds were starting to appear in readiness for a good night out. A rowdy group of five lads were heading in his direction but they didn't faze Kenny Steel. His anger was such that he would have taken them all on without batting an eyelid. The lads didn't speak to him but all knowing who he was, politely steeped aside as he passed. Kenny Steel was well aware that he instilled fear into all that knew him. Even though his business was carried out mostly in Essex he was still a well known face in the East End. His size alone was enough to scare most but the Steel name carried more kudos than anything else. Ali Celik the owner of the Istanbul kebab house was in the middle of loading up the doner as Kenny went by the window. He waved as Kenny passed but the greeting wasn't reciprocated. Placing his key in the lock Kenny wearily made his way inside. The sound of the door closing brought Zena round from the sleepy trance she had fallen into. Sitting bolt upright she checked to make sure that everything was right with the shotgun. Placing the stock to her shoulder she held it as steady as she could manage. The gun was heavy but above all else her nerves were kicking in and she prayed that she wouldn't drop the Purdey before she'd had the chance of revenge. Kenny was deep in thought regarding his mother's harsh words as he walked in but when he saw Zena Cartwright sitting in the centre of the room with a double barrel shotgun aimed directly at him he stopped dead in his tracks. As Zena rose from the chair he immediately raised both arms in the air in a show of submission.

"Kick the door closed with your foot and sit down behind the desk."

"Come on now love you don't....."

"I said sit down!"

Kenny noticed that her hands were shaking and as he couldn't see if she had released the safety catch didn't want to take any unnecessary chances. Doing exactly as he was told he sat down heavily in the leather swivel chair. Zena studied him for a few seconds and the one thing that struck her more than anything else was his piercing blue eyes that were as cold as ice.

"You don't know who I am do you?"

"You got me there sweetheart but if I was to hazard a guess I'd say Zena Cartwright."

"Give the man a fucking prize! On second thoughts don't because this man wrecks people's lives, takes everything from them and then like a piece of fucking shit discards them."

Zena Cartwright had begun to pace the floor and was holding the shotgun in both hands. Kenny knew that she was about to snap. He remembered back to his army days and seeing other soldiers behave in exactly the same manner. They were unpredictable and he knew he had to calm the situation quickly and in any way that he could.

"Look darling it's not me you want its Charlie. He's the one who got you to do the........"

"Shut the fuck up!"

Zena was now standing directly opposite him and the only thing separating them was the desk. Swiftly she raised the gun to her shoulder and walked around to the other side. Kenny pushed away so that his chair was now touching the back wall.

"Open your mouth now!"

303

Desperate to keep her calm Kenny did exactly as he was asked in the hope that there might be just a split second where he could grab the gun away from her. Zena was too fast for him and in the blink of an eye she had pushed the barrel into his mouth and pulled the trigger. The impact from the gun being fired at such a close range was horrific and half of Kenny Steels head was blown clean away. Bone blood and brains splattered the map that hung on the wall behind Kenny's chair and Zena with her head tilted to one side, watched mesmerised as they began to run downwards forming a sickening kind of abstract pattern. It never crossed her mind that someone would hear the gunfire and report it to the police and as luck would have it no one did or if they had heard then they didn't want to get involved. Calmly she retook her seat and opening the gun fished in her pocket for a replacement cartridge. As shed only discharged one shell from the double barrel she still had two spares but Zena very much doubted she would have a need for both of them now. Placing the gun by her side she once more sat in wait.

Back at the Steel family home Michelle had begun to sweat profusely and Sandra knew that her daughter was getting a fever. She wanted to call an ambulance but at the same time didn't want to move her daughter until Kenny came home. Oh Sandra knew that her harsh words would have bothered her son but she also knew he wouldn't be able to stay away for long, her boy loved his family far too much for that. Pacing the floor she was deliberating whether to phone for help when she heard the front door open. Assuming it was Kenny the disappointment on her face when Charlie and Vic walked in didn't go unnoticed. Charlie instantly made his way over to his sister and placed a palm on her forehead but Vic remained in the doorway.

"Well, nice to see you too mum!"

"I'm really sorry Son but we've had a bit of an upset here today. Me and Kenny's had a row but I'll tell you all about that later. Your sons in the kitchen, poor little bleeders been stuck in there for most of the afternoon."

"Vic! Vic! Get over here and have a look I don't think our Shells too good do you?"

Vic Steel did exactly as his brother had done a few minutes earlier."

"Fuck me mum she's burning up you need to get an ambulance and fast."

Sandra knew she couldn't wait any longer for Kenny and grabbing her mobile she dialled the emergency services.

"Charlie you stay with mum and Shell until they get here and then go and find Kenny. Got any idea where he is mum?"

"No but I would imagine the office. He always seems to end up there when he's in a strop."

Vic placed an arm lovingly around his mothers shoulder and pulled her to him.

"It's all ok mum. Once they get her admitted she will be fine trust me. Now I'm going to get little Vic home and then I'll join you all at the hospital. Please don't worry everything's going to be alright I promise."

Sandra kissed him on the cheek and then went and sat on the bed to hold Michelle's hand. Charlie followed his brother into the kitchen and witnessed the display of affection when little Vic spotted his dad and ran into his arms. Vic bent down and embraced his son at the same time Charlie placed a hand on his brother's shoulder.

"She don't look too good does she?"

Vic shook his head as he stood up.

"No, but mum don't need to hear that kind of talk. Now whatever you do make sure you find Kenny because if anything happens to our Shell and he aint there, well I don't even want to fucking think what he'd be like."

"Ok and Vic."

"What?"

"Oh it don't matter I'll talk to you later."

Vic Steel began the short walk home with his son. Once he'd sorted the boy out and got him settled he knew he was in for a long night back at the hospital. As they entered the flat the place was in darkness and at first Vic thought Deidre was out. Flicking on the light switch he was surprised to see her sitting on the sofa. Her eyes were still black from crying but there were no signs of alcohol anywhere.

Deidre was terrified and was expecting a beating for her earlier behaviour. When her husband smiled she felt a stab of guilt until she realised he didn't know anything about it. Deciding to get her side of the story over first she stood up and walked over to him but didn't acknowledge her son.

"Hi Vic! Now before you start I ....."

"What are you on about?"

"On about? What happened round at your mums earlier of course, now I know you're....."

"Look I aint got time for your shenanigans tonight. Shells really bad and I need to get to the hospital. I take it that for a change you aint had a skin full and can look after your child for once? As soon as I have any news I'll let you know."

Deidre now acted over the top in her affection towards little Vic and as she hugged him to her he tried desperately to wriggle free. Her fake show of love didn't have any impact on her husband but she hoped that with all that was going on she would get away with the appalling nastiness she had shown to Michelle. Shaking his head at her actions Vic left the flat and drove back over to his mother's house. He prayed that they were already at the hospital but as he hadn't had a phone call he doubted it. He was wrong and in fact the ambulance had arrived within five minutes of Vic leaving, a record by all standards for London and especially the East End. Seeing that all the house lights were turned off Vic continued straight on to the hospital. As soon as he'd seen his sister and mother into the emergency department Charlie Steel had set off for the office. He had dialled Kenny's number several times but it kept going to voice mail and that alone concerned him. No matter what he was doing Kenny always answered and Charlie was now worried. Pulling up outside the building he didn't bother to find a free parking spot and if he got a ticket then so be it. The High Street was now full of youngsters and he pushed passed them as he made his way inside. Once again Zena heard the door being opened and as if on auto pilot she sprang to attention and was instantly sitting bolt upright in her seat as the handle turned. The first thing Charlie saw was Kenny's body with half his head and face blown away. A second later and he spotted Zena out of the corner of his eye. For a split second he didn't relate the two things together but when it did begin to sink in and as Charlie Steel fell to his knees he started to moan. It was slow at first but then rapidly building to a crescendo of terrible screams. "What the fuck! Oh Zena what have you done you stupid bitch? Oh no Kennnnnnny!"

As Charlie stepped forward Zena Cartwright cocked the gun and once more moved it up to her shoulder but her eyes never left Charlie Steels face for a second.

"Put your hands on your head!"

"Come on babe don't be like this I know I've let....."

"I said put your hands on your head you bastard!"

308

Charlie Steel immediately obeyed and did as she asked. He studied her face and there was something that he had never seen before, a coldness that he couldn't get his head around.

"So what now Zena? Are you going to blow my head off as well?"

Charlie began to shake. After seeing his brother with half his head missing he knew that she must have lost the plot and the idea that he was about to end up the same way was paramount in his mind. Zena didn't answer the question; she only stood up and walked closer to the man that she had risked everything for. After studying him for a few seconds she finally spoke.

"Oh no Charlie I wouldn't do that. I've got something far better in store for you! Take off your clothes."

"What?"

"You heard me take off your fucking clothes!"

Charlie Steel slowly stood up and began to undress. Unlike before when they were back at Zena's flat after a night out and he had stripped off without a second thought, he now felt vulnerable. Finally he was down to his socks and pants and Zena studied him. As if seeing Charlie for the first time she couldn't for the life of her understand what all the fuss had been about, why she had even wanted him so much in the first place.

"All of them!"

"Look babe we can sort this out, I can help you get

rid of the body! Oh come on Zena this is your Charlie taking don't be silly now."

"I said all of them Charlie! There's no going back from any of this."

Charlie Steel slowly peeled off his underpants and then his socks. He was embarrassed and covered his penis and testicles with his cupped hands. Zena removed a knife from her pocket, the filleting knife that Linda had used on so many occasions to prepare the fish that her husband had caught.

"Now put your hands back onto your head."

Charlie could feel the sweat on his palms as he obeyed her command.

"Open your mouth Charlie."

Zena was calm, very calm as she placed the shotgun under his chin. The pressure of the cold steel barrel against his skin made him rise onto his toes.

"You know I love you Charlie, always have and probably always will. You do know that Charlie don't you?"

"Don't do this Zena please!!!! I'll do anything I promise."

"Tut tut Charlie! Now if I was you I wouldn't move too quickly. I'm really not that strong you know and its liable to go off at any given second."

With one hand on the trigger and the other holding the knife against his face Zena quickly moved her hand and placed the blade inside Charlie's mouth. Without warning she moved her hand sideways and the razor sharp tip slashed through his cheek and out of the other side.

"Arghhhhh you bitch!"

Charlie quickly moved his hands up to protect his
face but with the shotgun still pressed firmly under
his chin Zena swiftly moved the knife down to his
groin area. Placing it perfectly onto his balls Zena
sliced upwards in one quick movement. There was
no hesitation and she had a calmness about her that
she hadn't felt before. Charlie again screamed and
desperately clutched at his testicles. His inner
thighs and legs were rapidly deepening in colour as
the blood began to flow freely.

"I really did love you Charlie so I had to make sure
you would never again be able to fuck anyone over,
especially a woman. I've taken away your looks
and hopefully your sex drive if the hospital cant
stitch you up, fingers crossed hey?"

Zena's eyes were glass like as she gave him one last
smile. Placing the Purdey under her own chin and
with the chambers loaded she pulled both triggers.
This time the noise was heard and people did take
notice. Ali Celik ran to his shop window and when
he saw that people had stopped outside and were
staring up at the first floor he called the police. A
patrol car came screeching to a halt within a few
minutes. The street door was forced open and
when the blood bath was discovered the area was
immediately cordoned off. Charlie was now
unconscious and at first the policemen didn't think
there were any survivors. Bob Chilvers had been a

bobby on the beat for the last ten years but the gruesome sight that he was now looking at was new to him. Bending down he was about to feel for a pulse when he noticed Charlie's chest rise and fall slightly.

"Quick! Phone an ambulance this one's still alive!" The paramedics arrived swiftly and after a few minutes of working on Charlie they were able to stem the blood loss. Charlie Steel was rushed to hospital to undergo emergency surgery for his injuries and for once he'd been lucky, far luckier than Kenny.

CHAPTER TWENTY EIGHT

At the Mile End hospital Michelle Steel was checked over by the consultant who had initially treated her. Luckily he was still on duty after a long shift but he was now very tired and not in the best of moods. After severely reprimanding Sandra for taking her daughter home in the first place, Michelle was once more admitted to hospital. To Sandra's relief the consultant informed her that it was only a mild infection and nothing that a course of intravenous antibiotics wouldn't sort out in the next few hours. After his earlier run in with Kenny Mr Framingham's tone was authoritarian as he told Sandra in no uncertain terms that this time her daughter should be left at the hospital until he deemed her fit to return home. Sandra Steel didn't argue and was just glad that her baby was going to be alright. Vic was relieved but he couldn't for the life of him work out where his brothers had got to. It wasn't like Kenny to miss anything that concerned Shell. He didn't voice his worries to his mother as he didn't want to cause her any more stress, so after they both kissed Michelle goodnight Vic took Sandra home. There was little conversation as they drove back to Boreham Avenue and Vic put his mother's reluctance to chat down to tiredness. After seeing her safely inside he was looking forward to getting back to his own flat and checking on little Vic. It had been a long day what with all the travelling and family upset and Vic was feeling washed out. About to pull away from the curb he looked into the rear view mirror and saw two policemen walking up the path to his mother's house. He quickly turned off the engine and ran to the front door before the police had time to knock.

"Can I help you officers?"

"And who might you be Sir?"

"My mother lives here and we've just got back from the hospital, my sister is sick."

The two constables looked at each other and Vic had a gut instinct that whatever they were about to say wasn't going to be good.

"Is it bad news?"

Dave Hampton who had been in the force the longest out of the two slowly nodded his head.

"Well then I would like to be with my mum when you break whatever it is you've got to tell her."

Vic let himself in with the spare key that he always carried and the officers followed close behind.

"Mum! Mum where are you?"

Sandra Steel appeared in the kitchen doorway with a glass of brandy in her hand.

"Hello boy I thought you'd be well on your way by now. Did you forget...."

Sandra suddenly spied the two policemen standing behind her son.

"What? What's going on? Please don't tell me its Shell we've only just left her!"

As the three men walked towards her Sandra backed into the kitchen. The colour had drained from her face and she felt sick but didn't know why. "Mrs Steel I'm afraid we have some very bad news. There has been an incident at premises on Pimlico High Street. I am sorry to inform you that a gentleman by the name of Kenny Steel has been killed and another named as Charlie Steel has been taken to hospital with serious injuries."
As if in slow motion the glass containing her brandy dropped freely onto the tiles and smashed. Sandra who was now in an emotional mess threw herself to the floor and began to wail.
"My boys, my boys, my beautiful beautiful boys!!!! God no, oh please god heaven not my Kennnnny!"
Vic knelt down and took his mother in his arms. Looking up at Dave Hampton he asked what had happened.
"I'm afraid we don't have any further details yet but I can tell you there was a third person involved. A woman also died at the scene but as yet she's still unidentified."
Vic was baffled as to whom it could be and the idea that Deidre could be involved somehow fleetingly crossed his mind but he dismissed the notion straight away. Holding his mother close he kissed the top of her head. He was worried about Charlie but even more so about his old mum. Sandra had always been the strong one especially in a crisis but now she seemed childlike and lost. Standing up Vic

315

gently lifted Sandra to her feet.

"I know this is hard mum but there's nothing you can do for Kenny now. Its Charlie and Shell who need us and we can't let them down. Come on sweetheart I'll drive you back down to the hospital so we can find out what's going on."

It was now getting late and as Vic and Sandra Steel entered the Mile End emergency unit a patrol car was pulling up outside the home of Linda and Stan Cartwright in Southend. They were so worried about their missing daughter that they hadn't gone to bed but had both managed to fall asleep on the front room sofa. The car door closing woke Linda and she was up and looking out of the window in seconds.

"Stan! Stan wake up its the police!"

Running to open the front door Linda was dreading what they had to tell her. By the look on the woman police constables face she could tell straight away that it was bad news. WPC Emma Gatling led Linda back into the room where Stan was trying to stand up but was having difficulty managing it.

"Please Mr Cartwright stay seated."

Linda sat down beside her husband and they both stared at the woman longing for her to tell them what all this was regarding but scared at the same time about what they were going to hear.

"I'm sorry to inform you Mr and Mrs Cartwright but the body of a young woman has been found and we have reason to believe it is that of your daughter

Zena."

It was Stan who spoke first and his words ran into each other as he asked.

"What!!!!!! I don't understand, what do you mean, no it can't be, not our Zena I ..."

"I'm not able to tell you much very much Mr Cartwright only that it was at an office in Pimlico and a firearm was involved."

Stan immediately began to howl and clutching his head in his hands he rocked back and forth with tears streaming down his face. The enormity of what they'd been told didn't hit Linda straight away and to begin with she was more concerned about her husband. Stroking his back just as shed done to Zena as a child she softly whispered 'there there love'. A few minutes later and there was another knock at the door. The young policeman who had accompanied WPC Gatling and who had never before attended a death notification went to answer. His face was ashen as he opened up to Detective Templeman. Clive Templeman had been the bearer of much bad news during his time in the force and he straight away recognized the look on the young policeman's face.

"Take a break Son and grab a bit of fresh air."

As Detective Templeman entered the front room Stan was still sobbing and Clive coughed loudly as he approached the couple. Nodding in the direction of WPC Gatling he began to speak and she noticed how kind and sympathetic his voice sounded.

It was something they had all been taught how to do in basic training but being able to manage it when needed was another matter.

"I am deeply sorry for your loss. Now I realise this is a difficult time but I do need to ask you both a few questions if we are to find out why your daughter died."

The loss of Zena was slowly sinking in for Linda and she sat staring into space as tears rolled silently down her face. From somewhere deep inside Stan heard Clive's words and he instantly stopped crying and looked up.

"Find out why she died! You're looking in the wrong place mate. The reason this has happened is all down to Steel Security. They already set her up with all them drugs and I'd bet my life on it that those bastards somewhere along the line had a hand in her death!"

Detective Templeman was now more than intrigued. It was the second time in a day that he'd heard the name Steel. A few hours earlier his department had received a call from the landlord of the Stags Head over in Hoxton. Apparently the man had gone through an attack of guilt regarding the death of Mickey Sandish and had offered up Kenny Steels name as the culprit. Clive was about to pay Kenny a visit when the call had come through about the shootings. After arriving at the scene he had until now thought that was the end of things. His D.C.I had asked him to drive over to

Southend as a matter of routine but now things looked a whole lot more complicated. Maybe Detective Templeman should have looked into Zena Cartwright's history before calling on her parents but he couldn't worry about his oversight at the moment.

"Mr Cartwright do you have any idea if your daughter would have access to or know anyone with a shotgun?"

Linda and Stan looked at each other and Clive heard her softly mouth the words Oh no. Standing up Linda made her way into the hall and climbed the stairs. As she entered her bedroom she prayed that everything would be in place and when she found the key still taped to the bottom of the drawer, thought it was. Now a little less worried she opened up the wardrobe and then the gun case. Linda Cartwright let out a loud gasp when she found that the cabinet was empty. Turning round she saw that WPC Gatling was standing in the doorway.

"He hadn't used it in years well not since Zena lost interest; well you know what they're like as teenagers. Time and time again I've asked him to get rid of it but my old man's as stubborn as a mule. I hate guns do you know I think all this will finish my Stan."

Emma Gatling gently placed her hand on Linda's arm and led her back down the stairs. When they re-entered the lounge Stan's eyes were once more pleading as he looked at his wife. Linda slowly shook her head and her husband's wailing began all over again. Detective Templeman knew this case wasn't over by a long way but whether he could get to the bottom of things was another matter. After telling the constable to remain with the Cartwright's Clive was soon in his car and heading back to London and the Mile End hospital.

Michelle had yet to be informed of her brother's demise. Sandra knew it would be too much for her to handle in her fragile state. Together she and Vic once more waited in the relative's room as Charlie underwent emergency surgery for his injuries. As Clive Templeman walked along the corridor he saw the surgeon enter the room and hoped that it was, for want of better words, good news. It may have seemed callous to some but Detective Templeman was only too aware that if he left things to go cold then everyone would clam up. As it was cases were hard enough to deal with in the East End at the best of times. Leaning against the wall he waited for a few minutes and when he didn't hear the sound of sobbing and the surgeon had once more left the room he made his way inside. Sandra and Vic were seated on the sofa and Vic had his arm around his mother. Looking up he instantly recognised Old Bill when Clive walked in.

"I'm sorry to bother you at such a sad time but I'm leading the investigation into the shootings and as a matter of urgency I need to ask you both some questions."

Vic knew it was useless to argue as he'd have to speak to the law at some point and he wasn't worried about what his mum would say as Sandra knew nothing of what had gone on.

"Fire away detective but I don't think either of us will be able to help you."

"Have you any idea why your brothers would have been at the office with a young woman?"

"Charlie and me only got back from Spain today and when my sister got taken to hospital Charlie went out to look for our older brother. Other than that I don't know a thing. Mum can you add anything?"

Sandra Steel shook her head. Vic was right shed been kept in the dark regarding what her boys were up to but even if she had have know she wasn't in the habit of talking to the Old Bill. Clive Templeman recognised the signs and knew he wouldn't get any further at least not with the two people sitting in front of him.

"Fair enough but I will get to the bottom of this Mr Steel I promise you. Two people have lost their lives and someone needs to be accountable. I'll call back tomorrow when your brother is awake and maybe he can shed more light on things."

Vic was inwardly glad but he didn't show it. Surely this plod knew how things worked, knew that no East Ender worth his salt would ever offer up information freely to the law. Detective Templeman said good night to them both and then left the hospital. He had served in the force for over twenty years and the last ten had been spent in the East End. Just as Vic thought he knew how things worked and was under no illusions that he would get any further with the case but he had to try if only to justify things to himself. When she was sure they were alone Sandra turned to Vic and spoke.

"What the hell's going on Son and what the fuck was Charlie and Kenny doing at the office with a woman at this hour of the night?"

"I don't know mum really I don't."

Vic had long since realised that the woman in question must have been Zena Cartwright but it wasn't something he could admit to his mother. Strangely he wasn't heartbroken at Kenny's demise it was something which he knew had been on the cards for a long time. He wasn't aware that his brother had been the instigator of Stan Cartwright's beating and that was the reason Zena had lost her mind. As for Charlie, well he guessed it was a case of wrong time wrong place but then surely he would have been Zena's main target after he'd set her up. Whether his younger brother could shed any more light on things was another matter but he needed to speak to Charlie before the plods come back again tomorrow.

"Mum the surgeon said he'll be fine so I think it's best if we get off now. You have to get some sleep if you're going to keep your strength up. They are

322

both going to need us in the morning and its going to be tough for the next few days. Fuck me I forgot our Shell don't even know yet does she?"
"Oh no Vic! This is going to kill her!"
The realisation brought a fresh onslaught of tears from his mother and he sighed at his own stupidity. Leading her gently back to the car Vic Steel drove his mother home. After he had poured her a large measure of brandy and reassured her that he would be back within the hour ,Vic once again set off for the hospital. Slipping onto the ward he gently shook his brother's arm.
"Charlie! Charlie mate wake up!"
Charlie Steel slowly stirred and opened his eyes. For a few seconds he didn't realise where he was but when reality struck his eyes filled with terror.
"He's dead Vic our Kenny's dead!"
"I know mate but you have to listen to me. The Old Bill are sniffing around and I've told them we were in Spain until today. I said you had gone to find Kenny because our Shell had been taken into hospital and in all honesty that aint a lie. Now I gather they will if they aint already, find out that Zena was your girlfriend. You are going to have to spin a tale about her getting all possessive or something. Charlie I don't really give a fuck what you say but it had better be good as mum can't take much more upset and you getting into bother with the law would just about tip her over the edge."
Charlie's eyes felt heavy as he hadn't fully come

round from the anaesthetic yet but he had heard what his brother had said In a sleepy voice he muttered don't worry I'll sort it and then drifted off into a deep sleep. Vic was certain that he wouldn't let the family down and after deciding not to pop in and see his sister as he wasn't a good enough actor for that he headed back to his mother's house for a night of more sobbing and tears from Sandra.

CHAPTER TWENTY NINE

Two weeks had now passed and strangely both
funerals were held on the same day. Zena's cortege
had only two mourners in attendance, her mother
and father. There was no family to invite but Linda
had contacted her daughters work colleagues. All
had promised to attend but on the day hadn't
bothered to show up. It had hurt Linda and Stan
deeply but they knew what with the drug
smuggling charge and now the murder none of
them wanted to be tarred with the same brush. The
turnout for Kenny was a different matter and the
church was full to capacity. Security firms from all
over the smoke had come to pay their respects as
well as a few unsavoury gangland faces. Sandra
had been surprised that none of her son's old army
buddies had shown up but she was too busy coping
with Michelle to dwell on the thought for long.
Since the moment she had been informed that
Kenny was dead Michelle Steel had gone into melt
down. She didn't want to talk to anyone, wash or
change her clothes. Sandra was constantly on her
back and she hated having to do it but there was no
way she was about to let her family fall apart.
Every night she would sob herself to sleep but she
didn't let anyone least of all her children know that
fact. Charlie had been released from hospital in
time to see his brother off but he couldn't walk and
was pushed into the church by Tommy Bex. To all

it had seemed that Tommy had taken Kenny's demise hard but at the same time unbeknown to anyone else, he was also seeing the possibility of taking over the firm. Deciding to let the dust settle and see what the Steels had planned for the future he now portrayed the grieving friend. Vic had kept strong for his mother and sister but in all honesty couldn't wait for the day to be over. Since that terrible night he had thought constantly about Zena and what his family had put her and her parents through. There were a few hours between both services and he had contemplated attending Zena's if only out of a sense of guilt. Accepting that her family wouldn't welcome him he decided to stay away. The one thing he did do was send a wreath though he didn't sign it. Vic wasn't missing Kenny like he thought he would or should have done and those thoughts bothered him deeply. Entering the church the family portrayed a sorry sight and Deidre was a total embarrassment to everyone. Vic was desperately trying to hold his mother and Shell up and little Vic walked quietly beside his father. Deidre Steel on the other hand had been on the bottle all morning and swayed from side to side as she walked to the family pew. She reeked of wine and as the coffin was carried in she sobbed so loud that the vicar's words were drowned out. Vic Steel felt no compassion and he knew that after this day was over his marriage would finally come to an end. It wasn't the embarrassment but purely down to the fact that he now couldn't stand the evil bitch he'd married, couldn't even bear to be in the same room as her. Everyone thought Vic was in the dark regarding his wife's affair with his brother but nothing could have been further from the truth. After only a few months of marriage and when he had still been in love with her Vic had returned home from work early. As he'd climbed the stairs to his maisonette he had heard the groans of pleasure coming from the front room. Kenny hadn't seen him and he was grateful for that but as he saw his wife take his brothers penis in her mouth he felt sick. Quietly Vic had descended the stairs and both his brother and Deidre had been none the wiser but from that day onwards he looked at her differently. When little Vic was born it had crossed his mind that maybe the boy wasn't his but he reasoned that he always wanted a child and he would love him no matter what. Now sitting beside the woman who he had sworn to love for the rest of his life he wished she was the one lying in the coffin instead of his brother. Vic Steel wasn't a bad man but he had been dealt a bad hand when it came to his choice in women. Deciding to just let Deidre make a fool of herself he placed an arm round little Vic and pulled him close. Thirty minutes later and the service was finally over. After Kenny's body was placed in the hearse and before the family left for the crematorium everyone gathered outside in the church grounds. People were hugging and kissing

but deep down both Charlie and Vic knew that it was false. Tommy Bex wheeled Charlie over to a quiet area and placed the brake onto the wheelchair.
"Wos the matter Tom?"
"Nothing why?"
"Well you aint wheeled me over here for the good of me health now have you?"
"Well now you come to mention it I was hoping to have a quick word with either you or Vic but I can see your brothers got his hands full at the moment. Fuck me that Deidre's a right mess I don't know how he puts up with her."
Charlie was starting to get annoyed and turning round in his seat glared at Tommy Bex.
"Keep your fucking nose out of my brother's marital affairs! Now say what you've got to say will you."
I was just wondering what plans you and Vic had for the business?"
"Fuck me Tommy! We aint even laid my brother to rest yet and you're thinking how you can get your fucking hands on his business? I'll tell you this for nothing, I don't know what our Vic's got planned but as far as I'm concerned its business as usual. Now wheel me back to my family you cunt!"
Tommy Bex did what was asked but he knew there and then that Steel security would soon be his. Vic Steel had never been that interested and was now too wrapped up in his family to take any real interest. As for Charlie, well Tommy had always looked upon him as a necessary evil and if it came

328

down to a fight the boy and that was all he was, wouldn't be of any great concern.

Michelle had been silently standing next to Sandra when Julie Sullivan walked up. Taking her friend in her arms she hugged her and Michelle Steel started to cry when she felt the love emitting itself from her friend. For the first time ever she reciprocated Julies embrace which made Julie Sullivan smile with happiness but also a great deal of sadness that it had taken something so sad to bring them together.

"Oh Shell! I'm so so sorry about everything that's happened to you."

Taking her friends hand in hers Michelle squeezed it gently.

"It's me who should be sorry Jules, I was a right bitch to you. You have only ever been kind and loyal to me and I treated you so badly. I wouldn't blame you if you never wanted to have anything more to do with me."

They were still holding hands but now it was Julie Sullivan who had tears in her eyes.

"Don't be daft we're mates aint we?"

"Mates don't treat each other like that please forgive me."

"Honestly Shell there aint nothing to forgive."

Suddenly Michelle Steel hung her head as she spoke.

"I was having a baby you know?"

Julie couldn't think of what to say. Sorry seemed so empty and worthless and nothing else sprang to mind. Looking into her friends face she saw Michelle's eyes were glassy and she was staring into space like she wasn't even there. Julie Sullivan hoped that wherever her friends mind had wandered to it was a much happier place than here in the churchyard.

Two months later Charlie was now up and about but he still needed a cane to walk. Numerous times over the last few days he had tried to talk to his brother about getting back to work but Vic wasn't the least bit interested. True the lads had done a good job in keeping things ticking over these past weeks but it was, as far as Charlie was concerned time to get back into the saddle. His mother was consumed with making sure her Michelle was alright and didn't seem to have an interest in anyone else. He had wondered if she blamed him for all of this but what happened to Michelle was totally separate. Charlie wasn't aware that Vic had told his mother all about Zena and what Kenny and Charlie had done to her. Sandra felt ashamed that two of her own children had so little regard for another human being. She hadn't broached the subject with her youngest son but it was only a matter of time before she did. Charlie Steel had spent another day alone in his room and when he decided to join his mother for a cupper and she had walked out as soon as he sat at the table he realised he had to do something. An idea sprung to mind; tonight he would re-establish the Steel name in the world of security and make his mother proud of him again. With difficulty he dressed in his best designer gear and after ordering a taxi made his way over to the Sugar Hut. Hobbling up to the entrance he was greeted by Jock Denman but it wasn't overly friendly.

"Hi Mr Hop along and what brings you here tonight?"

The man's words made Charlie's blood boil. If Kenny was still alive Jock wouldn't have dared speak to him in that way. Suddenly and after all this time the realisation that Kenny was gone hit home.

"What brings me here? You cunt! This is my family's business and you'd better not forget it!" Making his way inside Charlie spotted a few potential lays and cane in hand he approached a slim blonde who would normally have been an easy conquest. What Charlie conveniently forgot was the fact that not only had he been off the scene for almost three months but he now sported a horrendous scar across his cheek. The young woman didn't have a clue who he was and in all honesty his scar turned her off big time. Charlie found the rejection hard to take but shrugging it off he moved onto his second choice.   When once again he got the same result he realised that things were never going to be the same again and that realisation made him angry. He was angry at Kenny for dying, angry at Vic for not helping him out but most of all he was angry at Zena for taking away the life he had, a life he had loved. Making his way to the office Charlie Steel wasn't in a good mood.

Entering he saw Tommy Bex seated behind the desk and he was in the middle of a conversation with Mattie Singer. Tommy like Mattie had never liked Charlie and had only put up with him for one reason and one reason only, he was Kenny Steels little brother. With Kenny no longer around he now didn't feel he needed to show the man any respect. Swiftly glancing in Charlie's direction Mattie nodded his head but soon turned his attention back to his new boss and the slight didn't go unnoticed by Charlie Steel. Tommy Bex could feel the tension rising and even though Charlie was no match for Mattie he knew that the situation could soon get out of hand if he didn't do something. Standing up he walked around the desk and placed a hand on Charlie's shoulder.

"Look Son I....."

"Who the fuck are you calling son and who said you could sit in my brother's chair."

Tommy was fast becoming fed up with Charlie's attitude and decided that in this case honesty would definitely be the best policy.

"Charlie boy you've asked for it so now I'm going to give it to you fucking straight. I was sad when Kenny died and I won't deny that but now it's every man for himself. You aint got the balls to run things

332

you never did have. Now if you feel like taking me
or any of my and I do stress my crew on, then give
it your best fucking shot because I guarantee it'll be
your fucking last. Do yourself a favour and walk
away with a bit of dignity. If you don't then I have
no doubt that Mattie here will take great fucking
pleasure in throwing you out!"

Realising that he was beaten Charlie Steel turned
round and limped out of the club. When he was out
of sight of anyone he broke down and cried like a
baby. Several minutes later and after Charlie had
dried his eyes he was now angry again, angrier than
he'd ever been before but he was also aware that he
didn't stand a chance on his own. Deciding to ask
for his brothers help one last time he ordered a cab
and headed over to Canning Town and Vic's flat.
Vic had just settled his son down for the night and it
was getting late. Since all the family upset little Vic
had started to play up. His manners had all but
disappeared and Vic knew that before long he
would have to take his son in hand. Deidre was
passed out on the sofa, which was becoming a daily
occurrence since Kenny's death. He knew she was
grieving like they all were but whereas he and his
mother were trying to move on Deidre refused to do
the same. His sister was in world of her own most
of the time but Michelle's grief Vic could accept
unlike his wife's. Charlie rang the bell and after Vic
buzzed him up he struggled to climb the stairs.
When he at last made it onto the landing and into

the flat he saw Vic sitting alone at the kitchen table. "You'll never fucking guess what that cunt Tommy Bex is doing over at the Sugar Hut!"

Vic shook his head. He didn't have the slightest interest in what his brother had to say or any interest in Tommy Bex and the clubs. He could see Charlie was struggling but at the same time realised that it was about time his brother accepted that things were never going to be what they were and for all intent and purpose the Steels were no longer in the security game.

"Look Charlie it's about time you faced facts and let go. We were never anything without our Kenny and I for one aint sad that it's over."

Charlie sneered at his brothers words and as he turned to leave couldn't help but give one last insult.

"You're a gutless bastard Vic you never did have any balls!"

Vic Steel heartily sighed.

"Maybe you're right but you know something? I like myself my conscience is clear and I can sleep well at night, can you say the same Charlie or have you conveniently forgot about the poor little Cartwright girl?"

Charlie Steel didn't reply. As he drove back to his mothers he was enveloped in rage. He now hated Zena with a passion and blamed her totally for how his life had turned out.

Three months later on the day that Kenny's last will

334

and testament was finally formalised, it sent shockwaves through the family. Charlie and Michelle had been left absolutely nothing. A small amount of money had been placed in trust for Sandra to make sure she didn't go short in her old age but the bulk was left entirely to Vic. With the house now on the market and the money Kenny had stashed away Vic Steel was set for a life of luxury except that wasn't what he wanted. In the last couple of months he had desperately tried to help Charlie and Deidre get back on track. All offers of help both financial and emotional had been thrown back in his face. Vic Steel and his son had moved into Sandra's house while his wife still resided at the maisonette on Rutland Road. She didn't enquire after her boys well being and neither did her mother or sister. To Vic it was as if their son never even existed as far as Deidre and her family were concerned. Her days were spent in an alcoholic stupor and just recently Charlie Steel had begun to spend more and more time in his sister-in-laws company. It was after one particularly nasty showdown when Vic had called at his former home to collect clothes for his boy that he had come to a monumental decision.

Sandra had been in the kitchen when she heard the front door slam and went into the hall to see who it was. Vic was angry and the entire colour had drained from his face, a sign to his mother that whatever was bothering him was serious.

"Hello Son. I can tell by that look that something's up, want to tell your old mum all about it?"

"Do you know something mum? I've just about had it up to here with those two wankers. I tried to be civil even tried to strike up a fucking conversation but the pair of them were out of their heads on booze. I know you probably aint going to like this but I've decided to move away."

Sandra's eyes instantly misted over and he knew she was about to cry which was the last thing Vic Steel wanted to see.

"I'm going to buy a place in the country with room for a few animals for the boy. I know it's a lot to ask mum but I want you and Shell to come with us."

Sandra was now laughing and crying at the same time. For a minute she thought she was about to lose another son and her grandson to boot. Looking round at the beautiful home Kenny had provided she realised that it meant nothing without her family.

"I think that's a fantastic idea Son. When do you think we can go because tomorrow wouldn't be soon enough for me. I hate this bastard city and all that it's taken from me!"

Vic Steel hugged his mother to him as he hoped that maybe just maybe, for once things were going to turn out alright for the remainder of the Steel family.

THE END

EPILOGUE

MAY 2013

A week after Zena's funeral Stan Cartwright had suffered a stroke. The doctors didn't think it had anything to do with stress but Linda knew differently. Zena had been their life, Linda was always telling them that they were like two peas in a pod and now since her death it was as if her husband was only half a man. After weeks spent in hospital and numerous amounts of physiotherapy and rehabilitation he had at last been allowed home. Stan hadn't progressed as well as the specialists had hoped for and they finally informed his wife that he was probably as well as he was ever going to be. Now confined to a wheelchair he was reliant on Linda for even the smallest of tasks. Reluctantly they had sold their dream home in Southend and within months had moved to a specially adapted bungalow in a quiet village on the Suffolk coast. They both knew that their lives would never, could never be the same again but Linda Cartwright was determined that they would claw back some kind of normality. If they didn't then Zena's death would have all been in vain and nothing would make sense. Linda Cartwright desperately needed to make sense of her life.

Julie Sullivan was planning on making a few visits to see her old friend while she was still living in

Canning Town. Once Michelle moved away from the city she knew that their friendship would dwindle to just swapping the odd Christmas or birthday card but Julie didn't mind that much. Oh she would miss Michelle but she realised there wasn't really any such thing as a true friendship, well only with her mum at least. Julie and Ruby Sullivan wouldn't ever dream of leaving Canning Town let alone London. As her mother was always telling her, they were true East Enders. If Ruby ever got to the stage where she couldn't look after herself or Julie then their roles would be reversed. Julie Sullivan wouldn't mind in the least because when it came down to it family was all that you had and the only people you could truly rely on.

Deidre Steel didn't try to follow her husband and the only time she contacted him was if she had spent her monthly allowance early. Vic was only too happy to send her a few quid as long as she didn't try and have any contact with their son. For Deidre it wasn't something she ever even thought about but the threat was always there and she knew this would assure her of a comfortable income. When his mother's house had been sold Charlie had moved in with his sister-in-law and together they became alcoholics. There was, at least to begin with, nothing sexual in their relationship. As time moved on and Charlie Steel had regained his libido but had received rejection upon rejection due to his facial disfigurement, he had begun to look more favourably on Deidre. She was no oil painting but having someone to cuddle up to on a cold winter's night was better than nothing. For Deidre it was slightly different. In Charlie she could see a resemblance of her Kenny and when Charlie was on top of her and was groaning in the throes of passion she could at least imagine that he was Kenny, the one true love of her life.

As for Vic, Sandra, Shell and little Vic? Life slowly started to turn around and the purchase of a small holding in the tiny village of Snowshill in the Cotswolds helped matters immensely. Vic Steels life was now a complete contradiction in terms to the one he'd lived back in London. Scanning the ten acres that he now called home and dressed in dungarees and wellington boots he was the epitome of a country bumpkin. As he stood ankle deep in pig shit he couldn't have been any happier. Staring down at his son he smiled and winked.

"Fancy seeing if the chickens have lain?"

"Oh yes please daddy."

"Right I'll race you over to the hen house."

His son had just had his sixth birthday and was the apple of his father's eye. Only trotting along Vic let the boy win and when they reached the hen house he acted as if he was out of breath and had been beaten easily. The Burford Browns over the past month had been slow to lay but Vic had been reluctant to get rid of them as little Vic loved them like pets. After a minute of sifting through the straw he at last found one solitary egg.

"Here we go Son! They knew you was coming and laid one just for you. Let's go see if your Nan will cook it up before you go to school.

Sandra was busy wiping down the table when her son and grandson entered the kitchen. The room was stifling as the AGA billowed out heat that wasn't needed. The stove had frightened her to death when they had first viewed the property but she had sworn that it wouldn't get the better of her, to date the AGA was winning hands down. Sandra glanced at the door and when she saw the mess her son was in her face was filled with a look of horror. "Victor Steel! Don't you dare come into my kitchen in that state. Now outside the pair of you and take those dirty boots off."

"A bit of pig shit never hurt anyone mum and besides little Vic's got a present for you."

Sandra walked over to her grandson and kneeling down gave him her warmest smile.

"What you got for me darling?"

Little Vic gently placed the egg into the palm of her hand.

"That one's special Nan and Gertie laid it just for me."

"Did she now? Well you get washed up and I'll put the pan on. An egg that special is going to taste really good especially if it's got a few soldiers to dunk into it."

Vic looked over to where his sister sat on the sofa staring blankly into space. Turning his face in the direction of his mother his eyes were pleading but

Sandra Steel could only shake her head sadly.
"No change son."
Vic Steel tenderly squeezed his mothers shoulder as he kissed her on the cheek.
"Give her time mum give her time. The poor little cows been through so much but with our help shell come through it."
Sandra smiled as she looked into her boys face and she couldn't help but notice he had tears in his eyes.
"You're right son. We're Steels and we don't ever give up!"

Printed in Great Britain
by Amazon.co.uk, Ltd.,
Marston Gate.